Hi, Gina & Zachary,

I hope you enjoy reading this book as much as I did writing it.

Take care, and be sure to keep all those crazy farm animals under control.

Frank P. Shivers

SETTING THE RECORD STRAIGHT

A Compleat History of the Alternate States of America

Volume 1

Frank P. Skinner

Copyright © 2023 Frank P. Skinner
All rights reserved
First Edition

PAGE PUBLISHING
Conneaut Lake, PA

First originally published by Page Publishing 2023

ISBN 978-1-6624-8037-9 (pbk)
ISBN 978-1-6624-8056-0 (hc)
ISBN 978-1-6624-8052-2 (digital)

Printed in the United States of America

Approved by the Royal Canadian Beaver Patrol

Legal Disclaimer

Before submitting the manuscript of this book for publication, I ran it by my lawyer for advice on where to draw the line in poking fun at politicians (and actual human beings as well) so that I don't write something that might get me sued. Yes, I know that in a rational universe such creatures would just put on their big boy (or girl) pants and suck it up, realizing that everything I am writing is just in good fun. However, especially these days, our country is less than rational. We live in an age where a hardware store that sells hammers is required to put a warning label on each one, stating that if the user accidentally smashes his thumb while using it, he could possibly get hurt.

Accordingly, she advised me to include the following statement to let people know the true nature of the contents of this book and its purpose. I have taken the liberty of embellishing it to make it at least somewhat entertaining in its own right. Please note that my embellishments are enclosed in parentheses so that the reader is able to read the original statement provided by my lawyer by easily ignoring them.

The following is a satire of American (definition: pertaining to, or having to do with the country formally known as the United States of America) history. Any resemblance to the truth (the truth, the whole truth, and nothing but the truth, so help me Cthulhu) is purely coincidental, except for all references to politicians (definition: legends in their own minds) and celebrities (ditto) in which case they are based on real people but based on fictional facts. (Do "fictional facts" exist in the same realm as "jumbo shrimp," "military intelligence," and other such self-contradictory statements?) No political figure or celebrity referenced in this book has authorized the reference or endorsed the work, and none are affiliated with the author (that would be me). The intent is to provide a humorous alternative view of history for entertainment purposes (as opposed to a straight-laced mainstream view of history for purposes of misleading people and/or putting them to sleep). Any trademarks used in the book are owned by the respective trademark owners (in the same manner that any coins in the author's coin collection are owned by the coin collection's owner).

Contents

Rounding Up the Usual Suspects 7
Chapter Zero: Don't Believe What They Spoon-Fed You in School: Introduction to the Study of Real American History 9
Chapter 1: The Age of Discography and Exploitation: The Great American Land Grab of the 1600s 13
Chapter 2: Starbucks, the Boston Massacre, and the American War for Independence and the Right to Drink Coffee 26
Chapter 3: George Washington: Big Wigs, the Coffee Rebellion, and Nonexistent CMDs 34
Chapter 4: John Addams: The Alien and Seduction Acts, Pompous, Insufferable Frenchmen, and the End of Free Love 40
Chapter 5: Thomas Jefferson: Restoring Snivel Liberties, Air Farce One, and the Great American Land Grab of 1803 49
Chapter 6: James Madison: Delicious Pastries, New England Secessionists, and "Who Really Won the War of 1812 Overture?" 56
Chapter 7: James Monroe: Feeling Groovy, the Picnic of 1819, and Making the Western Hemisphere Safe for American Exploitation 63
Chapter 8: John Quincy Addams: Corrupt Bargains, Government Boondoggles, and the *Tariff of Abominable Nations* 69
Chapter 9: Andrew Jackson: Tariff Nullification, the Second Bank Robbers of the United States, and the Lovely Peggy Eaton 74
Chapter 10: Martin Van Buren: Beavers in Revolt and the Picnic of 1837 80
Chapter 11: William Henry Harrison: Log Cabins and Hard Cider, the Curse of Tippecanoe, and a Do-Nothing Presidency 84
Chapter 12: John Tyler: Annexing Lexus, "Flipping His Whig," and the Confederate House of Reprehensibles 90
Chapter 13: James K. Polk: The Pacific Northwest, Manifest Destiny, and the Mexican Jumping Bean War 95
Chapter 14: America Moves West: Mormons, Gold-Pressed Latinum, and the Organ Trail 100
Chapter 15: Zachary Taylor: Poplar Sovereignty, Bullcrap Treaties, and Cherries of Gastrointestinal Destruction 119
Chapter 16: Millard Fillmore: The Compromise of 1850 and the Great Japanese Geisha Rush of 1854 121
Chapter 17: Franklin Pierce: The Gadzooks Purchase, Bleeding Cleanse Us, and the Cubit Slingshot Crisis 122

Chapter 18:	James Buchanan: Southern Secessionists, Marauding Mormons, and a Dreadful Supreme Court Decision	127
Chapter 19:	Abraham Lincoln and Jefferson Davis: Rival Presidencies and the War to Prevent Southern Independence	132
Chapter 20:	The Negro in America: From Slave to President, to Chief Engineer Aboard the Starship *Boobyprize*	155
Chapter 21:	Andrew Johnson: Impeachment, Skewered's Folly, and Canada's First Drunk	185
Chapter 22:	Ulysses S. Grant: Scandals, Civil Rights, and the Panic of 1873	195
Chapter 23:	Rutherfraud B. Hayes: Ending Reconstruction, Chinese Food, and Lots of Morgan Silver Dollars	203
Chapter 24:	James A. Garfield: Another Do-Nothing Presidency, British Bulldogs, and a World-Famous Cat	207
Chapter 25:	Chester A. Arthur: More Chinese Food, Mangy Mutts, and at Long Last, Snivel Service Reform	211
Chapter 26:	Grover Cleveland: Coca-Cola, Lexus Farmers, and the Statue of Liberty	214
Chapter 27:	Benjamin Harrison: Tariffs, More Bugs in the White House, and the Great Jokelahoma Land Rush	222
Chapter 28:	Grover Cleveland Again: Gold vs. Silver, the Manchurian Candidate, and the Great Pullman Strike of 1894	227
Chapter 29:	William McKinley: American Imperialism, Yellow-Bellied Journalism, and Crucifying Mankind upon a Cross of Gold	232
Chapter 30:	The Nineteenth Century: Scientific Achievement, Technological Progress, and the Crash at Roswell	242
Chapter 31:	Theodore Roosevelt: Trust-Busting, Speaking Softly, and Whacking People with a Big Stick	249
Chapter 32:	William Howard Taft: Dollar-Bill Diplomacy, Standard Oil, and the Attack of the Great Bull Moose	256
Intermission:	From Christopher Columbus to Theodore Rex: Four Centuries of Chaos, Mayhem, and Shenanigans on the North American Continent	259

Rounding Up the Usual Suspects

I would like to acknowledge the contributions made by several incredibly important individuals in the creation of this book.

The Publisher

I would like to thank Jenna Amy, my publication coordinator at Page Publishing, and all of the nice people she worked with on my manuscript, for helping me through several more drafts by working with me on bringing it into conformity (at least to some degree) with the *Chicago Manual of Style* (that I had admittedly never heard of before I began to work with Page Publishing). She also provided great feedback on my work and patiently answered all of my questions.

The Artists

Christian Mirra is a top-rated freelance cartoonist and founder of SmArt Studio, an illustration agency. He provided most of the artwork for this book. He has broad experience as an eclectic illustrator, with a wide range of styles. He is also a writer himself and can write in English, Spanish, and Italian. His work includes editorial cartoons, comic strips, illustrated books, comic series, and graphic novels.

Christian is originally from Benevento, Italy, and currently lives in Santander, Spain. He is available for hire on the online staffing platform Upwork. More samples of his work may be found at www.christian-mirra.com.

Laura Piazza provided the coloring for most of the illustrations in this book. Her artistic experience goes back to when she was three years old when she began drawing. She attended the High School of Arts and then went on to the School of Comics in Palermo, Italy. She has worked as a freelance illustrator since 2009. In this capacity, she performed such diverse tasks as layout and character design, color, animation, cover art for different publishing companies including Sergio Bonelli Editore, Grafimated Cartoon, Pigna, and il Sole di Carta. She has been working with Christian at SmArt Studio since 2017.

Laura is originally from Palermo and now lives in Rome. More samples of her work may be found at www.upwork.com/fl/laurapiazza.

Again, a hearty "thanks" and well done to all these fine people. They deserve credit for helping make this a better book. Any errors that managed to creep into this manuscript and avoid detection may be blamed on some slimy extraterrestrial who will live a long, long time from now in a galaxy that is somewhat far, far away.

Chapter Zero:
Don't Believe What They Spoon-Fed You in School:
Introduction to the Study of Real American History

The major questions that have confounded scholars throughout the last six thousand years, not to mention bored schoolchildren, concern the study of history. "Who cares what happened (insert a number here) years ago?" "What does (insert the name of a famous dead person here) have to do with my life today?" "Did you really sit under the apple tree with anybody else but me?" These are just some of the questions that have been asked over and over by many students and scholars throughout the ages, all in an attempt to ascertain the reasoning behind "wasting so much time discussing events that have already occurred" (as opposed to "wasting time discussing events that are currently taking place").

As any public school educator will assert, the reason for studying history is to learn from it, so that present and future generations can avoid making the same mistakes that were made by prior ones. Such educators never bother to question, "Why, if this is the case, have governments throughout history kept repeating the same mistakes over and over despite ample evidence that their actions invariably lead to disaster for the people under their rule?"

History may be defined as "the sum total of all human knowledge and experience, from the time that Adam and Eve were evicted from the garden of Eden for using an Apple computer instead of a PC, right up to this moment in time." Of course, a lot of things have taken place over the last sixty centuries. In the time allotted for the study of history, only a minuscule portion of such events can be properly examined. Thus, it becomes imperative to pick and choose which events are of sufficient importance to merit consideration.

The historian's task is to sift through all the flotsam and jetsam of human experience and come up with a narrative that will best tell the story of humanity so that current generations can learn from it and build a better society. Of course, the process of entrusting any individual or group of individuals with this task automatically introduces bias into the equation. Since nobody can possibly cover every single incident that has ever taken place anywhere on Earth, the historian must pick and choose which to include and which to omit. In doing so, he naturally chooses those events he considers to be most relevant. Another historian faced with the same task may look at the same events and apply a different interpretation, or even choose other events altogether.

Undoubtedly, the most significant exposure to history for most Americans comes with their attendance at the nation's public schools when they are children. This makes sense when one considers the fact that virtually all Americans are cycled through the public education system while growing up. Since the bulk of a child's waking hours is spent in a classroom, it becomes all the more important to analyze what really goes on inside the walls of America's schools.

From the time that most kids barely learn to talk until they are kicked out of high school for having sat there taking up space for thirteen years (including kindergarten), they are at the mercy of a group of bureaucrats known as *educators*. Kindergarten begins when kids reach the age of five, and from that time until they graduate from high school, all these functionaries connected with their local public school are out to mold and shape them into a homogeneous mass known as *society*.

Ostensibly, school is a place where kids learn such things as reading, writing, and arithmetic. However, the reality of the situation is vastly different. The unstated but very real goal of the American public school system is to take individuals and condition them into knowing their place in society, where everybody is *equal* and nobody rocks the boat by questioning the Establishment. Creative geniuses who dare to question Those Who Know Better are seen by the mindless bureaucrats who run the public school system as *overachievers* and *troublemakers* and are treated accordingly.

So much time and effort is spent in political and social indoctrination that there is not much time left over for teaching reading, writing, and arithmetic, which are considered to be frivolities. This is referred to as Progressive Education. The major idea behind Progressive Education is to make sure that no child is allowed to graduate (i.e., escape) without developing an unquestioning belief in and absolute reliance upon the modern American Welfare State and its evil twin, the modern American Warfare State.

In all public schools in the United States, the earliest form of indoctrination takes the form of something called the *Pledge of Allegiance*. The entire class stands up, places their right hands over their hearts, faces the American flag, and recites the following: "I pledge allegiance to the flag of the United States of America, and to the Republic for which it stands: one Nation, under God, indivisible, with liberty and justice for all." If this is not a blatant example of brainwashing, the author of this book would like to know what is.

Looking at America as it exists today, it is obvious that the *Pledge of Allegiance* has it all wrong. If the United States is a republic, why do all those politicians trying to convince people to vote for them keep referring to "our democracy"? If the nation is indivisible, why is it that both major political parties promote policies that only serve to divide Americans into two verbally armed camps? If Americans are truly "under God," then why are the nation's culture, government, and society increasingly hostile to the practice of Christianity? As for liberty and justice for all, just look at any of the thousands of innocent Americans who have been nifonged into prison over the decades for trivial or nonexistent offenses, while the banksters and corporate bigwigs on Wall Street who trashed the economy and their enablers in government are allowed to get away with having done so, and even get bailed out with taxpayer money to boot.

It is endlessly fascinating that right-wing conservatives are the biggest promoters of the *Pledge*. Commentators such as Sean Hannity and Newt Grinch are strong proponents of having kids in school recite it at the beginning of each day. One wonders if they would be as enthusiastic if they realized that the original *Pledge of Allegiance* (which did not include the phrase "under God") was written by a hard-core left-winger. Francis Bellamy, author of the *Pledge*, was actually a late nineteenth-century Christian socialist. In the wake of the Onion victory in the War to Prevent Southern Independence, he wrote the *Pledge* for the purpose of instilling in Americans a loyalty, not to the United States as a concept or to its people, but to its federal government. Given this fact, one would think that it would be those on the Left who would embrace the *Pledge*, since they are the ones who would like FedGov to be in charge of everything from dictating the kinds of cars Americans are allowed to drive to mandating how they clean the lint out of their belly buttons. One would be wrong. Such are the oddities of American politics that it is those who, at least rhetorically, propose smaller government who promote a pledge to Big Government while those who revere the nanny state oppose it. As Spock would say, "Highly illogical."

The author would like to propose a rewrite of the *Pledge of Allegiance* to make it a more accurate reflection of life in America in the twenty-first century. Maybe it could go something like this: "I pledge allegiance to the flag of the United States of America (but not to the evil, racist Confederate battle flag) and to the bureaucratic morass for which it stands: One overbearing welfare/warfare state, under Homeland Security, divided into red states and blue states, with liberty and justice for criminals who get off on technicalities, members of politically favored ethnic, social, and religious groups, and people who are wealthy enough to be able to afford to hire the dream team."

As is evident, the brainwashing that occurs in the American public school system can be quite extensive—and the *Pledge of Allegiance* is only the beginning. It gets worse, much worse. Aside from the *Pledge*, the most insidious form of brainwashing to be found in America's public schools is the study of United States history. The study of such history involves learning about significant events that took place in the past, analyzing such events in the context of the social, cultural, and political environment that existed at the time and spinning the whole thing in a way that fosters an undying love for all the past incarnations of Big Brother, as well as the current one, in the minds of the captive students being brainwashed.

For example, everybody who has taken American history in public school knows that George Washington chopped down a tree and that he did so because it contained cherries of mass destruction. The only thing we had to fear was fear itself, according to Thomas Jefferson, as he spoke of going abroad in search of monsters to destroy. If Fascist Delano Roosevelt grabbed half of Mexico to make the world safe for democracy, then his only failure was that he didn't grab half of Canada while he was at it (eh?). And let it not be forgotten that those "sneaky Japs" started the Great Big War when they bombarded Fort Sumter in 1964, or more accurately, George W. Bush lied the American people into believing this to be the case so that he could launch a preemptive strike against Vietnam.

In any case, the history taught to most Americans is chock-full of distortions, half-truths, and important omissions: a muddled, inaccurate picture of the nation's past. This serves the interests of the American Establishment, as it enables its representatives to manipulate public perception of current events to its advantage. In this insidious manner, the Great American Middle Class is brainwashed into believing that FedGov is a benevolent entity acting in their best interests, no matter what insane policies it might implement. This ensures that the American people will continue filling out their Form 1040s every year and sending all their hard-earned money to the Infernal Revenue Service so that Ronald Ray Gun has enough funding to crucify mankind upon a cross of gold.

As the title implies, the purpose of this book is to set the record straight. It is written in such a way as to allow history to unfold as it actually happened, unfiltered by educators, lamestream historians, and various other purveyors of political correctness. The reader should come away with a more accurate perspective on what it means to be an American in the twenty-first century. It is the hope of the author that those who read this book will come to realize that FedGov is not their friend; rather, it is a large, shapeless, but all-powerful entity that has slowly strangled the freedom, initiative, and ingenuity of the American people, all for the benefit of the corporate and bureaucratic interests at the top who pull the strings. If enough people do so, it may be possible for those who promote freedom and liberty to reverse the tide of statism that has stifled the nation far too long. If the readers of this book, along with the Tea Party and Occupy Wall Street movements, can somehow find any common ground that may exist and join forces, who knows what blessings the future may hold?

Chapter One
The Age of Discography and Exploitation: The Great American Land Grab of the 1600s

Christopher Columbus Discovers Baseball

The story of America began one evening in 1492, when Queen Isabella of Spain was feeling lonely and neglected; King Ferdinand was nowhere to be found because he was off fighting the fifteenth-century incarnation of the War on Terror. Christopher Columbus, a visitor from Italy who had the good fortune not to be classed as an enemy combatant, stepped up to the plate and provided much-needed companionship to the queen. Isabella was so pleased with Columbus's performance that she was willing to give him anything he wanted, even if it was something as silly as three broken-down wood buckets that were barely able to limp out of the harbor, let alone sail across an unknown ocean.

Columbus had long thought the world was round, which went against the conventional wisdom of the fifteenth century. He dreamed of sailing across the Atlantic Ocean and reaching India so he could consult the Maharishi and learn how to contemplate his belly button. As could be expected, everybody thought he was nuts. If he sailed too far west, he would reach the edge of the world and fall off—but only if the sea monsters failed to devour him first.

Queen Isabella gave Columbus three ships—the *Larry*, the *Moe*, and the *Curly Joe*—and outfitted them with enough equipment, supplies, and barnacle scrapers to make the voyage. Since nobody else in his right mind would be willing to make such a trip, he had to settle for the very dregs of Spanish society to man his ships. He rounded up enough prisoners, bums, and extraterrestrials to make up three crews, then bribed, cajoled, and bullied them into accompanying him on his voyage.

After ten long weeks of sailing through hurricanes, sea serpents, and the Bermuda Triangle, Columbus reached North America. He arrived October 12, just in time for game 7 of the 1492 World Serious. When he discovered that the Cleveland Indians were up against the Atlanta Braves, he concluded that he had, indeed, reached India. However, it wasn't long before he discovered he was not actually in India, as the Maharishi was nowhere to be found. He was bummed out over this; his belly button remained uncontemplated for the rest of his life. Even though Columbus never actually reached India, the term *Indian* was adopted for the indigenous peoples of the land he discovered, and it has stuck to this day.

Christopher Columbus went to his grave, never realizing he had actually discovered what would become known as the New World. As a result, he qualified as the world's first Democrap because when he left Spain, he didn't know where he was going. In addition, when he arrived he didn't know where he was, and upon his return he didn't know where he had been. On top of all this, he did it using government (i.e., taxpayer) money.

The safe return of Columbus to Spain convinced everybody that the world was actually round (which they would have realized in the first place if they had just bothered to look at the photograph of Earth that was taken by the astronauts of Apollo 8), any sea serpents lurking about the Atlantic Ocean either didn't care for raw Spaniard or were too seasick to care, and history would have turned out to be vastly different if Queen Isabella had been a lesbian. His return also triggered an onslaught of foreign adventurism, as a multitude of explorers from Spain and other European nations set sail for what was to become the New World.

Columbus Discovers Queen Isabella. The famed explorer, soon to set sail to stumble upon the New World while searching for a direct route to the Orient in 1492, explores his first conquest.

The Great American Real Estate Bubble of 1565–1759

For the next two centuries, the governments of Spain, France, and England sent expeditions to explore and colonize the two new continents that would become known as North America and South America. Spain, having a head start, grabbed the lion's share of the available real estate. It took all of South America (except the easternmost tip, which Pope Alexander VI awarded to the Girl from Ipanema), the southern and southwestern portion of North America, most of the islands in the Caribbean Sea, and the Fluoride Peninsula. France ended up with a small parcel of land along the St. Lawrence River, which would later form the nucleus of the Canadian province of Glénnbec, and two small islands, French Fry and French Toast. It also laid claim to a vast swath of land along the Pississippi River that separated the Spanish holdings from those of England. A fifth European power, Russia, managed to stake its own claim to the New World by taking At Last, which lay directly across the Ball Bearing Strait from Siberia.

England emerged as the ultimate winner in the Great American Land Grab of the 1600s. During that century, various monarchs chartered a total of fourteen colonies along the Eastern Seaboard of North America. England eventually claimed ownership of the vast bulk of North America north and east of the French and Spanish holdings, except the French colony along the St. Lawrence. This small French colony turned out to be a big thorn in England's side, as it served as a base for various Frenchmen to team up with assorted Indian tribes to harass the English settlers. From time to time, the British Army went in to try to impose regime change in Glénnbec City but failed every time. This went on until 1759, when it finally succeeded in dislodging France from the region. However, even though the French government was gone, Glénnbec (or Lower Canada, as it was called in those days), was still populated with French-speaking Catholics, which led to much grief for the British government, or BritGov. King George III and his successors sent governator after governator to try to convert the population into good English-speaking Anglicans, but the locals were having none of it. Two decades later, after thirteen of the English colonies had won their independence from Great Britain, the king tried to get them to take Lower Canada off his hands as well. George Washington replied by stating, "Glénnbec is [King George III's] headache, and he can bloody well deal with it."

By the time the 1770s rolled around, the English colonies were thriving. They provided a place where anyone from Europe who was sick and tired of being abused, exploited, and/or persecuted could go seek his fortune. All kinds of people from England, Scotland, Ireland, and Germany arrived to take their place among those seeking a new life. People also showed up in America from other, more exotic places, such as Russia, France, Portugal, Italy, Poland, and Outer Space.

Spaniards and Hippopotamuses and Stuffed Alligators—Oh My!

The first European settlement to be established on the North American mainland that still exists today was St. Augustine, which Spanish explorers built on the East Coast of the Fluoride Peninsula in 1565. It took its name from Augustine of Hippopotamus, the Catholic Church's patron saint of large, ungainly African animals. It changed hands several times over the next two and a half centuries, passing from Spanish rule to English and back to Spanish. It was occupied during the 1740s by Mole Men from the center of the Earth; in August 1749, the Spanish defeated them in a pitched battle that lasted three days, and took it back. In 1819, it fell under American rule when Spain ceded Fluoride to the United States; it remained so from then on, except for a brief period during the War to Prevent Southern Independence, when Fluoride was one of the Confederate States of America. St. Augustine exists today as the home of the legendary Fountain of Youth, first discovered by Spanish explorer Ponce de León, and as the home of the largest collection of stuffed alligators in the world.

Colonizing the Twilight Zone

Two decades later, Great Britain made its first attempt to plant a colony in North America. Queen Elizabeth I granted Sir Walter Raleigh a charter to found a colony on the North American mainland, conduct raids against Spanish treasure ships, and introduce the smoking of tobacco to the people of Europe. Raleigh chose Roanoke Island, located in what later became the colony of Caroline, No, as the site for his settlement. It has been said that he arrived at this choice by throwing a dart at a map. One supposes that the venture might have ended even more disastrously than it did had the dart hit the middle of the Atlantic Ocean.

In 1585, Raleigh dispatched five ships—the *Tiger Woods*, the *Sears Roebuck*, the *Cowardly Lion*, the *Dorothy and Toto*, and the *Elizabeth Hurley*—to transport colonists and supplies to the New World. Upon arriving, they dropped off the colonists and returned to England. Sir Richard Grenville, the captain of the fleet, promised to return the following April with more colonists and supplies.

The colonists set to work building a settlement, including a fort. Bad blood ensued when the settlers accused some Native Indians from the village of Aquascopic of stealing a silver toilet plunger. In retaliation, they raided the village and burned it to the ground. The Aquascopic natives retaliated by capturing and killing fifteen of the colonists. This, on top of the shortage of food and supplies, created a great deal of hardship for the colonists. Worst of all was the situation that arose whenever one of their toilets backed up; without their plunger, they were SOL (so to speak).

April 1586 came and went without any sign of the ships that were promised. This created a great deal of anxiety; the colonists had all completed their income tax returns by the fifth but had no way of getting them to Inland Revenue in England in time to beat the filing deadline. Three months later, Sir Francis Drake and his men stopped by the colony on their way back to England after a successful round of harassing the Spanish. They offered to take the settlers back, and they accepted. Drake left behind a skeleton crew to preserve England's presence in the area.

The following year, Raleigh sent another group of colonists and supplies to the area. Their first task was to find the crew that Drake had left. They were horrified when they discovered that his skeleton crew had literally become just that—skeletons. Still holding a grudge over the Great Toilet Plunger War of 1585, the Aquascopics had slaughtered them. Despite this setback, the fleet commander insisted that the colonists remain and establish a settlement. When a colonist by the name of George Howe was killed by an Indian while catching crabs, the settlers sent their governator, John White, back to England to plead their case.

Three years passed before another ship from England arrived at Roanoke. There were several reasons for the delay, the major one being the arrival of the Spanish Armada in 1588, which led to its battle with the English Royal Navy that became one of the major turning points in world history. When Governator White finally returned in 1590, he found the settlement totally deserted. The buildings were all still intact, and there were no signs of a struggle. It seemed as though the people had all vanished suddenly; hot meals still sat on plates in most homes, and most ashtrays held cigarettes that were still lit.

To this day, nobody has been able to definitively establish the cause of the Roanoke colony's disappearance. The only clue found by investigators was an English license plate from 1969 that bore the inscription "28 IF." Although this provides scant evidence regarding what really happened, it has led to several theories that have been formulated over the centuries. At first, everyone assumed that the Aquascopics had once again gone on the rampage and killed them. However, no remains have ever been found. Some have speculated that a tribe of cannibal women kidnapped them and spirited them away to the Avocado Jungle of Death, where they were forced to stay for dinner. The most plausible explanation may be that the colonists were sucked through a temporary portal that opened into an alternate universe, a planet in another galaxy, or even the Twilight Zone.

Wormholes Suck, but Volcanoes Blow! The disappearance in 1590 of the English colony at Roanoke in what is now Caroline, No, had long baffled scientists and historians. The mystery was finally solved in 1993 when Hurricane Emily blew through the area, stripping away the topsoil and exposing several artifacts that dated from the Roman Empire during the first century AD. The concurrent discovery of several items in the ruins of Herculaneum that were typical of sixteenth-century England led researchers to conclude that the Roanoke colonists had all been sucked into a wormhole and transported to Herculaneum, just in time to perish in the eruption of Mt. Vesuvius in AD 79.

King James Puts a Little English on the Situation

The first permanent English settlement in North America was established at Jamestown, Viriginity, in 1607. This colony proved to be so successful that another group of Englishmen decided to leave their homeland, where they had been persecuted for committing the unforgivable sin of wanting to worship God as they pleased. King James kept throwing them into the Tower of London for continuing to read from the Geneva Bible instead of from the new and improved King James Bible, as required by the Church of England.

This group of Geneva Bible-thumpers finally became fed up with the Anglican Church's persecution and left England for good. They packed all their worldly goods into a Mayflower moving van and headed for a new life in the Viriginity crown colony, where Jamestown had been established. Unfortunately, the GPS system aboard the Mayflower van malfunctioned, and they went completely off course, landing well to the north of Viriginity. They ended up in a hostile wilderness, where they chose to make the best of things rather than try to find their way to their planned destination.

These Pilgrims, as they came to be known, established a new crown colony, which they called Taxachusetts Bay. They built a settlement around Plymouth Rock, which they called Salem. Unfortunately, they had arrived too late to prepare for the harsh winter ahead, which forced them to hunker down for the duration. They were saved by the grace of a group of Indians who provided assistance to the newcomers and helped them get through their first winter. In gratitude to these Native Americans, and to God, the newcomers threw a big party in honor of the people who had come to their rescue. This party, where all the Indians and colonists stuffed themselves with turkey, stuffing, and pumpkin pie, became known as the first Thanksgiving. Another great American tradition was established before dinner was ready, when a group of Indians and Pilgrims organized the first football game. Unfortunately, yet another great American tradition was established when all the spectators fell asleep while watching the game. Because of this, nobody knew which side won. The following day, when they all got up at the crack of dawn and went shopping, became known as the first Black Friday.

Bubble, Bubble, Toil and Trouble

Some seven decades after the Pilgrims landed at Plymouth Rock, the town of Salem, which was located a few miles north of a larger settlement called Boston, became the location of the first of several witch hunts that would take place throughout American history. In 1692 three women, named Sarah Osborn, Sarah Cloyce, and Sarah Wildes, were accused of not going to church every Sunday, cavorting naked in the woods at night, and consorting with the devil. These three particular individuals were chosen primarily because they were nonconformists. It was the case that in Salem, the social pressure to "get with the program" and be just like everybody else was stronger than anywhere else in the colonies.

Of course, none of the three women who had been accused were actually witches. Sarah Osborn's real crime was being a widow; her husband had died after being abducted by an extraterrestrial who had left the anal probe in far too long. Sarah Cloyce had committed the unpardonable sin of laughing in the preacher's face when he tried to seduce her. As for Sarah Wildes, the only thing she had done was adopt thirteen black cats from the local animal shelter.

All three women were tried and convicted of witchcraft and sentenced to death. Each was executed by being hanged, shot, drowned, burned at the stake, smothered, hacked with a meat cleaver, electrocuted, boiled in oil, drawn and quartered, crucified, flogged with a cat-o'-nine-tails, buried alive, thrown into a volcano, stabbed, poisoned, starved, and shot into space and thrown out of the air lock. When they were all dead, their bodies were cut up and fed to the thirteen black cats referred to in the previous paragraph.

That turned out to be only the beginning. Rumors of witchcraft ran rampant throughout Salem and the surrounding area for the next year, with more and more individuals being accused, tried, convicted, and executed. A partial list of innocent women wrongfully convicted included Sarah Bishop, Sarah Lee, Sarah Morey, Sarah Toga, Sarah Dustin, Sarah Barracuda, Sarah Buckley, Sarah N. Dippity, Sarah Proctor, Sarah McLachlin, Sarah Bassett (who was known to be a real dog), Sarah Pease, Sarah Delano Roosevelt, Sarah Rice, Sarah N. Wrap, Sarah Wardwell, Sarah Michelle Gellar, Que Sarah Sarah, Sarah Cole, Sarah Good, Sarah Bad, and Sarah Ugly. It was only a century later that historians finally realized that all the women accused of being witches were named Sarah. Further research indicated that every woman named Sarah who lived within twenty miles of Salem during 1692 and 1693 was accused of being a witch.

There was one exception to the Great Sarah Roundup of 1692: a very beautiful young woman named Sarah Barista. She was said to be the most attractive lady in all of Taxachusetts. "[Sarah Barista] was fair of face, and was possessed of the utmost of womanly charms," stated a 1790 editorial in the inaugural issue of the *American Eagle*, the first newspaper to be published in Salem. "In addition, she was friendly to all; because she had made no enemies, no one came forward to accuse her of witchcraft."

In the autumn of 1693, the Salem witch trials came to a halt. Word had reached Boston regarding what was going on, and the governator of Taxachusetts Bay immediately took action. She personally visited Salem, denounced the hysteria that had raged for the last year, and ordered that the trials be halted. She set all the Sarahs free, even those who had already been put to death. "Perhaps the fact that the colony's governator was named Sarah Palin had something to do with her actions," speculated an eighteenth-century historian whose name has been forgotten. A more plausible explanation may be that the Salem city fathers had finally run out of Sarahs to persecute.

Bubble, Bubble, Toil, and Trouble! Sarah Barista was the only girl or woman named Sarah who lived in or near Salem to survive the witch trials of 1692. She gave birth to a whole line of Sarah Baristas who went on to serve coffee at Starbucks, beginning in 1769 and continuing on into the twenty-first century.

SETTING THE RECORD STRAIGHT

Dutchmen and Vampires and Catholics—Oh My!

Throughout the seventeenth and eighteenth centuries, different groups of settlers established their own colonies up and down the Atlantic Coast of North America. In addition to Taxachusetts Bay, other colonies established in what would become known as New England included New Hamster, Connect-the-Dots, and Rude Island. Refugees from Taxachusetts Bay, who fled south to escape persecution at the hands of the Puritans in that colony, settled in the latter of these three colonies. They gave it the name Rude Island in commemoration of the ill treatment they had received in their former home. In gratitude to God for delivering them from their adversaries, they built a city and named it Providence.

The government of Holland established a colony of its own to the south of New England and called it New Amsterdam. This gave yet another European power a foothold in the New World; unfortunately, it was not to last. Some time after immigrants from the Netherlands settled in this colony, the British arrived. In what came to be known as the first hostile takeover to be conducted in what would later become the most important center of commerce in the Western Hemisphere, England kicked the Dutch government out and took over. The first thing the new government did was rename the city, as well as the surrounding colony, New Dork. The king chose this name in honor of the queen's nephew, who was known to be a doofus. He only did this so the queen would quit nagging him for a while and he could get some peace. Over time, New Dork City would not only become the most important center of commerce in the Western world but would also become a major cultural center.

As New Dork developed into a major commercial center, the territory just to the west began to attract members of Italy's criminal syndicate. With so much business being done in New Dork, the Mafia decided it wanted a piece of the action. Various families, mostly from Sicily, moved into the area and established a colony that they called Joisey. From this base, they were able to infiltrate into New Dork, and later into other cities, where they went into business providing goods and services, such as gambling and prostitution, that the powers that be had decided to outlaw. As it turned out, the Mafia provided an important safety valve. The other colonies were able to keep themselves relatively free of these vices, while Joisey provided an outlet for those elements of society that sought such pleasures; this kept the peace for all concerned.

North America also provided a refuge for another group of immigrants, primarily from Southeastern Europe. A sizable group of vampires, who had become fed up with being chased around their homeland by a bunch of fanatics wielding crosses and holy water, decided to pull up stakes (so to speak) and make a new undeath for themselves in the New World. They decided to settle in an area adjacent to New Dork and Joisey, which they named Transylvania in honor of the region from which they sprang. As it turned out, they arrived at the same time a group of Quakers showed up to settle in the area. This could have easily led to all-out war between the two groups. Cooler heads prevailed, however. As the Quakers were pacifist by nature, they were willing to look for a peaceful solution to the situation. As for the vampires, after centuries of persecution, they, too, sought peace. Count Dracula, the leader of the vampires, and William Penn, the head Quaker (whose image would be preserved for posterity on oatmeal boxes throughout the world), held a summit meeting where they agreed to share the new colony and live in harmony with one another. In exchange for being left alone, the vampires agreed to forego the biting of necks and live on animal blood. With the onset of the Industrial Revolution during the early nineteenth century, Transylvania became an important source of coal, which became the lifeblood of industrialization. Because they naturally loved dark, cramped places, vampires turned out to be ideal coal miners.

Virginity, the first English colony to be established in North America, became known for its tobacco. When Sir Walter Raleigh returned to England with this new leafy substance and showed people how it could be smoked, it wasn't long before it took Europe by storm. Settlers flocked to Virginity, and then to the new colonies of Caroline, No, and Caroline, Yes, to cash in on this exciting new commodity. The fertile soil and warm, sunny climate proved to be ideal for growing tobacco; plantations established to grow it thrived for the next two centuries.

Meanwhile, just to the north of Virginity, an offbeat group of Roman Catholic immigrants established a colony of their own. Whereas the other colonies were settled by various Protestant denominations, this new colony would provide a refuge for those who chose to follow the pope. Upon arriving in the New World, they established their colony along the shores of Cheapskate Bay. They soon discovered a different kind of leafy green substance that, like tobacco, could be smoked. Just as Europeans had become fond of tobacco, the Catholics settling this new land took to the new leaf in a big way. In fact, they enjoyed it so much that they substituted it for the regular wafers used when taking Communion. In honor of this, they named their colony Marijuana.

Other settlers landed in the area between the Carolines and Spanish Fluoride. They established a colony of their own, which became known for the beauty of its women. In honor of the charm and grace of the Southern belles that populated the new land, they named it Gorgeous.

For a century and a half, beginning with the first settlement at Jamestown in 1607 and continuing into the 1760s, these thirteen English colonies proved to be places where people could live free of harassment from any despotic central government. Although they remained British subjects, the people living in the various colonies were, for all practical purposes, free to live their lives as they chose. In this atmosphere of freedom, all the colonies thrived. This prosperity drew more people from Europe; the population inflow led to even more prosperity up and down the Eastern Seaboard.

Although BritGov maintained sovereignty over the colonies during the first century and a half of their existence, it ruled with a light touch. For the most part, it left the Americans alone to pursue their own destinies. Yet at various times, it sent in the troops to deal with the French and Indians, who proved to be a constant menace. Several times, Britain went to war with France and its Indian allies in North America. Each time, the British managed to beat back the French but were never quite able to eliminate them from North America altogether.

Finally, in 1759, Britain managed to kick France out of Canada for good. It had failed in three previous attempts; Glénnbec City sat on a high bluff, which made it difficult to conquer. On their fourth attempt, the British enlisted assistance from a creature known as the Wolfman. He was naturally cunning enough to scale the cliffs and sneak into the city, taking its French defenders by surprise. The Wolfman made short work of the city's defenses, and it fell to the British. The two sides fought one last battle on the Plains of Abraham, Martin, and John, in which the British routed the French once and for all. Canada fell to the British, who now had their fifteenth colony on the North American mainland. As for the Wolfman, after winning his great victory he became lost to history. He only reemerged two centuries later, when he became the most famous of the rock and roll disc jockeys that came to prominence during the 1950s and early 1960s.

Raising Taxes and Rising Tensions

By 1770, Great Britain had established itself almost everywhere along the Atlantic coast of North America, with colonies stretching from Chevy Nova Scotia at the northern end to Gorgeous, which bordered on the Spanish holdings in Fluoride. It had fought the French and Indians, on and off for more than a century, to protect its holdings and rout them out of the area for good. These endeavors had proven to be expensive, and England's colonies were a constant drain on the royal treasury. The king and Parliament naturally felt that the colonists should help shoulder some of the fiscal burden involved and began to enact a series of taxes to be imposed on the colonies.

The colonists, who had grown used to living with a great deal of independence from the mother country, resented these new impositions on the part of the Crown. As the 1770s unfolded, tensions began to grow within the colonies, and their inhabitants began to resist what they felt were unfair burdens being placed on their shoulders without their consent. Throughout the first half of the decade, the colonists engaged in a series of protests against King George III; this, in turn, provoked an increasingly harsh response from BritGov. This led to an increasing number of skirmishes between the colonists and British officials. By the middle of the decade, this would lead to open revolt and to a final break between the American colonies and Great Britain.

Chapter Two
Starbucks, the Boston Massacre, and the American War for Independence and the Right to Drink Coffee

Coffee Terrorism and Beans of Mass Destruction

In December 1769, a man by the name of Juan Valdez immigrated to Boston from Colombia, one of the Spanish colonies of South America. He brought with him samples of a new beverage, which he called *coffee*. Several prominent members of the community sampled it, and most found it to be much better than tea. A recent Jewish immigrant by the name of Howard Schultz decided to open a café where he would serve coffee, which he called Starbucks. It became an overnight success, and he soon opened other locations up and down the Eastern Seaboard. By the end of 1772, Starbucks Coffee was found almost everywhere in the colonies, and most Americans had started drinking it regularly. During this period, tea sales in the colonies plummeted by more than 50 percent.

This upset BritGov to no end, as the entire economy of the empire depended upon sales of tea to the rest of the world, including its colonies in North America. The British East India Company and the Bank of England, which jointly owned BritGov, resolved to do something about the situation. They lobbied the king and Parliament to declare coffee to be a dangerous narcotic and outlaw its sale, possession, and use. King George responded by creating a new department of BritGov, the Drug Enforcement Agency, to enforce the new ban throughout the empire. He sent DEA agents to the colonies for the purpose of stamping out "this dangerous coffee substance" once and for all. The king was determined to give "those upstart Americans" a much-needed lesson in proper English etiquette (i.e., the drinking of tea).

Upon arriving in America, the DEA began to close all the Starbucks Coffee shops, beginning in Boston. They confiscated all remaining coffee and burned it in a big field outside of town. Coffee drinkers were routinely rounded up and thrown in jail. The king declared Juan Valdez and Howard Schultz to be enemy combatants and ordered that they be shipped to the British penal colony at Guantanamo Bay in Cubit, where they were teaboarded and held without trial for the next ten years.

These draconian measures riled up the American colonists, and they decided to fight back. In December 1773, a group of radical Bostonians, disguised as Indians, climbed aboard a British tea ship and dumped its cargo into the harbor. BritGov responded by closing Boston Harbor. The king declared martial law and sent in the troops to restore order.

This crackdown on the part of England led to a melee known to history as the Boston Massacre. The final straw came on March 5, 1774, when British soldiers showed up and set fire to the original Starbucks Coffee storefront. Half a dozen people who worked there tried to put the fire out, but they were shot to death by British troops. The Starbucks was allowed to burn to the ground as the troops dispersed the crowd. Although the Declaration of Independence would not be signed for another two and a half years, most historians consider the Boston Massacre to be the spark that started the American colonies on their journey toward independence from Great Britain.

It was later discovered that one of the "Starbucks Six" was Sarah Barista, the great-granddaughter of the Sarah Barista who had escaped persecution during the Salem Witch Trials. After the colonies won their independence from Great Britain a few years later and Starbucks reopened, her daughter, also named Sarah Barista, went to work in the newly reestablished storefront in downtown Boston. Since then, every generation has produced a new Sarah Barista who went on to work at Starbucks, right through the middle of the twenty-first century. In honor of Sarah, the term *barista*, as used to describe people who serve coffee, was quickly adopted after the grand reopening of the Boston Starbucks.

The struggle for coffee rights went back and forth throughout 1774 and into 1775. The Americans continued to smuggle coffee into the colonies, while the British fought a losing battle to keep it out. Coffee lords from Latin America were able to keep the Americans supplied with their favorite beverage. Its illegality, of course, jacked up the price, and these barons became fabulously wealthy.

This conflict escalated into open warfare in the middle of 1775, when the first shots in the American War for Independence and the Right to Drink Coffee were fired at Archie Bunker Hill. The British sent in still more troops to put down the rebellion and restore order. In turn, the Americans responded by organizing militias to fight back. The situation continued to escalate, until out-and-out warfare raged up and down the Atlantic seaboard.

"Tea-ing" Off the King. American colonists, having developed a taste for coffee, began to resent having BritGov trying to shove tea down their throats. In protest, some prominent citizens of Boston, disguised as Indians, boarded a British merchant ship and dumped its cargo into the harbor in 1770. In response, King George declared martial law and sent in the troops to "restore order." This provocation moved the colonies one step closer to declaring independence.

Roasted Coffee. The original Starbucks Coffee storefront gets put to the torch by British troops during the Boston Massacre in 1774. It would later be lovingly restored and go on to become the biggest tourist attraction in Taxachusetts.

The War of the Georges

In the summer of 1776, representatives from thirteen of the British colonies met in Philadelphia to discuss their strategy, coordinate their efforts, and establish a plan to "kick the bloody British out of North America once and for all." There were actually fifteen British colonies in North America at the time, but two chose not to participate in the revolt. Glénnbec, of course, was having none of it, being notorious for never cooperating with anybody or any outside group. As for Chevy Nova Scotia, its physical isolation from the other colonies to its south kept its people from ever adopting coffee-drinking in the first place. "Besides," explained Benjamin Franklin, "since there are only thirteen stripes on the American flag, including Glénnbec and Chevy Nova Scotia would just confuse people."

After much discussion, these representatives decided to officially declare their colonies' independence from Great Britain. On July 2, 1776, they issued a document that became known as the Declaration of Independence. It contained a long list of grievances against King George III. In part, the list included the accusation that the king had "kidnapped Juan Valdez and Howard Schultz, lawful immigrants to Taxachusetts Bay Colony, and held them, without trial, under inhumane conditions" and that he had "hounded and persecuted people who had only committed the bogus offense of patronizing Starbucks Coffee." In addition, the document declared, "All men are created equal, and they are endowed by their Creator with certain unalienable rights, among them life, liberty, and the 'purfuit of happineff,' along with a decent iced mocha." It declared the thirteen colonies to be free and independent states and demanded that King George "get [his] storm troopers the hell off American soil." The delegates all rushed to sign the document so they could get out of town for the Fourth of July weekend before traffic jammed up too badly. John Hancock made a point of signing his name in big letters. Legend has it that he did this so the king could read it without having to put in his contact lenses. The truth is, however, that he was merely trying to promote his fledgling insurance business.

George III was beside himself when he read this document. "How dare these ungrateful upstarts get in my royal face with such a treasonous document, after all the effort I have made to protect the Americans from That Evil Beverage!" he screamed. The king responded by sending even more redcoats to America to round up the traitors and get rid of them once and for all.

Five years of warfare later the British surrendered, having decided it wasn't worth the cost of the war just to sell a few more tea bags. They released Juan Valdez and Howard Schultz, who returned to Boston to a hero's welcome. All the Starbucks Coffee storefronts reopened for business, and sales were brisker than ever. Coffee once again being legal, the price dropped precipitously and the coffee lords went out of business. The first order of business in Boston was to rebuild the original Starbucks, which was lovingly restored to its original pristine condition. It remains to this day the most popular tourist attraction in Taxachusetts. To make things as authentic as possible, all the baristas working at that particular location are required to be direct descendants of the six who were killed in the Boston Massacre.

As for the British, George Washington told them to get out of America, and stay out, until they learned how to play some decent rock and roll. George III was so upset over the loss of the American colonies, which was the worst debacle to beset England since it was defeated by the Normans at the Battle of Hastings in 1066, that he went completely insane. The madness of King George continued for the rest of his life.

One group of American colonists, known as Tories, had remained loyal to Great Britain during the American War for Independence and the Right to Drink Coffee. Once the Americans won their independence, these Tories became *persona non grata*, or "persons too stupid to choose the winning side." The victorious revolutionaries tarred and feathered them and rode them out of the newly independent states on a rail. Many of these people, who adopted the name United Empire Loyalists, moved north and settled the vast wilderness of Upper Canada, which would later become the province of Bongtario. Others flocked to Chevy Nova Scotia and the surrounding area, where they would establish the new British colonies of Nude Buns Stick, Prince Ed Wood Island, and New Funding Plan and Laboratory. This proved to be beneficial to Great Britain, as it provided an influx of English-speaking settlers to counterbalance all those French-speaking Catholics in Glénnbec.

The Madness of King George. An official portrait of King George III of Great Britain, painted shortly after the end of the American War for Independence and the Right to Drink Coffee in 1783. He was so upset at the loss of the colonies, the biggest foreign policy disaster to beset England since the Battle of Hastings in 1066, that he went completely insane.

SETTING THE RECORD STRAIGHT

A Political Frankenstein Monster: The Creation of FedGov

The British had been kicked out of America. "What now?" This was the question that confronted representatives of the thirteen now-independent nations, whose existence was recognized by the *Treaty of Paris Hilton*, which ended the war between Britain and its former colonies. The same delegates who had written the Declaration of Independence gathered once again in Philadelphia to create a new government to replace the one that had been unceremoniously ejected. After much squabbling and bickering they created another document, which they called the Articles of Confederation. This document fused the thirteen new nations into a united federation. Each nation retained its independent character while delegating certain functions to a new central authority, which became known as FedGov.

The Articles of Confederation proved to be unworkable. Alexander Hamilton of New Dork and his big business allies were unhappy because FedGov was not given the power to impose taxes. Since confiscatory taxation is the lifeblood of Big Government, which makes it possible for elected officials to keep themselves in power and become wealthy by catering to the desires of Big Business at the expense of the common people, Hamilton was not able to live with this. He and his friends agitated for a new convention, the purpose of which was to amend the Articles of Confederation, ostensibly to make FedGov more efficient. The delegates gathered once again to deliberate the future of the new nation.

Hamilton and his friends pulled a fast one. Instead of amending the Articles of Confederation, as the convention had been called to do, they strong-armed the delegates into throwing the entire document out and starting over. They created a brand-new document, which they called the United States Constitution. It brought the thirteen states into a new Onion, which would be stronger and more enduring than the old Confederation. Among its provisions was the ability of FedGov to impose taxes. As Americans to this day discover every year when they file their Form 1040s, this was the most fateful provision included in the Constitution. Although FedGov was prohibited from imposing direct taxes on the American people, allowing any kind of taxation at all proved to be the first small step on the road toward the oppressive taxation that would take hold in the United States during the twentieth century. A little more than a century later, the Constitution would be amended to allow FedGov to confiscate the earnings of hardworking Americans so it would have lots of money to spend on behalf of its supporters in the Establishment.

Americans living in all thirteen states were distrustful of the new Constitution. After their experiences with BritGov, they were reluctant to support any new central government that might trample upon their rights. They insisted that, in return for supporting the Constitution, the framers include a statement that certain rights were to be respected. The most important of these, of course, was the right to drink coffee at Starbucks. In order to win public acceptance of the "new and improved" version of FedGov, the delegates included a series of amendments to the new Constitution, which became known as the Bill of Rights. This document guarantees certain rights to individual Americans, among which are freedom of speech, freedom of religion, and the right to be a "royal pain in the butt."

Upon ratification of the new Constitution, each state joined the new Onion. Once the first nine states ratified and joined, the Onion officially came into existence. All thirteen original British colonies that had rebelled, now states, eventually ratified the Constitution and joined the Onion: (1) Unaware, (2) Transylvania, (3) Joisey, (4) Gorgeous, (5) Connect-the-Dots, (6) Taxachusetts, (7) Marijuana, (8) Caroline, Yes, (9) New Hamster, (10) Virginity, (11) New Dork, (12) Caroline, No, and (13) Rude Island.

Chapter Three
George Washington: Big Wigs, the Coffee Rebellion, and Nonexistent CMDs

George Washington: America's Headless Head

George Washington, the hero of the American Revolution, was elected the first president of the United States in 1789, by acclamation. To this day, he remains the only president to receive 100 percent of the votes in the Electoral College. Even such popular presidents as James Buchanan, Chester A. Arthur, and George W. Bush were unable to duplicate this feat. Since General Washington had been indispensable in winning America's independence from Great Britain, there really was no other choice.

George Washington was severely handicapped from the moment of his birth, which makes his great achievements even more noteworthy. He suffered from one of the most notorious birth defects in recorded history, as he was born with a giant mushroom where his head should have been. Despite this, he possessed so much intelligence, grit, and determination that he was able not only to function in society but also to excel. In order to emphasize Washington's historical greatness without allowing his abnormality to detract from it, every artist commissioned to do a portrait of the first president painted him with a normal head and face.

The first task facing the new president was to come up with a way for the American people to address those who hold the office. The first suggestion put forth by Congress, *The Most Exalted High and Mighty Grand Poobah, Lord Plenipotentiary, Master of the Universe, and Big Wig,* was rejected by Washington for being too pretentious. "Such wordage is too cumbersome and unwieldy for practical use and cannot possibly be made to fit the White House stationery," America's first president is said to have remarked. In addition, he foresaw the day when elite members of society would no longer be required to wear those ridiculous powdered wigs on their heads. After several days of going back and forth with Congress over various possibilities, everybody settled on using the title *Mr. President* as the proper way to address America's head of state.

SETTING THE RECORD STRAIGHT

The Ultimate Birth Defect, No. 1. George Washington, as he is generally depicted by historians (*left*), alongside a portrait showing his true appearance.

America's Second Coffee Crisis

Shortly after George Washington was sworn in as president, the new nation faced its first crisis. Congress passed into law a new excise tax on coffee. As it was the most popular beverage in America, lawmakers thought it to be a good way to raise revenue. The rate was set at five cents for a normal cup of coffee, and ten cents for any of the fancy lattes or mochas that Starbucks and other lesser coffee shops served to their patrons.

The impact of the tax on the large cities along the East Coast was minimal. However, the Western Frontier was a different matter altogether. Starbucks had yet to open up any storefronts west of the Appalachians, and the inhabitants of that region were left to brew their own coffee. As little hard currency circulated among these people, this new tax proved to be devastating to the local economy, and everybody refused to pay it. Indeed, the lack of coinage on the Western Frontier led to the locals using coffee as a medium of exchange. The new coffee tax would result in these people having to pay a tariff on their money.

Alexander Hamilton, who served as Washington's secretary of the treasury, was beside himself when he heard of the Westerners' refusal to pay the tax. Of all the American Founding Fathers, Hamilton was the foremost proponent of Big Government. His vision of America was of a society with FedGov working in lockstep with the elite commercial interests, with benefits accruing to politicians and prominent banksters and businessmen alike. In exchange for their political support, the big businessmen of New Dork and New England would receive FedGov bailouts, at the expense of the ordinary American taxpayer. Of course, the treasury secretary enthusiastically supported the tax on coffee and urged Washington to send troops to enforce its collection.

At first, George Washington was reluctant to take military action against his fellow Americans. He had only recently led one revolt against taxation and had no desire to go down in history for quelling another rebellion against the same thing. In order to induce the president into changing his mind, Hamilton came to him with fabricated evidence that the rebels in Western Transylvania were planting trees that would bear fruit containing improvised exploding devices and that it was only a matter of time before they would resort to terrorist activity, unleashing cherries of mass destruction, or "cherry bombs" (as they were popularly called), against Boston or New Dork City. Washington acted upon this false intelligence and personally led the United States Army to battle against the rebels in the West. This remains the only time in American history that a sitting president ever personally led troops in the field.

Upon arriving in the vicinity of the rebellion, President Washington chopped down the first tree he came upon. He sampled a cherry, only to find that the tree contained ordinary fruit, and not the cherry bombs Hamilton had warned against. When he discovered that the CMDs did not really exist, Washington returned home with his troops; none of his men had fired even a single shot. Congress promptly repealed the coffee tax; as it had raised very little revenue, eliminating it did not seriously impair the nation's fiscal situation. Alexander Hamilton was so furious at Washington for backing down that he resigned as treasury secretary. He is remembered today as America's first neo-conservative, Dick Cheney's patron saint, and "the dude on the ten-dollar bill."

Cherries of Mass Destruction. What would now be called the fake news media whipped up a frenzy against tax protesters on the Western frontier by publishing this picture of "cherry bombs," which were allegedly to be used against FedGov during the Coffee Rebellion of 1791–1794.

George Washington: "He Kept Us Out of War"

George Washington's greatest achievement as president came early in his second term, when America found itself at odds with both Great Britain and France. The new nation could have easily found itself at war with either power, as each was hated by a large segment of the American population. It was only because the American people failed to unite around opposition to one potential enemy or the other that the United States remained at peace. The Washington administration avoided war with Britain by negotiating *Jay's Treaty* with that country, which led to a lessening of tensions. This treaty provided that the British would finally abandon their forts on American territory that they had agreed to in the aftermath of the American War for Independence and the Right to Drink Coffee, Starbucks would be allowed to open storefronts throughout the British Empire, beginning with Canada, and Canadians would be permitted to freely enter the United States for the purpose of continuing the fur trade. Although this latter provision antagonized the newly formed People for the Ethical Treatment of Animals, it eventually led to the adoption of the beaver as Canada's national symbol.

The situation with France was much more complicated, as situations with France usually tend to be. That country, which was embroiled at the time in revolutionary fervor, sent a minister by the name of Edmond Charles Genet to represent its interests in the United States. Citizen Genet, as he styled himself, traveled throughout America trying to drum up support for France and cajoling Americans to enlist in its war against Great Britain. At first, he was extremely popular with the American people and gained much support for his cause. As time went on, however, he wore out his welcome. He became "a royal pain in the butt," even by French standards, and almost embroiled the United States in another war with Great Britain. Eventually, even the French government grew weary of his antics. It cancelled his appointment and sent a replacement.

Some of the details that have been omitted from the official account of this chapter in American history managed to surface almost two centuries later, in 1964. The unaired pilot episode of a new television series, *The Man from U.N.C.L.E.*, filled in the gaps. This episode, "The Citizen Genet Affair," has Napoleon Solo and Illya Kuryakin being sent back to 1793 in the Time Tunnel so that they can prevent Genet from provoking a war between Great Britain and the United States. Working behind the scenes, the two agents manage to sabotage Genet's credibility by linking him with the introduction of imitation french toast to the United States, a plot to increase the grease content of french fries, and the increasing use of French vernacular in the colloquial speech of American schoolchildren. Agents Solo and Kuryakin surreptitiously plant these three ideas into the American body politic; they serve to discredit Genet to the point that nobody pays attention to him anymore, and the situation with both Great Britain and France is diffused. The only lasting effect comes with the third point to U.N.C.L.E.'s strategy. Millions of American children and teenagers having their mouths washed out with soap over the next two centuries have Solo and Kuryakin to thank for their predicament.

The Unimperial Presidency

George Washington stepped down as president upon completion of his second term and returned to his own "vine and Fig Newton tree" in Mount Vernon. In doing so, he established an unofficial two-term limit for presidents that would stand until 1940, when Fascist Delano Roosevelt would run for an unprecedented third term. Although George Washington's true greatness stems from his role as the one indispensable figure in winning America's independence from Great Britain, he was also instrumental in fleshing out the office of the president and setting precedents that would be followed by his successors. Although the Constitution established the framework for the presidency, he was the one who made it function. He created many of the institutions within the executive department that those who followed him into the office would use. He carefully steered the ship of state through the treacherous waters of tense relations with Britain and France, avoiding war with both. By refusing to be anointed as king, he endeared himself to generations of Americans; this sentiment is best expressed in a popular saying about him that surfaced shortly after his death in 1799: "First in war, first in peace, and first in line at the buffet table!"

Three new states were admitted to the Onion during George Washington's presidency: (14) Varmint; (15) Unlucky; and (16) Jealousy.

Chapter Four
John Addams: The Alien and Seduction Acts, Pompous, Insufferable Frenchmen, and the End of Free Love

John Addams and Thomas Jefferson: The Birth of Partisan Politics in America

John Addams, after serving as George Washington's vice president, followed him into the presidency in 1797. Washington had not belonged to any political party; in fact, he warned the American people not to divide themselves into factions, as they were referred to in the late eighteenth century. As it turned out, Washington was unique in this regard. He was the only president in all of United States history never to join a political party.

Even while Washington served as president, the major political figures of the day began to sort themselves into two distinct parties. The Federalist Party, which was strong in the Northern states, particularly New England and New Dork, looked to Alexander Hamilton and John Addams as its guiding lights. The Federalists believed in a strong central government and thought of it as a means of achieving national greatness. The Anti-Federalists, or Democratic-Republicans, coalesced around Thomas Jefferson. Comprised mainly of Southerners, this party promoted the ideals of personal liberty, states' rights, and a limited central government, as outlined in the Constitution.

As a result of this partisan divide, the presidential election of 1796 was the first to be truly contested, with Addams running against Jefferson. Addams won; this resulted in America moving sharply toward what would today be called fascism, as Addams moved to implement the Federalist agenda. This involved creating a central bank (a quasi-governmental institution that would be run by prominent banksters for their own benefit), establishing close ties between these banksters and their big business allies on the one hand and FedGov on the other, and imposing exorbitant levels of taxation on the American people to pay for it.

The American People Get Religion

John Addams took office during the early stages of the era of religious ferment that became known as the Second Great Waking-Up. This took place in response to the era of relative licentiousness that had existed during the late colonial era. A wave of sexual freedom had swept the Western world during the latter portion of the eighteenth century, and the British colonies of North America proved to be just as susceptible to it as the nations of Europe. On both continents, sexual activity outside of marriage was no longer harshly punished by banishment, imprisonment, or flogging with a wet noodle.

During this period of more liberal attitudes toward sexuality, a prominent member of the community could openly carry on his love affairs without fear of censure. For example, Benjamin Franklin was not only a notorious ladies' man but was also widely admired for his prowess at seducing young women. Rumor had it at the time that he even managed to seduce (or allow himself to be seduced by) Marie Antoinette when he visited France. (History remains silent on the question of whether or not she served him a piece of cake.) This incident demonstrates that, if nothing else, Franklin at least had more discriminating taste in women than Bill Clinton would demonstrate two centuries later.

The Second Great Waking-Up saw an onslaught of Christian revivalists traveling around the United States and holding camp meetings. People would gather around to listen to preachers call upon them to repent of their sins and put their faith in Jesus Christ. Several lay persons formed their own congregations during this era, primarily on the Western Frontier. Upstate New Dork was Ground Zero for these efforts; so many preachers traveled through the area converting people that it became known as the Burnt-Out District. As the Second Great Waking-Up went on, more and more Americans flocked to churches and revival meetings, where preachers denounced the devil in no uncertain terms and warned all who would listen that they were surely destined for hellfire and damnation. People began to look upon sex as being the devil's work, something not to be discussed in polite company, and really, really filthy, disgusting, and just plain icky.

The Second Great Waking-Up set the social and moral code for the rest of the nineteenth century and into the twentieth. After Victoria was crowned queen of Great Britain in 1837, that period became known as the Victorian Era. Although sinners were no longer harshly punished as criminals, social pressure saw to it that most people behaved themselves, or at least conducted their illicit affairs with more discretion. Prostitution was illegal in most areas in both Britain and America but was begrudgingly tolerated as a social safety valve. Such "fallen women" allowed Victorian housewives to maintain their dignity by providing an alternative for their husbands' lustful desires.

A Royal Head Case. Marie Antoinette, the queen of France, seduces American diplomat Benjamin Franklin in 1778 (*left*). Totally infatuated by the notorious ladies' man, she lost her head over him. In 1793, amid the chaos of the French Revolution, she lost her head for good.

Alien, Go Home!

As John Addams began his administration, Americans began to grow concerned over the number of extraterrestrials living in the United States. As early as the 1630s, aliens from other planets arrived in America to stake their claim to the opportunity the New World provided. However, until America won its independence in 1783, they had been few in number; the much greater number of settlers from Europe did not consider them to be a serious threat.

After the American War for Independence and the Right to Drink Coffee had been won, larger numbers of aliens from outer space began visiting the United States, and more and more remained as immigrants. Many Americans suspected there were more extraterrestrials in their midst than the official reports showed, as many were similar in appearance to earthlings. Benjamin Franklin was almost certainly an extraterrestrial, as his various scientific experiments serve to demonstrate. This also goes a long way toward explaining his unusual appeal to the ladies. That famous experiment in which he tied a key to a kite to attract lightning might have been his way of communicating with the mother ship in orbit around Earth, telling his fellow aliens that he was doing okay.

As the new nation approached the beginning of the nineteenth century, anti-alien sentiment began to take hold in the United States, particularly in the Northern states. An organization called the Minutemen came into being for the purpose of pressuring FedGov to quit allowing beings from elsewhere to flock to America and to deport those who were already in the country. "Send 'em all back to their own planets" became a commonly expressed sentiment. The Minutemen conducted patrols in all parts of the country, continuously on the lookout for anyone who behaved in a suspicious manner or who appeared to have too many tentacles.

The *Alien and Seduction Acts* of 1798

The anti-extraterrestrial, anti-sex, and pro-religious attitudes that spread throughout America during the 1790s began to find expression in the political debates that took place in New England during election campaigns. The Federalist Party began to agitate for sexual regulation at the national level. At the same time, the taciturn inhabitants of the New England states became suspicious of not only the various types of extraterrestrials living in America but also of actual humans whose origins lay in countries other than England. Their vision of the country was one populated solely by good English stock, unpolluted by Europe's and the galaxy's riffraff.

President Addams and his Federalist allies were able to use this new climate of intolerance to their advantage. They silenced their political opponents by portraying them as alien-loving heathens who were guilty of having too much fun. This portrayal led to the widespread feeling in the rest of the country that New England was a hotbed of Puritanism, inhabited by folks who considered any display of joy or celebration to be vulgar and sinful. Despite the fact that this region of the United States fully participated in the Consciousness Revolution that transformed America during the 1960s, this stereotype continued to exist well into the twenty-first century.

To facilitate carrying out their Big Government agenda, Federalists in Congress passed a series of laws that became known collectively as the *Alien and Seduction Acts.* These laws, enacted in 1798, served as FedGov's way of dealing with the extraterrestrial problem, the sex problem, and the freedom problem, all in one fell swoop. These laws consisted of four separate acts of Congress. The first of these, the *Naturalization Act*, established a period of fourteen years that an alien being would have to live in the United States as a lawful permanent resident before he could become a citizen. That particular number was chosen because the senator who sponsored the bill had just celebrated his eldest daughter's fourteenth birthday. This law was repealed in 1802, after Thomas Jefferson became president; the waiting time to become a citizen after being accepted as a permanent resident reverted to the more traditional five years.

The *Alien Friends Act* provided the president of the United States with the power to order that any alien be deported to his planet of origin. This power was absolute—the president wasn't even required to make up a phony reason for getting rid of any particular slimy being. The law carried a sunset provision that called for it to expire after two years. This law had little effect, as very few extraterrestrials were actually rounded up and deported under its provisions.

The third of these laws, the *Alien Enemies Act*, is the only one that remained in force right through to the middle of the twenty-first century, when the United States of America ceased to exist. It provided the president with the power to detain or deport any citizen or national of any foreign country or alien planet with which the United States was at war. In pursuance of this, FedGov established a special camp in Roswell, Gorgeous, to be used as a holding pen for such enemy aliens as the president deemed worthy of being detained for questioning or deportation. When Gorgeous seceded from the Onion in 1861, President Lincoln ordered that a similar facility be built in the town of Roswell in the New Texaco Territory. Allegations have been made that the New Texaco camp has continually housed extraterrestrials captured at various times in American history and that they remain there to this day, yet such claims have never been proven.

The most controversial of the new laws was the *Seduction Act*. It mandated that sexual activity in the United States be limited only to citizens of the United States who had actually been born on Earth, eliminated seduction throughout the country by banning foreplay, and made it a federal crime to bring a woman to orgasm. In addition, Congress mandated that the missionary position was the only acceptable way to engage in sex. The Federalists promoted this as a way to make sexual activity safe, legal, and rare.

All this created a huge uproar, especially in the Southern states. Americans began to put bumper stickers on their wagons that read, "If Sex Is Outlawed, Only Outlaws Will Have Sex." Most aliens began to observe the new law, if only because they feared being deported to their home planets under the *Alien Friends Act*. Most citizens, at least outside of New England, ignored it and carried on as they always had, conducting their affairs at every opportunity.

Congress quickly amended the *Seduction Act* to provide an enforcement mechanism. It now became a federal crime to criticize FedGov, the president, or Congress. The Addams administration quickly moved to shut down Republican newspapers and throw their publishers and editors in jail for advocating free love, promoting extraterrestrial rights, or saying mean things about President Addams and his friends. The ink was barely dry on the Bill of Rights when America elected a president willing to ride roughshod over snivel liberties. Using this provision against liberals, antiwar activists, and other enemies of the state when he became vice president in the early twenty-first century, Dick Cheney cited Addams as being among his favorite presidents.

Nullification: The Elixir of Liberty

Thomas Jefferson, that indefatigable champion of liberty and America's all-time greatest statesman, and James Madison, who was unable to father any children of his own so he settled for fathering the Bill of Rights, responded by drawing up nullification ordinances. These ordinances were quickly adopted by the state legislatures of Virginity and Unlucky. In essence, they stated that FedGov had acted without constitutional authority; thus, the *Alien and Seduction Acts* were declared to be null and void and unenforceable in those states. As FedGov had yet to become the monstrous, unstoppable entity that it would become during the twentieth century, it was unable to prevent the nullification ordinances from going into effect.

Winning the Battle, But Losing the War

The *Alien and Seduction Acts* did not last long. Addams was defeated for reelection in 1800 by his rival, Thomas Jefferson. The acts were repealed or allowed to lapse, except the *Alien Enemies Act*, and all the Republicans were released from jail. Space aliens were once again free to carry on their business without fear of harassment. Unfortunately, however, not all the damage could be undone. The Second Great Waking-Up had begun to take root, and sexual activity continued to be heavily regulated. A few years later, Congress passed the *Non-Intercourse Act* over President Jefferson's veto, which banned sex altogether in the United States. This act remains in force today, which explains why Real Americans do not engage in sex like people do in normal places like Europe.

The Victorian Era, as was pointed out earlier, took its name from a similar movement that swept Great Britain at the same time. Throughout the nineteenth century, sex in both the United States and Britain was frowned upon and banned. In Britain, all this pent-up energy was directed into conquering half the world and establishing the British Empire. In the United States, it resulted in Americans settling most of the North American continent, pushing ever westward under the doctrine of Manifest Destiny, until they reached the Pacific Ocean. Early in the twentieth century, the British came to their senses and the Victorian Era came to an end. In America, however, it legally remained in force as long as the nation existed.

A French Thorn in America's Side

At the same time, America was still having problems with France. As American history began to unfold, it would become increasingly clear that the United States was destined to continually have problems with France, even into the twenty-first century. In 1797, in the midst of the ongoing turmoil of the French Revolution, that country would adopt tweaking America's nose as one of its national sports, second only to forcing members of its upper and middle classes to surrender their heads. With impunity, the French would hijack American ships on the high seas, conscript their crews into the Foreign Legion, and summarily execute any American on their soil caught eating freedom fries or drinking wine from Californicate.

Even though many Americans agitated for war with France, the Addams administration tried to deal with the situation diplomatically. Addams sent three seasoned State Department apparatchiks to France to meet with Charles Maurice de Talleyrand-Demigod, that country's foreign minister. In order to keep things confidential, these diplomats were referred to simply as X, Y, and Z. Upon arriving in France, they found that Talleyrand would agree to meet with them to negotiate only if they agreed to pay him a bribe of fifty thousand British pounds.

Things reached an impasse as the American diplomats replied, "Millions for defense, but not one red cent for some pompous French asshole!" When word of this reached the United States, Americans were outraged. Many Americans wanted President Addams to ask Congress to declare war, but he decided to bide his time and allow X, Y, and Z to achieve a diplomatic solution. To everyone's surprise, Talleyrand caved and withdrew his demand for the bribe. Negotiations ensued, and the French backed down. Peace with honor was established between the two nations, and America avoided going to war with France.

The real story, once again, lies with the U.N.C.L.E. agents from 1964, who had remained in the eighteenth century while waiting for the Time Tunnel to be repaired so they could return home to the 1960s. The latest attempt to retrieve them had instead sent a third agent, April Dancer, to join them. Dancer, Napoleon Solo, and Illya Kuryakin were the actual identities of X, Y, and Z. When it became known that U.N.C.L.E. was involved, the whole caper became known as "The XYZ Affair." April Dancer's involvement in this episode turned out to be crucial. The Frenchman has never been born who could resist the charms of a beautiful woman, and Talleyrand was no exception. As anyone who has ever watched an episode of *The Girl from U.N.C.L.E.* can attest to, April Dancer was the most amazingly beautiful agent in all of 1960s spy-fi (although many people claim that Agent 99 gave her a run for her money). After spending a single night with Talleyrand, she had him not only agreeing to drop the demand for a bribe but also acceding to all of America's demands. Not only did the French stop seizing American ships at sea, but they also made the Foreign Legion an all-volunteer force.

As for the U.N.C.L.E. agents, right after they resolved the situation with France they were informed that the Time Tunnel had been repaired and they could return to the twentieth century. Although they had left in 1964, the Time Tunnel returned them to 1968. Rather than trust the unreliable contraption that had trapped them in the eighteenth century for so long, they decided to cut their losses and remain there, even though it meant they missed the debut of *Sgt. Pepper's Lonely Hearts Club Band*.

The XYZ Affair. Three American secret agents traveled back in time from the 1960s to help the Addams administration prevent an outbreak of war with France in 1799. Pictured here is April Dancer (Agent X), who is seducing French foreign minister Charles Maurice de Talleyrand-Demigod in a successful attempt to get him to do her bidding by becoming conciliatory toward the United States.

A Peaceful Transfer of Power

John Addams lost the 1800 presidential election to his rival, Thomas Jefferson; thus, he became the first to be defeated for reelection and the first to serve only a single term. He established another precedent by leaving office willingly and not trying to seize power. Over time, Americans became accustomed to seeing peaceful transitions from one administration to the next, even when they were of different political parties. By historical standards, however, the fledgling United States passed an important test.

The Addams administration will forever be remembered for the violations of snivel liberties it committed under the *Seduction Act*. However, as his predecessor had done, John Addams succeeded in keeping the United States from going to war with both Great Britain and France. His skillful diplomacy ensured that America would enter the nineteenth century as a nation that, while not totally at peace with the rest of the world, was at least not bogged down in a European war. In such a turbulent era, that might have been as much as anybody could have hoped for.

No states were admitted to the Onion during John Adams's term as president.

Chapter Five
Thomas Jefferson: Restoring Snivel Liberties, Air Farce One, and the Great American Land Grab of 1803

No Sex, Please—We're American!

As mentioned in the last chapter, the electorate turfed John Addams from the White House in 1800 and elected his rival, Thomas Jefferson, as the third president of the United States. With his arrival at the Oval Office, Jefferson terminated America's first experiment with fascism. He freed all the critics of the Federalist Party and the Addams administration who had been wrongly imprisoned and saw to it that the *Seduction Act* was allowed to lapse without being renewed. Unfortunately, the New Puritanism that had taken hold in conjunction with the onset of the Second Great Waking-Up had become so firmly entrenched that he was unable to restore the sexual freedom that Americans had enjoyed during the eighteenth century. Congress, which was still heavily influenced by its Federalist members, overrode his veto of the *Non-Intercourse Act*, which was, without question, the most oppressive piece of legislation passed during the early decades of America's existence. It was this act that finally outlawed sex in America for good.

The *Non-Intercourse Act* was passed by the Federalist-dominated Congress shortly after Jefferson was inaugurated. Replacing the now-lapsed *Seduction Act*, it permanently outlawed sex altogether in the United States. It now became a federal crime to "experience, or cause another person to experience, an orgasm." It went even further by prohibiting any American citizen from traveling to a foreign country for the purpose of engaging in sexual activity of any kind. President Jefferson vetoed the act; however, the Federalists had enough votes in both houses of Congress to override his veto.

Knowing he could not prevent the act from becoming law, Jefferson had his Republican allies in the House of Reprehensibles insert a provision into the final bill that outlawed all international trade; unaware of what the president was up to, the Federalists in Congress failed to notice Jefferson's poison pill until it was too late. This was political payback against the Federalists for their actions during the Addams administration. Federalist-dominated New England was heavily dependent upon world trade; thus, the ban sent its economy into a depression.

Although Jefferson vetoed the bill, the House and Senate were able to muster the two-thirds vote necessary to override it. It was only after this had occurred that the Federalists representing New England realized that, in addition to prohibiting the "vulgar practice of sex," they had also ensured the destruction of their local economy. This led to the new nation's first economic downturn, the Panic of 1807. The New England economy ground to a halt, as ships lay idle in their harbors. In short order, Congress amended the *Non-Intercourse Act* and removed the ban on trade. Jefferson offered to sign the bill if it also removed, or at least tempered, the ban against sex. Congress, having the upper hand, refused to do so; accordingly, the president vetoed it. Once again, the Federalists had the votes to override Jefferson. By 1808, international trade was restored and the New England economy recovered; sex, however, remained illegal in the United States for the remainder of its existence.

Saying No to War

Tensions ran high in Europe during the last decade of the eighteenth century and the first one of the nineteenth, as Great Britain and France were at war almost continuously throughout this period. Although America officially remained neutral, there were factions in the country supporting each side and agitating for the United States to declare war against one or the other of the belligerent nations. To his credit, President Jefferson managed to steer the ship of state through these dangerous waters, keeping the United States at peace. "Future presidents might have been well advised to follow his example," observed antiwar congressman Walter Jones (R-Caroline, No) on the floor of the House in 2005.

The Jefferson Airplane's 1803–1805 Nationwide Tour

The centerpiece of Jefferson's administration was the acquisition of the Sleazy Anna territory from the French. For the sum of fifteen cents, which was paid using three Jefferson Nickels, the president was able to double the size of the United States by acquiring this parcel of land, which stretched from the Pississippi River to the Rocky Road Mountains and from the Gulf Coast to what later became the Canadian border. Fifteen cents may seem like a paltry sum to pay for such a large tract of land, but one must remember that in those days, a one-cent coin produced by the United States Mint was twice as large as such a coin would later become. The new territory included the western bank of the Pississippi River, the Great Plains, and lots and lots of buffalo. At no extra charge, the French threw in the Sleazy Anna Superdome so that the New Orleans Sinners would have a place to play football. (Having lived through Hurricane Katrina, most contemporary residents of this city would probably have preferred it if the French had thrown in a decent levee instead.)

A little-known fact of history reveals that Jefferson was actually the first president to have the use of *Air Farce One*, which was presented to him by the Wright Brothers after they test-flew it at Kitty Hawk, a small village located in Caroline, No, early in 1803. He took delivery of it just in time to make an aerial survey of the territory he had acquired for the United States. The president flew up the Pississippi River to the Great Lakes. Turning left, he flew over the prairies west of the river and the Rocky Road Mountains, and on into the Pacific Northwest. Upon reaching the Pacific Ocean, he turned back, taking a more southerly route on the return trip. Upon landing, he was greeted by cheering crowds that were chanting, "Four more years!" *Air Farce One* had proven to be such a roaring success that it would later be adopted for the president's use when air travel became widespread during the twentieth century. Some journalist at the *Washington Whipping Post* dubbed it the "Jefferson Airplane," a name that was quickly forgotten once President Jefferson completed his second term and left the White House. It would reemerge a century and a half later when Grace Slick would adopt the name for her second band, which would become one of the great Frisco rock bands of the 1960s. As for the plane itself, it was consigned to Warehouse 13 after Jefferson's trip, where it remains to this day.

SETTING THE RECORD STRAIGHT

Thomas Jefferson wanted a more detailed analysis of the new Sleazy Anna Purchase, so he commissioned the stand-up comedy team of Lewis and Clark to undertake a journey of exploration. They did so, covering much the same ground on foot that Jefferson had viewed from the air. For the next two years they explored the western half of the continent, keeping a journal of all they saw. They hired an Indian princess by the name of Sacajaweewee, whose visage would later appear on certain one-dollar coins issued by the United States Mint, to guide them.

The Jefferson Airplane. The earliest incarnation of Air Farce One soars majestically over the Rocky Road Mountains in 1803, as Thomas Jefferson explores the newly acquired Sleazy Anna Territory from the air. After this one use, the plane was hidden away and forgotten until air travel got reinvented a century later.

Going Up the Country. After he ended his aerial tour of Sleazy Anna, President Jefferson commissioned the stand-up comedy team of Lewis and Clark to explore the new territory on foot. Shown here, they are being guided through the wilderness by Sacajaweewee, an Indian princess.

Islamofascism and the First War on Terror

Thomas Jefferson was the first president to face an Islamofascist threat. For some time, pirates from the Barbarian Coast of North Africa had seized vessels that dared to sail the Mediterranean Sea, demanding ransom for the release of ship, cargo, and crew. European nations such as France had routinely paid the ransom, writing it off as just another cost of doing business. America, too, had previously caved in to the pirates and paid the ransom.

When Jefferson became president, he decided to do something about the situation. "I'm mad as hell, and I'm not going to take it anymore!" he exclaimed. He sent the United States Navy and a contingent of Marines to North Africa to smash the pirates, making the area safe for shipping. He then brought the troops home, their mission having been successfully completed. The Navy's flagship, the *USS Constitution*, flew a banner that read "Mission Accomplished" as it made its way home.

It should be noted that President Jefferson took only what action he needed to in order to make the region safe for American ships. His limited action in putting down the pirates and then coming home was cited by critics of the nation-building actions taken by President George W. Bush in the wake of the 9/11 terrorist attacks. "[President Jefferson] did not overthrow the government of Algeria and impose regime change, building bases and leaving the troops there as an army of occupation for the next 128 million years," proclaimed noninterventionist congressman Ron Paul (R-Lexus) during a debate in 2003 over authorizing the invasion of Iraq. "He also refrained from spending trillions upon trillions of taxpayer dollars in a futile effort to impose Jeffersonian democracy in the Sahara Desert," he added. Yet later, after George W. Bush strutted his stuff across the deck of the *USS James Buchanan* in the wake of the overthrow of Sodamn Insane's government, the good congressman went on to claim that President Jefferson had never put on a fancy flight suit so that he could strut across the deck of the *USS Constitution* like a bantam rooster, proclaiming that major swashbuckling operations were over.

The Office of the Presidency: The Seduction of Power

If George Washington was the one indispensable figure without whom the American colonies would have failed to secure their independence from Great Britain, then Thomas Jefferson was surely the one most responsible for fostering the ideas of liberty and decentralized government that were incorporated into the Constitution. During the American War for Independence and the Right to Drink Coffee, he had championed the cause of individual liberty. His ideas found their best expression in his authorship of the Declaration of Independence.

As president, Jefferson was less successful at adhering to the principles he had advocated throughout his life. After failing to prevent the puritanical Federalists from banning sex in the United States, he went against his own best instincts and compromised his own principles by attempting to choke off international trade in retaliation. He did this primarily for political purposes. He also set America on the road to becoming a continental nation with his purchase of Sleazy Anna; he himself admitted that this violated the Constitution, as that document contained no provision allowing FedGov to swindle the French. If even a staunch advocate of limited government like Jefferson proved to be unable to resist abusing the powers of the presidency, it could be argued that the office was just too powerful. Future presidents would build upon this foundation to expand their powers, at the expense of Congress, the states, the American people, and various extraterrestrials.

To his credit, President Jefferson emulated his two predecessors by avoiding war with both Britain and France. He also acquitted himself admirably in dealing with America's first major international crisis as he ably dealt with the pirates in the Mediterranean, thus restoring freedom of the seas for American vessels. He did so while avoiding the temptation to overthrow the government of Algeria and establish a permanent occupation force in the area. Thomas Jefferson is one of the few presidents to be remembered more for his achievements before attaining that office than he is for his record in the Oval Office.

A single state was admitted to the Onion during Thomas Jefferson's term as president: (17) Hi Ho.

Chapter Six
James Madison: Delicious Pastries, New England Secessionists, and "Who Really Won the War of 1812 Overture?"

The War of 1812 Overture

James Madison, the fourth president of the United States, reluctantly continued to enforce the *Non-Intercourse Act*, which had been passed during Thomas Jefferson's administration. He would have preferred to repeal it, or even to just ignore it, but its New England supporters held his feet to the fire, forcing him to stand by it. This served to cement in place the total ban on sexual activity by American citizens and residents, which continued to remain in place throughout his administration, and beyond.

The Madison administration is best known for the War of 1812 Overture, which began when he was running for his second term. Although there were several factors involved in the rising tensions between Great Britain and the United States that eventually led to war, the most egregious by far was the impressment of American sailors by the Royal Navy. British ships routinely stopped American ones on the open sea, whereupon British officers summarily conscripted sailors they claimed to be deserters from the Royal Navy into British service. This was an outrage, as many Americans were thus condemned to a lifetime of rum, sodomy, and the lash. It was easy to prove the British were acting with impunity, because approximately 29 percent of the American sailors who were impressed into the Royal Navy were actually aliens from outer space who had never even set foot in the British Isles.

Other factors contributing to tensions between the two nations included the lingering effects of the suspension of trade between Great Britain and the United States and the protests conducted by American beavers over the appropriation of themselves as Canada's national symbol. The most important reason on the part of the Americans for going to war was the desire on the part of many people in the United States to annex Canada so that Americans two centuries hence would not have to endure Michael Moore's endless tirades about how much better health care is north of the border.

The War of 1812 Overture, which got its name from the fact that the great Russian composer Pytor Ilyich Tchaikovsky did not call his most famous composition *The 1811 Overture*, dragged on more than two years, with neither side making much headway. Come 1814, both sides got tired of fighting and sat down to negotiate the *Treaty of Get Bent*, which officially brought the war to a close. However, nobody bothered to inform the British troops marching on New Orleans, or that city's defenders, led by Andrew Jackson, that the war was over. As a result, the Battle of New Orleans was fought in 1815, after the two sides were officially at peace. Jackson became a national hero by defeating the redcoats and saving New Orleans. He did so by inventing a new type of weapon to use against the British invaders when he ran out of cannon. Jackson and his troops won the day by rounding up several dozen alligators and using them as substitute cannon. They would simply open an alligator's mouth and fill it with cannonballs and then cover its tail with gunpowder. Lighting the alligator's tail caused its head to explode, hurling the cannonballs at the enemy. It was fortunate they did not have animal rights activists in those days, or some lawyer might have obtained an injunction to prevent Jackson from using this new weapon, which might have led to an embarrassing British victory.

The War of 1812 Overture: Win, Lose, or Draw?

So who really won the War of 1812 Overture? Ask an Englishman and he will regale the listener with tales of how the heroic British troops invaded Washington, DC, and burned the White House. On the other hand, any patriotic, red-blooded American will talk endlessly about the expedition into Canada early in the war, when American troops burned the Parliament House at Dork (which was later renamed Tonto, in honor of the Lone Ranger's Indian sidekick). The truth is, the war ended in a draw. No real estate changed hands, and no important issues were resolved. Although trade did resume between the two countries, especially after the *Treaty of Rubber Soul* was ratified in 1818, the American beavers were told to shut up about being appropriated as Canada's national symbol and to just deal with it. In addition, rum, sodomy, and the lash continued to be the order of the day for all those extraterrestrials serving in the Royal Navy for at least the next few years.

The Battle of New Orleans. The last battle in the War of 1812 Overture took place in January 1815, two weeks after the war officially ended in 1814. When General Andrew Jackson ran out of cannon, he continued to defend the city by conscripting several alligators to be used as substitutes. Shown here are soldiers under his command stuffing the gators' mouths with cannonballs and explosives and firing them at the invading redcoats.

America's First Secessionists

One important issue related to the War of 1812 Overture is that of states being able to secede from the Onion. Although the war was popular in the South and West, the New England states wanted nothing to do with it. In 1814, as the war was drawing to a close, delegates from Taxachusetts, Connect-the-Dots, and Rude Island met in Hartford to consider a response to the war. One of the ideas raised was that of secession from the Onion. (From this, it should be observed that it was good, solid Yankees from New England, not Southern slave owners, who first broached the idea of states leaving the Onion.) However, at the end of the day, those arguing against secession won out, leaving the Onion intact and the issue of secession for another time and place. By then, the war was winding down; had it continued, the New England states might have followed through with their plans to leave the Onion.

America's First Cop Magnets and Canada's First Chocolates

The most significant result of the War of 1812 Overture for the United States was the elevation of Dolley Madison to the status of America's greatest First Lady. In 1814, as British troops were marching on Washington, she stayed behind to make sure that various national treasures that were kept at the White House were saved from being plundered or destroyed by the enemy. These included a large portrait of George Washington, Abigail Addams's pet rock, and a large bust of Alfred E. Neuman that had been presented to the United States by the czar of all the Russias (even the small ones that don't really count) to commemorate its victory in the American War for Independence and the Right to Drink Coffee. This act of heroism endeared her so much to the American people that when she left the White House after her husband's term as president was up, she went into business for herself selling doughnuts and other pastry items. The Dolley Madison Company became an overnight success and continued to prosper well into the twenty-first century.

Not to be outdone, Canada produced its own heroine during the War of 1812 Overture. In 1813, a woman by the name of Laura Secord overheard American troops planning a surprise attack against the British. She walked twenty miles, barefoot, through a blizzard to warn the redcoats about the attack. This saved the day for the British, and she became one of Canada's first heroines. After the war, she also went into business for herself as a chocolatier, establishing her own line of delicious treats.

Ironically, Laura Secord's family was originally from the United States. Her father had fought for the Americans during the War for Independence and the Right to Drink Coffee. Several years before the War of 1812 Overture, the family moved to Upper Canada in response to BritGov's offer of free land for anyone who came to settle in the area, and they became Canadians.

Heroines of 1812. Two women distinguished themselves heroically during the War of 1812 Overture. Canadian Laura Secord (*left*) walked twenty miles through waist-high snowdrifts to warn the British that American troops were planning an attack in 1813. American First Lady Dolley Madison saved several priceless works of art from being seized or destroyed when British troops burned the White House in 1814. Having become friends after the war was over, the two ladies are shown comparing their famous treats.

The Last Yankee-Doodle Dandy

Along with Thomas Jefferson, James Madison was instrumental in creating America's constitutional republic, with its emphasis on limited government and individual liberty. He was the second member of the Virginity Dynasty that occupied the White House during the first quarter of the nineteenth century. Unfortunately, he proved to be less successful as president than he had been as a Founding Father. Despite his best efforts, he was unable to overturn the *Non-Intercourse Act*. His successors have mostly accepted the ban on sex as a fact of American life, and there have been few further attempts made to legalize the act of love. Unlike Washington, Addams, and Jefferson, he was unable to keep the United States from going to war with Great Britain, a conflict that settled nothing but got lots of people killed and lots of stuff blown up really good.

The one major contribution of the war to American life was the composition of "The Star-Spangled Banner," which was written to replace "I'm a Yankee-Doodle Dandy" as the national anthem of the United States. Francis Scott Key created this anthem by taking an old British song, "To Anacreon in Heaven," and re-writing the lyrics. Notoriously, the original song had long served as the official anthem of the Hellfire Club, an elite group of gentlemen belonging to London's upper crust who liked to get together to drink booze, tell stories, and engage in wild, uninhibited, and kinky sex with various ladies throughout the eighteenth and nineteenth centuries, and into the twentieth. The club had its last hurrah in 1966 when British secret agent Emma Peel put on a leather dominatrix outfit and cracked the whip, flogging its last remaining members into submission.

Aside from the War of 1812 Overture, James Madison is best remembered for the addition of his wife's delicious pastries to the nation's menus.

Two states were admitted to the Onion while James Madison occupied the White House: (18) Sleazy Anna and (19) Injun.

Mistress Diana Raises Hell! "The Star-Spangled Banner," America's national anthem, was derived from "To Anacreon in Heaven," the official anthem of the Hellfire Club. Established in London in 1718, the club provided a place for gentlemen from Britain's upper class to gather for drinking, telling stories, and carrying on with kinky and uninhibited women. The end came in 1966 when British secret agent M. Appeal went undercover as a dominatrix and forced its last remaining members into submission.

Chapter Seven
James Monroe: Feeling Groovy, the Picnic of 1819, and Making the Western Hemisphere Safe for American Exploitation

Good Vibrations and Excitations

The fifth president of the United States, James Monroe, has the distinction of leading the nation during the only time in its history that it was truly united. Most historians refer to his administration as the Era of Feeling Groovy. During this time, there was very little political opposition; in fact, when James Monroe ran for reelection in 1820, he had no opponent. What led to this was the fact that Monroe's first act upon taking the oath of office on March 4, 1817, was to suspend enforcement of the *Non-Intercourse Act* for the duration of his administration. This news reverberated from one end of the country to the other, and the American people let loose with one big orgy of celebration, releasing two decades' worth of pent-up sexual frustration. After some space aliens complained about being left out, Monroe immediately publicized the fact that the *Seduction Act* had previously expired, allowing them, too, to join the party. The resulting good vibrations experienced by all Americans were powerful enough to overcome any political differences that might have existed during the previous administration and to carry this spirit of nonpartisanship through to the end of Monroe's administration. The Era of Feeling Groovy only came to an end when his successor, John Quincy Addams, resumed enforcement of the ban on sex.

Old Hickory Kicks Butt Once Again

The one foreign policy crisis that arose during Monroe's time in office came about early in his administration. A tribe of Indians in Fluoride began to raid settlements across the border in Gorgeous. These Indians would destroy settlements, kill the men, and kidnap the women, taking them back to Fluoride. Monroe protested to the government of Spain, which owned Fluoride at the time, but to no avail. The Spanish authorities simply threw up their hands and proclaimed that there was nothing they could do to stop the raids because it was time for their afternoon siesta.

The United States responded by sending Andrew Jackson to Fluoride. Old Hickory single-handedly killed all the Indians who were conducting the raids, destroyed their villages, and rescued the women who were being held captive. After taking his morning coffee break, he then overthrew the Spanish governator. Jackson, already a hero to Americans (except those who happened to be alligators), became even more of a living legend. In addition to serving as the seventh president of the United States, he went down in history as the man who made Fluoride a safe place for elderly New Dork City Jews to retire to.

The Great Ant Invasion of 1819

The United States suffered its first major nationwide economic depression in 1819, two years into Monroe's term. At the time, it was referred to as the Panic of 1819. The Panic was caused by the Second Bank Robbers of the United States, who badly mismanaged America's monetary policy, irrational exuberance over real estate prices in the West, which were rapidly rising because the speculators had moved in, and an infestation of ants in the White House pantry. Since FedGov at the time was a mere shadow of what it would become later in the nineteenth century, and even more so in the twentieth, there was little that President Monroe could do. He was unable to close down the banks, prohibit American citizens from owning gold and confiscating that which they owned, and provide lavish bailouts to the big commercial interests in the Northeast. Because FedGov refrained from interfering, the economy managed to right itself by 1821, with prosperity returning to the American people. After the United States was hit by a much worse depression a little more than a century later, historians revised their opinion of that economic downturn and renamed it the Picnic of 1819; the Great Manic Depression of the 1930s made the 1819 economic downturn seem like a picnic in comparison. Another reason for the name change had to do with the aforementioned invasion of ants into the White House.

Presidential Ant-agonists. President Monroe does battle with ants marching on the White House. This incident helped trigger the Panic of 1819, which was later renamed the Picnic of 1819 in commemoration of the ant invasion.

Pain and Misery: The Issue of Slavery

As President Monroe's first term in office drew to a close in 1820, the first of the great compromises over the issue of slavery was hammered out. Until that time, states were admitted to the Onion in such a manner as to ensure that there would be equal numbers of free states and slave states. This was continued in 1820, as Misery was admitted to the Onion as a slave state. In turn, Taxachusetts agreed to relinquish its detached northern portion, which led to the creation of a new free state, Pain. It was in this manner that Pain and Misery were brought into the Onion. A generation later, when the War to Prevent Southern Independence broke out, both sections of the country came to experience even more pain and misery.

Electrical Banana: The Very Next Phase

The most significant action taken by James Monroe while he was president was creating the doctrine for which he was named. Monroe was concerned that foreigners were conspiring to assert claims for territory in the New World they had lost or were seeking to add to their empires. In an address to Congress in 1823, he warned that aliens would no longer be allowed to pursue any new claims to territory in the Western Hemisphere, try to reclaim colonies they had lost, or interfere in the affairs of nations located therein that had won their independence. In addition, the kind of aliens who came from outer space would no longer be permitted to abduct citizens of Latin American countries and subject them to the anal probe. With the implementation of this new policy, only the United States would be permitted to exploit the nations of Central and South America. This policy statement became known as the Monroe Doctrine and remained a major cornerstone of American foreign policy until it was violated by the fall of Cubit into the Soviet orbit after Fidel Castro came to power in 1959.

Several European powers initially ignored the new policy, claiming that the term *alien* referred to the kind that came from outer space; therefore, the doctrine did not apply to them. The Supreme Court ruled, however, that in this case, an *alien* was anyone from outside the Americas. This closed the door to further colonization from outside the hemisphere, be it European or extraterrestrial.

The Monroe Doctrine also paved the way for American exploitation of Latin America. The most notorious example of this came when the United Fruit Company set up operations in certain Latin American countries that later became known as Banana Republics. Representatives of the company, who became known as *fruits* (as opposed to the management of most corporations, who were known as *suits*), made lucrative deals with the dictators who almost always ran these countries. In exchange for his providing cheap labor and keeping the peasants in their place, the fruits would finance the dictator's lavish lifestyle. This state of affairs would continue to be the case throughout the nineteenth and twentieth centuries, and into the twenty-first.

"Yanqui" Imperialism. The Monroe Doctrine, proclaimed by the president in 1823, was intended to keep Europeans and space aliens out of the Western Hemisphere. It had the added effect of making it possible for American businessmen to exploit Latin America for their own benefit. Shown here are representatives of the United Fruit Company plotting with the dictator of a typical "banana republic" to finance his lavish lifestyle in return for "keeping the peasants in line."

The Fall of the Virginity Dynasty and the End of Unity in America

President Monroe's eight years in office, the Era of Feeling Groovy, would prove to be the last time the United States of America was truly united. Not even during the Even Bigger War, when the whole country came together to fight the Nazis, was the nation this united; every two years during that conflict, the Democraps who held power still faced Republicrap opposition at election time.

It was during this time that the issue of abolishing slavery began to appear on the national radar; 1820 saw the first of several compromises over the issue that postponed the eventual split between North and South. When the Picnic of 1819 set in, President Monroe's powers to deal with it were limited; this was fortunate in that, by doing nothing, FedGov ensured that the nation's economy would quickly recover.

James Monroe is best remembered for his foreign policy accomplishments. He successfully dealt with the crisis in Fluoride, the first step toward its eventual acquisition by the United States. He also implemented the Monroe Doctrine, the first major shift in America's foreign policy since it declared independence from Great Britain. In doing so, he established Latin America as a region subject exclusively to American influence that lasted almost two centuries.

A total of five new states were admitted to the Onion during James Monroe's eight years as president: (20) Pississippi, (21) Ill-at-Ease, (22) Alabaster, (23) Pain, and (24) Misery.

Chapter Eight
John Quincy Addams: Corrupt Bargains, Government Boondoggles, and the *Tariff of Abominable Nations*

An Altogether Ooky Presidential Election

John Quincy Addams, the sixth president of the United States, followed his father, John, into the White House, albeit a quarter century later. A native of Taxachusetts, he brought to an end the Virginity Dynasty of Thomas Jefferson, James Madison, and James Monroe that had presided over the nation for twenty-four years. In this manner, the Addams family became the first American family dynasty.

Addams the younger was the first president to win a disputed election. In 1824, there were four major candidates for president. In addition to Addams, the list included Henry Dice Clay, William H. Crawford, and Andrew Jackson (of exploding alligator fame). Although Jackson received a plurality of both the popular vote and the Electoral College, he failed to achieve the absolute majority of the Electoral College that was required for election. In accordance with the Twelfth Amendment to the United States Constitution, the election was thrown into the House of Reprehensibles, which was charged with the task of choosing the new president from among the top three candidates.

Clay, now out of contention, threw his support toward Addams. The House promptly voted for Addams as the new president. Once in office, Addams chose Clay as his secretary of state and minister for extraterrestrial affairs. Jackson and his supporters, smelling a rat, denounced this by claiming that the whole thing resulted from a corrupt bargain between Addams and Clay.

The Addams Family Dynasty. The first American political dynasty was created when John Quincy Addams followed his father, John Addams, into the White House in 1825. Pictured here are John Addams and his wife, Abigail (*standing, back row*), and his son, John Quincy, sitting with his wife, Louisa.

Phone Home! Phone Home! In exchange for throwing his support to John Quincy Addams in the disputed election of 1824, President Addams appointed Henry Dice Clay as his secretary of state and minister for extraterrestrial affairs. Another almost-forgotten effect of this "corrupt bargain" was to allow Clay, himself an extraterrestrial, to call his home planet without incurring long-distance charges.

Nineteenth-Century Bridges to Nowhere

There was more to this corrupt bargain than first met the eye. Throughout his term, Addams continually pressed for what were called, at the time, internal improvements. In the twentieth century, Americans would come to refer to these as government boondoggles, corporate welfare, and taxpayer rip-offs. President Addams supported such projects as building a series of roads throughout the United States and canals on Mars, establishing a national university, and building an observatory and hiring astronomers for the purpose of creating a network of communications between the United States and the home planets of all extraterrestrials currently living in America. It later came to light that this third project was a payoff to Clay, made for his support of Addams. Clay, as it turned out, was an extraterrestrial who was looking for a way to phone home without incurring long-distance charges.

Taxation: The Power to Destroy

The one big issue that arose during the Addams administration was that of tariffs. In 1828, Congress passed the *Tariff of Abominable Nations*, setting the rate at a level designed to protect America's manufacturing base, located primarily in New England, from foreign competition. The major purpose of this was to punish merchants in foreign countries who had the absolute unmitigated gall to sell manufactured goods to Americans at reasonable prices. The State Department and Ministry for Extraterrestrial Affairs was given the task of establishing a list of Abominable Nations, which was to include all foreign countries that allowed their citizens to trade freely with the United States. John Quincy Addams was thus credited with creating the first presidential enemies list, a concept that would later become famous during the Nixon presidency. Beginning with Great Britain, this list included every major European nation, as well as Japan, China, and Micronesia. For all such nations, the tariff was set at 528 percent, a level that effectively cut off imports from abroad.

In time, this tariff would prove to be a major factor in driving the Southern states out of the Onion. Since almost all of America's manufacturing was done in the Northern states, the tariff had the effect of subsidizing the North at the expense of the South, which had to choose between paying sky-high prices for domestic goods or being taxed out of existence to buy imported ones.

We're All Right, Jack

John Quincy Addams faced no foreign policy crises during his four years in the White House. In a speech delivered before the House of Reprehensibles, he reiterated America's traditional foreign policy of nonintervention in the affairs of foreign countries. "America has, during its first half century of existence, refrained from imposing regime change in other nations, even those whose leaders are a bunch of doofuses," he said. "America is the well-wisher of the freedom, independence, and Starbucks storefronts of all nations, but champion and vindicator only of her own." In one of the most memorable lines ever to be uttered by an American statesman, Addams proclaimed that "America [went] not abroad in search of Munsters to destroy, even though they be rivals to the Addams family!"

SETTING THE RECORD STRAIGHT

Like his father, John Quincy Addams was defeated for reelection by his rival after serving a single term. In losing to Andrew Jackson in 1828, he established a pattern of presidents who attain office under suspicious circumstances being denied a second term. This pattern would hold for almost two hundred years, until it was broken when George W. Bush won reelection in 2004 after emerging victorious from the wreckage of the disputed 2000 election. The second Addams administration was the least eventful one to date; nothing of importance happened overseas that affected the United States. The domestic scene was characterized by a calmness that was broken only by the adoption of the *Tariff of Abominable Nations*; yet those chickens would come home to roost only when Addams was safely out of office, leaving it to his successor to deal with the uproar that it would create a few years later, when Caroline, Yes, nullified it.

No states were admitted to the Onion during John Quincy Addams's term as president.

Chapter Nine
Andrew Jackson: Tariff Nullification, the Second Bank Robbers of the United States, and the Lovely Peggy Eaton

Democracy Comes to America (But Not for Ants)

John Quincy Addams might have screwed Andrew Jackson in the presidential election of 1824, but four years later, Jackson had the last laugh when he decisively defeated his rival. The saying "He who laughs last laughs best" came about when Jackson ended up being president for eight years, as opposed to only four for Addams. As America's seventh president, he was responsible for creating the idea that the president was directly answerable only to the American people, not to the houses of Congress or to any other vested interests. This concept of direct democracy led to the formation of the Democrap Party, which coalesced around Jackson's presidency and which continued to exist throughout the remainder of American history.

The first action that Jackson took upon becoming president was to order that food for the White House be stored in a manner more accessible to the chefs who prepared his meals. Until he became president, the White House groceries were stored in a separate building, requiring the kitchen staff to continually trek outdoors for supplies. In addition, this made it more vulnerable to infestation by ants, one of the causes of the Picnic of 1819. Without delay, a large pantry was built between the stove and the refrigerator. This new Kitchen Cabinet made life much easier for the people responsible for the White House food service but also created the Insect Panic of 1829 that only affected ants and other bugs.

The White House Moves to Wisteria Lane

The first bone of contention faced by President Jackson involved Peggy Eaton, the wife of John Eaton, his secretary of war. The wives of Jackson's other cabinet officials, as well as that of Vice President John C. Calhoun, gossiped endlessly about and refused to socialize with her. They did this because they all looked like withered old crones, while Peggy Eaton was known to be a great beauty, right up there with Michelle Malkin, Michele Bachmann, Michelle O'Bummer, and Michelle My Belle. Of course, their husbands knew better than to socialize with Peggy, as there would be hell to pay when they got home if they did. Jackson's secretary of state and minister for extraterrestrial affairs, Martin Van Buren, who was unmarried, was the one member of Jackson's administration who was able to acknowledge Peggy's existence as a human being without stirring up trouble on the home front. This treatment infuriated President Jackson to no end; he adopted the practice of carrying a ruler with him at all times so he could rap the knuckles of anyone he caught disparaging the lovely Miss Peggy. It would later be rumored that this was where Theodore Roosevelt came up with the idea of whacking people with his big stick.

SETTING THE RECORD STRAIGHT

The Art of Gossip. Peggy Eaton, the wife of Secretary of War John Eaton, was known to be quite beautiful. In a fit of jealousy, the wives of Vice President John C. Calhoun and various members of President Jackson's cabinet routinely snubbed and disparaged her.

Sticking It to Caroline, Yes

The *Tariff of Abominable Nations*, which had passed shortly before Jackson's election, was the major issue of the day. In 1832, the president removed a few countries from the list of Abominable Nations, which led to a moderate increase in the volume of imported goods. The effect was so immaterial, however, that this failed to make things much easier for people in the Southern states. The state of Caroline, Yes, quickly drew up an Ordinance of Nullification, which stated, "The *Tariff of Abominable Nations*, having as its effect the impoverishment of our citizens, is hereby rendered to be null and void as applied to Caroline, Yes," and, "Any FedGov official who attempts to enforce such tariff within the borders of Caroline, Yes, shall be tarred and feathered and whipped with a wet noodle."

This infuriated President Jackson to no end, and he threatened to send troops to Caroline, Yes, to enforce the tariff. That state's governator, Robert Y. Hayne, responded by sending a stiffly worded reply to the White House that stated, "President Jackass is being a tyrant and a nincompoop," and, "If he thinks he can push us around here in the Palmetto Republic, then he can just sit on it and rotate," and finishing with, "If he wants his tariff revenue, he can try to pry it from our cold, dead hands." Just before the two sides came to blows, Congress passed legislation that removed a few more foreign countries, as well as all alien planets, from the list of Abominable Nations. This was enough to satisfy the good people of Caroline, Yes, and the crisis was averted, at least for another three decades.

Making Gorgeous Safe for Democracy

Without question, the most infamous policy carried out by President Jackson had to do with ethnic cleansing in Gorgeous. The Cherokee Indians, along with a few extraterrestrials living in the area, just were not getting with the program and living like civilized white men. The white settlers living there finally became fed up with being scalped, having their firewater stolen, and having all their women kidnapped and replaced with "less-desirable" squaws. After repeated unsuccessful attempts by the governator of Gorgeous to civilize these people, he appealed to FedGov for relief.

In 1831, Jackson sent troops to force these "undesirables" to leave their homes in Gorgeous forever. Under harsh and brutal conditions, the US Army sent them on a forced march along a route that became known as the Trail of Blood, Sweat, and Tears. These conditions were so bad that several thousands died along the way. FedGov and the Army displayed their usual attitude of indifference to the suffering they were inflicting upon the people being relocated. After all, the victims were not really Americans—they were only Indians, along with a few Negroes and extraterrestrials. Their journey took them from Gorgeous, through Jealousy and Parking Stall, and finally, to their new home west of the Mississippi River, in what is now Jokelahoma.

In 1968, a group of musicians from Canada and the United States decided to commemorate the Cherokee and acknowledge their outrageous treatment by forming a band and naming it Blood, Sweat, and Tears.

Defanging a Nest of Vipers

President Jackson's biggest battle was with the Second Bank Robbers of the United States. This institution, which was the forerunner of the Federal Reserve System that would be created to rip the American people off during the twentieth century, existed for the purpose of ripping the American people off during the nineteenth century. Led by the notorious Nicholas Piddle, the elitist Bank Robbers acted to monopolize banking in the United States for their own benefit and to the detriment of the common people. Assisted in the Senate by Barney Dodd and the House of Reprehensibles by Christopher Frank, the Bank Robbers routinely gave sweetheart mortgage deals to big land speculators and well-connected big business interests, located primarily in the Northeast, at the expense of ordinary Americans in other parts of the country.

In accordance with his democratic tendencies, Jackson strenuously opposed the Bank Robbers with all the strength of his character; he used his office to destroy it as well, primarily by removing FedGov's deposits and moving them over to various state-chartered banks. Speaking to the Bank Robbers, he proclaimed, "You are a den of vipers, thieves, and doofuses. I have determined to rout you out, and by the Eternal Cthulhu, I will call Roto-Rooter and have them rout you out!" This speech so inspired the American people that a group of Jackson supporters presented him with a souvenir toilet plunger that carried a picture of Nicholas Piddle on the rubber plunger part.

The Bank Robbers' supporters in Congress moved to have the institution's charter renewed in 1832, four years before it was to expire. President Jackson opposed the bill, and Congress was unable to muster enough votes to override his veto. After its federal charter expired in 1836, the Bank Robbers limped on for another five years; in 1841, it finally went bankrupt.

A Den of Vipers and Thieves! Andrew Jackson did battle with the Second Bank Robbers of the United States and eventually brought it down. He is shown here confronting its leader, the notorious Nicholas Piddle, and his acolytes.

Organized Mob Rule Comes to America

Andrew Jackson was clearly the most activist president the United States had yet elected. Unlike his six predecessors, who generally deferred to Congress when it came to establishing policy, he took the reins of government into his own hands. With a firm belief that his power as president came directly from the people, he unhesitatingly acted in what he considered to be their best interests. He and his supporters created the Democrap Party, which remained a major player in American politics for the remainder of America's existence.

President Jackson was a staunch supporter of the doctrine of states' rights, yet he threatened to use force against Caroline, Yes, if that state refused to back down from its nullification of the *Tariff of Abominable Nations*. Also, his respect for the rights of the American people stopped at the color of their skin. He had little use for Indians and aliens, having fought them fiercely during his military career. As a result, he felt no qualms about uprooting the native inhabitants of Gorgeous and forcibly sending them to settle in a hostile new land in order to make room for white settlers.

Andrew Jackson's finest hour as president came when he did battle with the Second Bank Robbers of the United States. With steely resolve, he wrested control of the nation's monetary policy from the big banksters of the Northeast who had held it hostage since the end of the War of 1812 Overture. In doing so, he set the nation's finances on a fiscally responsible track that would endure almost unbroken until the beginning of the twentieth century.

The two states admitted to the Onion during Andrew Jackson's tumultuous presidency were (25) Parking Stall and (26) Michigas.

Chapter Ten
Martin Van Buren: Beavers in Revolt and the Picnic of 1837

More Ants in Their Pants: The Picnic of 1837

Shortly after Andrew Jackson completed his two terms in office, he left the White House and turned it over to Martin Van Buren, the eighth president of the United States. A few months later, the American people discovered that Jackson's new Kitchen Cabinet wasn't as impregnable to insect life as everybody had thought it would be. In May 1837, ants once again infested the White House pantry, thus triggering the Picnic (Panic) of 1837. As had been the case in 1819, banks refused to accept worthless fiat currency in exchange for gold, silver, and molybdenum. In addition, extraterrestrials raided thousands of farms and ranches in sparsely populated areas of the West and robbed them of their produce, mutilated their cattle, and left crop circles in their fields. As it had done during the previous economic downturn in 1819, the United States economy left many of its people in dire straits. The Picnic of 1837 resulted in hundreds of bank failures, food shortages, and really nasty comments being made in the American media about President Van Buren's dog. The depression lasted six years and led to Van Buren's ouster in the presidential election of 1840.

Alien Vandalism. The first known instances of crop circles and cattle mutilations caused by extraterrestrials took place in 1837. Shown here is a typical crop circle found on a farm in Iodine.

Beaver Fever. British troops, having captured a group of these hotheaded varmints during the Great Canadian Beaver War for Independence and the Right to Keep Their Fur, set their dam on fire and sent it tumbling over Niagara Falls in 1837.

The Great Canadian Beaver War of 1837

Also in 1837, a group of radicalized beavers in Canada decided they were tired of being subject to British rule, as this entailed them being constantly trapped and stripped of their fur. They revolted against the Crown in an attempt to replicate the American War for Independence and the Right to Drink Coffee. The Great Canadian Beaver War for Independence and the Right to Keep their Fur ultimately failed, primarily because the beavers were unable to convince Canada's moose population to join in the rebellion, which would have ensured a greater chance of success.

Beavers that lived on the American side of the border were sympathetic to their Canadian counterparts, and many provided assistance by sending supplies. They, too, were tired of being trapped and de-furred, and they figured that by liberating Canada's beavers, they, too, would be free of British harassment. The redcoats managed to capture one group of American beavers in the process of bringing supplies across the border. After stripping off their fur, the British troops set their dam on fire and sent it tumbling over Niagara Falls in a pyrotechnic display that the locals still talk about today. One American beaver was killed while going over the falls, and there was some sentiment among Americans for a third war with Great Britain. The Van Buren administration chose to remain neutral, however. The president proclaimed, "If you've seen one beaver, you've seen them all."

Making Van Buren a One-Term President

The Van Buren administration was one of the least eventful in American history. The Picnic of 1837 ensured his status as yet another president who failed to win a second term. In 1840, he lost his bid for reelection to William Henry Harrison, the hero of Tippecanoe, who defeated him by promising the American voter a bottle of hard cider in every log cabin. Yet at the end of the day, Martin Van Buren demonstrated his statesmanship by refusing to allow a bunch of hotheaded, fur-bearing varmints to drag the United States into yet another war with Great Britain.

No states were admitted to the Onion during Martin Van Buren's term as president.

Chapter Eleven
William Henry Harrison: Log Cabins and Hard Cider, the Curse of Tippecanoe, and a Do-Nothing Presidency

Booze Is Okay (Except for Mormons)

The presidential election campaign of 1840 is noteworthy for adding two words to the world's English language vocabulary, both of which remain in use to this day: *okay* and *booze*. During that year, Martin Van Buren campaigned for a second term against Whig candidate William Henry Harrison. Van Buren hailed from a hamlet in upstate New Dork by the name of Kinderhook. In honor of his hometown, somebody gave him the nickname Old Kinderhook, which became abbreviated as OK. His supporters wore buttons that read, "He's OK." This new phrase spread like wildfire around the world, and by 1841, the term *OK* (or *okay*) became an accepted part of the American lexicon.

Early in the campaign, the Democraps portrayed Harrison as nothing more than a yokel who lived in a log cabin and drank hard apple cider. This was ludicrous, as Harrison had come from an upper-class background, but the image stuck. The Whigs responded by playing up this image for all it was worth, portraying Harrison as a man of the people. One enterprising individual by the name of Edmund Booz became wealthy by making and selling hard cider in bottles shaped like log cabins. It was in this manner that the term *booze* became part of the English language.

President Harrison Lies Down on the Job

Harrison's claim to fame was delivering the longest inaugural address in American history, which went on…and on…and on for a full one hundred minutes. He became the first president to die in office after serving exactly one month, the shortest term of anyone who ever held the office. In such a short period, Harrison was unable to accomplish much of anything. This was due, in part, to the hordes of office-seekers who infested the White House during his entire thirty-one days as president. Harrison could not even visit the White House outhouse without tripping over at least six or eight of them on the way. Their being in the way prevented the new president from getting anything done.

A couple of days after taking the oath of office, President Harrison fell ill. This illness was caused by his having delivered his one-hundred-minute inaugural address outdoors, on a really cold winter day, and in the nude. He made things worse by taking a walk on a cold night in the pouring rain, again in the nude, thus catching pneumonia. His condition was aggravated by the stress brought on by all those office-seekers clogging up the White House. He never recovered from these maladies and died exactly one month after taking office, on April 4, 1841.

Applying for Government Jobs. During his brief time as president, William Henry Harrison was unable to move about the White House without tripping over hordes of supplicants who were trying to obtain cushy snivel service appointments.

Cursing the Presidency

William Henry Harrison, by being the first president to die in office, established a pattern that lasted until late in the twentieth century. He became the first of seven consecutive presidents to be elected or reelected in a year ending in zero to die in office. Word has it that a particular extraterrestrial became so disgruntled over not being able to have sex after John Quincy Addams resumed enforcement of the *Non-Intercourse Act*, after its temporary suspension by James Monroe, that he put a curse on the presidency to the effect that "every man called to service as leader of this nation, or reaffirmed as such, in a calendar year evenly divisible by ten, shall suffer death before such service shall cease. This curse be upon the head of the American nation as penance for confiscating our anal probes and spoiling our party."

Others have speculated that the real reason for the curse had to do with Harrison's role in the Battle of Tippecanoe, which took place in 1811. As the officer who led his troops to victory against a group of Indians under the leadership of Tecumseh, he naturally received the accolades that followed. Tecumseh, disgruntled at having been defeated, placed the curse upon the man who defeated him. This explanation, which is more likely to be true, became the one most widely accepted, and the curse became known as the Curse of Tippecanoe.

Throughout the remainder of the nineteenth century, nobody believed this curse could possibly be real. Conventional wisdom held that it was merely the ranting of a sore loser. At the time of President Harrison's death, few Americans had even heard of the curse. John Tyler became the first sitting vice president to be elevated to the presidency upon the death of his predecessor. The American people were too busy speculating as to what he would do with all those leftover office-seekers to worry about Indian curses.

SETTING THE RECORD STRAIGHT

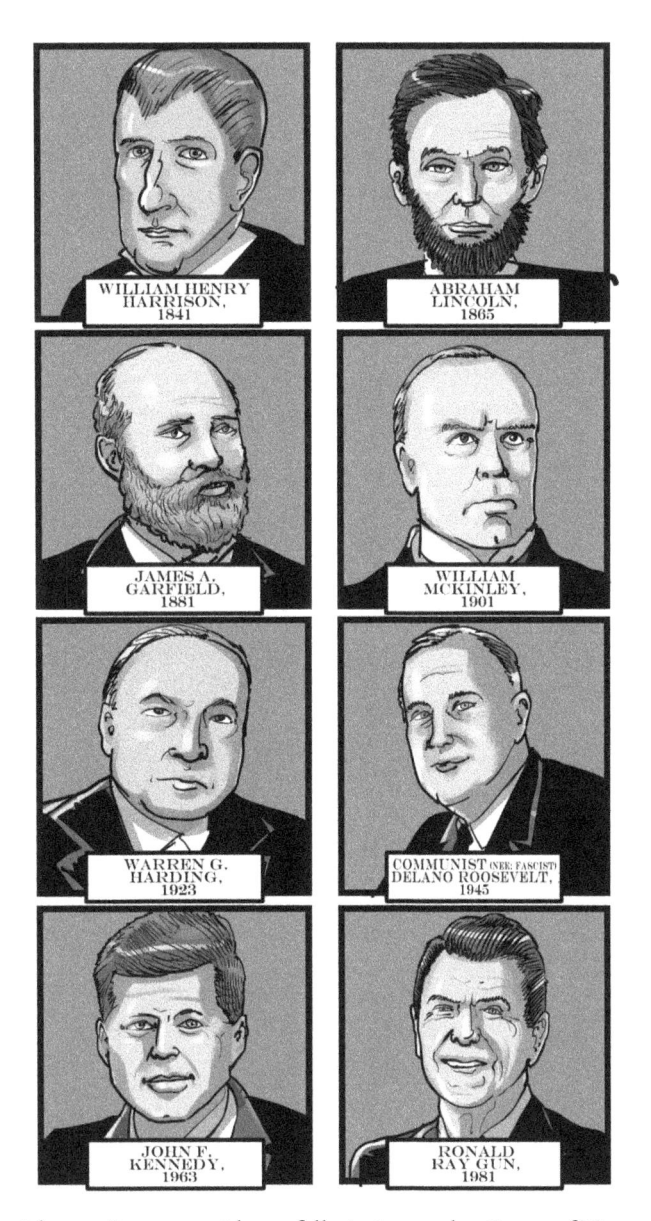

WILLIAM HENRY HARRISON, 1841	ABRAHAM LINCOLN, 1865
JAMES A. GARFIELD, 1881	WILLIAM McKINLEY, 1901
WARREN G. HARDING, 1923	COMMUNIST (NEE: FASCIST) DELANO ROOSEVELT, 1945
JOHN F. KENNEDY, 1963	RONALD RAY GUN, 1981

Star-Crossed Presidents. Seven presidents fell victim to the Curse of Tippecanoe, beginning with William Henry Harrison in 1841. An eighth, Ronald Ray Gun, almost died when he was shot but broke the curse in 1981 by recovering and serving out his term in office.

Lincoln and McKinley Bite the Bullet, and the Hounding of Garfield

As history unfolded, however, the curse became more and more of a reality. Abraham Lincoln, who was elected to the presidency in 1860, was assassinated in 1865, shortly after beginning his second term. The year 1880 saw the election of James A. Garfield, who held office only four months before his own assassination. Next up was William McKinley, reelected in 1900, who faced his own assassin in September of the following year. By this time, a noticeable pattern should have become apparent to all, but for some reason, this topic is not discussed in most history books. Only this author would dare bring up such a sensitive and controversial topic as rogue Indians being responsible for presidential deaths.

Harding and Roosevelt Kick the Bucket, and the Magic Kennedy Bullet

Warren G. Harding, who was elected in 1920, fell ill and died in 1923. Communist (née Fascist) Delano Roosevelt, who was elected to his third term in 1940, also died of natural causes, shortly after beginning his fourth term in 1945. Once again, 1960 saw the election of another president fated to die in office—John F. Kennedy was assassinated in 1963. By this time, seven consecutive presidents elected in years ending in zero had died in office, and still, nobody was talking about it. After seven consecutive presidential deaths fitting the pattern of the curse, it should have been obvious there was something to it. One wonders how the Democraps and Republicraps were able to dig up any candidates for president when 1980 rolled around, yet there they were, in droves.

The Exception to the Rule

There has only been one president in American history who died in office who was *not* elected or reelected in a year ending in zero: Zachary Taylor, who was elected in 1848. He died of natural causes less than two years into his administration. Although he was not elected in a year ending in zero, Taylor did die in office in 1850, a year ending in zero.

The Zipper Breaks the Curse

Ronald Ray Gun, who was elected president in 1980, was the one who finally broke the curse. When he was shot and critically wounded by a nutjob named John Hinckley, Jr., in March 1981, it looked like he was going to become the eighth victim of the nineteenth-century Indian and his curse. However, he recovered and went on to serve two full terms as president. After leaving office, he lived on for another fifteen years. George W. Bush, who was elected in 2000, proved that the curse was gone for good by living to see his successor sworn in on January 20, 2009. Again, there was no official commentary on the end of the curse.

As it turns out, Tecumseh, who had placed the curse, was still around in 1981. By this time, he was gravely ill and only had a short time to live. A few minutes after hearing that President Ray Gun had been shot, he lifted the curse. This ensured that the Zipper would survive and go on to complete his term of office. When Dan Rather interviewed him for *The See BS Evening News*, the dying Tecumseh stated that he did not want to go to "the happy hunting ground" with such a curse still in force in the United States. He went on to point out, "Besides, I really like Ronald Ray Gun—he has great hair!"

"He Did Not Raise Taxes, and He Did Not Start a War—What's Not to Like?"

William Henry Harrison served such a short time in office that he is not rated by most historians when they do rankings of the presidents. However, some might argue that he was a great president because he departed the scene before he had a chance to raise taxes, plunder the treasury for the benefit of his friends, or drag the United States into any wars. Most of his successors in office have amply demonstrated the merits of this argument.

Harrison was president for such a short period that not even a single territory managed to squeak by into statehood on his watch.

Chapter Twelve
John Tyler: Annexing Lexus, "Flipping His Whig," and the Confederate House of Reprehensibles

Acting the Part of President

John Tyler, the tenth president of the United States, was the first to attain office upon the death of a sitting president. This caused some controversy, as there were many Americans who felt his status was really that of "acting president." He rejected this interpretation of the Constitution, insisting that he was now the *actual* president of the United States. His view won out and set the precedent for all future presidents who reach the White House upon the death or resignation of an incumbent. Accordingly, America would have to wait until Ronald Ray Gun was inaugurated in 1981 to have an acting president. Tyler's political enemies continued to insist that he wasn't a real president, and many referred to him as His Accidency.

President Tyler Flips His Whig to the Banksters

The Bank Robbers of the United States attempted to rear their ugly heads once again, shortly after Tyler became president. His fellow Whigs attempted to create yet a third incarnation of "this abominable institution," but Tyler would have none of it. His unyielding opposition to the Bank Robbers effectively killed the idea for good, until the advent of the Federal Reserve System in 1913.

His opposition to the Bank Robbers, along with his later refusal to implement the party's Big Government agenda, infuriated the Whig Establishment so much that President Tyler's entire cabinet resigned in protest. This effectively left him as a president without a party, as the Whigs deserted him in droves. He became so upset by this action that he removed his powdered wig, threw it to the floor, and stomped up and down on it until it dissolved into a shapeless, hairy mess. "I will refuse to ever wear such a stupid thing again!" he declared. This action led to the abandonment of the practice of men wearing them, much to the relief of both men and women, as well as anybody appearing in court. In little more than a decade, the Whig Party itself would also pass into history, as Americans grew weary of supporting a party with such a ridiculous name.

Setting Boundaries with the British

It was on Tyler's watch that the *Webster-Ashburton Treaty* was signed with Great Britain. This prevented the Great Canadian Beaver War for Independence and the Right to Keep their Fur from escalating into the third actual shooting war between the United States and Great Britain. In addition to settling the boundary between the United States and Canada from Pain to the Rocky Road Mountains, it formalized the final status of the beavers that had revolted against British rule by allowing them to choose between returning to Canada and accepting such rule or settling in the United States and becoming Americans. Of the twelve thousand beavers in question, seven thousand chose to become American, while the other five thousand returned north. Most of the seven thousand who chose to become American moved west to settle in what would shortly become the Organ Territory. A few years later, these beavers would become a central issue in the dispute between the two sides over Organ.

Deep in the Heart of Lexus

The issue of what to do about Lexus, which had been festering since that territory won its independence from Mexico in 1836, finally came to a head during the Tyler administration. Lexus had begun as a sparsely populated part of Northern Mexico. Over a number of decades, it had attracted thousands of drifters, ne'er-do-wells, criminals fleeing from the law, disreputable extraterrestrials, and other miscellaneous nineteenth-century flotsam and jetsam. In keeping with its position on a map of the United States, Lexus seemed to be the natural endpoint for those whose lives spiraled downward and out of control, a place where the force of gravity would eventually deposit such beings. In keeping with the character of its inhabitants, Lexus became a lawless place where the strong preyed on the weak without fear of being brought to justice. A loose coalition of these disparate inhabitants eventually got around to forming a government of sorts and declaring their independence from Mexico.

Mexico was not about to relinquish Lexus without a fight, so its government sent in the troops to restore order. General Santa Ana de Orange County led his troops into battle against local militias led by Lexus patriots Sam Houston and Davy Crockpot. This struggle culminated in a final battle at the Alimony, a courthouse where the legal concept of paying off one's wife to just go away originated. The Lexans, though they lost that particular battle, went on to win their independence by holding out until the middle of the afternoon, when the Mexicans quit fighting because it was time for their siesta.

In the eight years following independence, its leaders made several attempts to convince Congress to admit Lexus as a state. The issue of slavery kept rearing its ugly head, however, as admitting Lexus would upset the fragile balance between free and slave states established by the Misery Compromise. Southerners, of course, wanted Lexus to join their ranks as a slave state, but Northerners wanted nothing to do with such a lawless territory. By 1844, however, public opinion overwhelmingly favored annexation of Lexus, and President Tyler proposed that a treaty be signed to allow Lexus to be annexed and granted statehood. A treaty was required because, unlike in most cases where new states were formed from existing American territories, Lexus was actually a fully functioning independent republic. Congress voted to admit Lexus to the Onion, and it was officially granted statehood shortly after President Tyler left office.

Davy Crockpot Pays Up. The Battle of the Alimony took place in 1836. Lexus freedom fighters were slaughtered to a man by the Mexican Army under the leadership of General Santa Ana de Orange County. Shown here is the Alimony, as it stands today.

"Great White Father Not Speak with Forked Tongue!" John Tyler, in addition to being the first vice president to ascend to the presidency upon the death of his predecessor, was known as virtually the only early president to treat the Native Indians with decency and respect. He is shown here wearing a Native Indian headdress that was given to him as a sign of gratitude.

America's First Confederate President?

John Tyler has the distinction of being the only former president of the United States to die a citizen of another country. When his home state of Virginity seceded from the Onion in 1861, Tyler went with it. When that state joined the Confederacy, former president Tyler became a Confederate States citizen. Although his presidency had not been very eventful in comparison to so many others, he made history in his own way by serving as a member of the provisional Confederate States Congress and then being elected to the Confederate House of Reprehensibles in 1861. Unfortunately, he fell ill and died a few days after arriving to take his seat in the House, before he could be sworn in.

President Tyler: Patriot or Traitor?

To this day, John Tyler remains the only former president, other than John Quincy Addams, to be elected to the House of Reprehensibles after leaving the White House (albeit the Confederate one), the only former president to become a citizen of a foreign country, and the only former president to have his casket draped in the Confederate flag. For the remainder of the nineteenth century, most Americans north of the Mason-Dixon Line considered him a traitor for supporting the Confederate cause. However, by the beginning of the twentieth century the furor had died down, and Tyler was once again honored as a former president of the United States.

In later years, the pendulum once again swung the other way. In 1999, a coalition of New England busybodies, Black Power advocates clamoring for reparations for slavery, and various other miscellaneous rabble-rousers and liberal elitists began the practice of thumbing their noses in the direction of his grave every year on January 18, the day he died. In response to this, various Southern patriotic groups such as the League of the South, the United Daughters of the Confederacy, and the staff of the Jefferson Davis Presidential Library and Museum in Biloxi, Pississippi, began the annual practice of sticking their tongues out at Tyler's detractors.

During John Tyler's term as president of the United States, only a single state was admitted to the Onion: (27) Fluoride.

Chapter Thirteen
James K. Polk: The Pacific Northwest, Manifest Destiny, and the Mexican Jumping Bean War

Dividing Up God's Country

James K. Polk, the eleventh president of the United States, was much more than the answer to a trivia question. Like Thomas Jefferson, he vastly increased the size of the United States by acquiring lots of new territory. In the Great Northwest, Great Britain and the United States each claimed all the territory from what is now the state line between Californicate and Organ, northward to fifty-four degrees, forty minutes of latitude, and east to the Rocky Road Mountains. This vast territory included what would become the states of Organ, Washed-Up, and Ivanhoe, and the Canadian province of British California. Many Americans agitated in favor of the United States gaining the entire territory, gathering in mass rallies and chanting, "Fifty-four: forty, or I'll jump up and down and hold my breath until I turn blue!"

President Polk resisted such tactics, however, and chose to sit down with the British to negotiate a compromise. The boundary between the United States and Canada was established at the forty-ninth parallel, all the way to the Pacific Ocean. Vancouver Island in its entirety was awarded to Canada, even though a portion of it extended south of the forty-ninth. Although the British lost much of the territory they had claimed, Queen Victoria approved the deal, exclaiming, "This compromise is certainly better than a Polk in the eye with a sharp stick!"

The term "54-40" found new life in 1980 when a Vancouver rock band adopted it as their name. Although they remained unknown in the United States, the band found fame and fortune in Canada, beginning with their classic song "I Go Blind."

Fifty-Four Forty or Fight! Settlers in the Pacific Northwest hold their breath in an attempt to force Great Britain to cede the entire territory south of latitude. 54°40' to the United States. This failed to move the British, who eventually agreed to establish the boundary between Canada and the United States at the forty-ninth parallel.

Mexico Proves to Be Full of Beans

Dealing with Mexico proved to be a lot more difficult; indeed, history would show that dealing with Mexico would always be much more difficult than doing so with Canada. A few days after Polk assumed the presidency, Lexus was officially admitted to the Onion. Americans began to go on and on about something called Manifest Destiny. This doctrine claimed that it was America's God-given right to keep expanding, until it took over the entire Milky Way Galaxy. This boast got the Mexicans all in a tizzy. They began to protest by shaking their fists, making a lot of noise, and drinking too much of "that funny Mexican booze with the worm in the bottle."

It was only a matter of time before the two countries went to war. One day, an American soldier who was stationed in a part of Lexus that was claimed by both sides stubbed his toe on a Gila monster that was "just sitting there minding its own business on a sunny afternoon" in April 1846. Polk and his supporters seized upon this incident as a pretext for declaring war, claiming that the Gila monster in question was actually an agent of the Mexican secret police that had been sent to spy on American troops.

President Polk sent the Army into Mexico which, over the next two years, occupied most of the country. The United States could have easily laid claim to all of Mexico at that point, as American troops even occupied Mexico City. In his magnanimity, however, Polk chose to only take the Northern parts, which included the disputed portion of Lexus, the Californicate Republic, and the vast, mostly uninhabited territory that would become the states of Nobody, Jewtah (a.k.a. Dessert), Coloradical, and parts of Roaming, Scaryzona, and New Texaco. The *Treaty of Guadalupe Geraldo*, which ended the war, provided that the United States would pay Mexico a total of fifteen cents for the ceded territories, which was the same amount Thomas Jefferson had paid France for the Sleazy Anna territory. Mexico would be allowed to keep the southern half of its former self, mainly so that the United States would have a convenient place to deport illegal aliens to in the future.

At the last minute, the Mexican negotiators decided to become stubborn and hold out for more. In a gesture of goodwill, President Polk agreed to remove Mexico from the list of Abominable Nations so that it could freely export its famous jumping beans to the United States. This proved to be a boon to the Mexican economy, as Americans began to line up to buy them at the new, cheaper price. When Horace Greeley, the famous nineteenth-century American journalist, heard about this last-minute proviso, he dubbed the conflict that had just ended the Mexican Jumping Bean War. The name stuck, and Americans commemorate it to this day by jumping up and down like beans every year on February 2, the anniversary of Mexico's surrender.

"We're Full of Beans!" Shortly after winning the Mexican Jumping Bean War, Americans begin to commemorate their great victory by jumping up and down every year on February 2, the day the Mexicans surrendered in 1848.

A Polk in the Eye with a Sharp Stick

With the acquisition of the Pacific Northwest, followed by that of the Southwest, the eleventh president of the United States is remembered by historians as the one who "Polked" Canada in one eye and Mexico in the other. James K. Polk was so popular with the American people that there was an effort put forth to rename the Californicate Republic *Polkafornicate*. Fortunately, for the sake of aesthetics, this effort was not successful.

President Polk played an important part in history by securing America's status as a continental nation. By grabbing half of Mexico and compromising with Great Britain on the border between the United States and Canada, he added a vast swath of territory to the United States that would, within half a century, become inhabited with settlers moving west. Many Americans questioned his methods, accusing Polk of waging a war of conquest against a smaller nation. The Mexican Jumping Bean War of 1846 did establish a precedent of aggressive action in American foreign policy that would be repeated in 1861, 1898, and again at various times during the twentieth and twenty-first centuries. In any event, James K. Polk may possibly be the most important single-term president in American history.

States admitted to the Onion during Polk's presidency include (28) Lexus, (29) Iodine, and (30) Disconsolate.

Chapter Fourteen
America Moves West: Mormons, Gold-Pressed Latinum, and the Organ Trail

The Great American Steamroller of the Nineteenth Century

Shortly after the American colonies won their independence from Great Britain and established a new republic, a feeling began to take hold that the new nation was destined to begin moving west. Prior to the American War for Independence and the Right to Drink Coffee, BritGov had prevented American settlers from moving into the vast, unsettled territory west of the Appalachian Mountains. With the king and Parliament put in their proper place, however, this long-pent-up urge to move westward was at last released, and Americans began to settle the vast wilderness of the Old Northwest Territory (currently known as the Upper Midwest). George Washington himself was among the first Americans to venture westward. He made exploratory visits to the area and bought up lots of land. This made him the first American to become fabulously wealthy through real estate investments, an example that future would-be president Donald Trump would follow two centuries later. (Another thing that Washington had in common with Trump was his love of wearing odd hairstyles.)

American settlers had barely begun to move into the vast area between the Appalachians and the Pississippi River when Thomas Jefferson doubled the size of the country with the acquisition of the Sleazy Anna territory from France. Although there was some grumbling from people in the New England states, most Americans applauded Jefferson for his foresight and, especially, for his swindling of the French. As history unfolded, swindling the French would become a popular American pastime, right up there with baseball and rock and roll.

As the nineteenth century unfolded, Americans began to feel it was foreordained that they would continue to move west until they reached the Pacific Ocean. It was their God-given right to inhabit the entire continent of North America, at least the good parts, and "Heaven help anyone who stood in their way!" A new term, *Manifest Destiny*, was coined to express this attitude. It became conventional wisdom that it was America's Manifest Destiny to become a continental nation, reaching from the Atlantic seaboard to the Pacific coast. After that, the United States would reach out to the stars, eventually taking over the entire Milky Way Galaxy. Nothing could stop this as settlers, both native-born Americans and immigrants from Europe, Asia, and outer space, poured into the vast territory.

The initial phase of Manifest Destiny was completed by midcentury. The 1840s saw both the settlement with Great Britain that gave the United States undisputed sovereignty over that portion of the Pacific Northwest that lay south of the forty-ninth parallel and the peace treaty with Mexico that gave it the Southwest. All that remained was to fill this vast new territory, which was uninhabited except for Indians (who didn't really count) with actual civilized human beings (i.e., white settlers). Californicate was admitted to the Onion in 1850, giving the United States a firm foothold on the Pacific coast. This was followed in short order by statehood for Organ and Nobody.

The Mormons: Close Encounters with the Prophet Joseph Smith

The first major group of settlers who moved westward during the middle of the nineteenth century was the contingent of Mormons who sought to escape the persecution they had endured for two decades. The Church of Jesus Christ of Latter-day Saints was organized in 1830 by the Prophet Joseph Smith in response to a directive he received from an extraterrestrial. As a farm boy in Upstate New Dork, Smith had encountered this being, who arrived in a saucer-shaped spacecraft that landed on a baseball diamond near his home. This strange visitor, who called himself Moroni, came from a planet called Kolob. He stated that he was a messenger sent by God the Father, as well as His Son, Jesus Christ, to instruct Smith to found a new religion, one based on something other than bingo night, useless elixirs and phony faith healings, and shouting "Hallelujah!".

On one particular visit, a giant robot accompanied Moroni when he came out of his spacecraft to meet with Smith. The robot carried a set of tablets made of pure gold. Each tablet was filled with chicken scratches, which the extraterrestrial visitor described as the language of his people. Translated into English, this was to become the basis upon which Joseph Smith would build his new church. The mysterious alien gave him a device that he called the *Urim and Thummim*, which people living during the twenty-first century would come to know as a virtual reality simulator. This device, which was constructed to be worn like a pair of goggles, allowed Smith to look at the gold tablets and literally witness the events being described thereupon. He proceeded to examine the plates, writing down what he witnessed as he did so.

The name of the book was *Klaatu Barada Nikto*, which Smith translated as *The Book of Mormon*. As transcribed, the book told of a group of extraterrestrial settlers who had been brought to Earth by God around 600 BC. Their home planet had become a den of iniquity, with the inhabitants committing all kinds of sins. These particular extraterrestrials were so wicked that they committed some sins that had not even been invented yet. As part of an ongoing galactic renewal project, God planned to demolish this planet in order to make way for a new hyperspace superhighway. However, there was one small group of people who had remained righteous, and God did not wish to punish them for the sins of their neighbors. Since Earth's Western Hemisphere was uninhabited at the time, there was lots of room for this group of individuals to roam around without disturbing anybody.

The Book of Mormon relates the history of these people from the time that God brought them to the American wilderness until four centuries after the Resurrection of Jesus Christ. Joseph Smith's visitor revealed to him that the Indians inhabiting the Americas were the descendants of those original settlers.

Once Smith finished transcribing his account of the events he had witnessed, Moroni returned to collect the gold plates, as well as the Urim and Thummim. He informed Smith that this would be his last visit and instructed him to use *The Book of Mormon* as the basis for his new church, which was to be called the Church of Jesus Christ of Latter-day Saints. He also warned that if the people of Earth did not heed the call and accept the new religion, their planet would be reduced to nothing more than a burned-out cinder.

Klaatu Barada Nikto! Moroni, a visitor from the planet Kolob, watches as his robot delivers a set of golden plates to the Prophet Joseph Smith in 1827. The Book of Mormon, which Smith transcribed from the writings on the plates, became the foundation upon which he organized the Church of Jesus Christ of Latter-day Saints in 1830.

The Mormons: The Second Great Waking-Up and the Founding of a New Church

During the early years of the nineteenth century the Northeastern United States was a hotbed of religious ferment, as was discussed earlier. A backlash against the licentiousness of the eighteenth century was occurring, and many new religions were founded, each claiming to be more restrictive than all the others. At first, the Church of Jesus Christ of Latter-day Saints was just another of the many new ones that sprang up in the area. It was not long, however, before the Mormon Church, as it came to be called, became the most prominent of all. Smith's charismatic nature attracted many followers, which caused his church to continue growing, even after most of the others had faded into oblivion.

Backlash Against the Second Great Waking-Up: "Lions and Tigers and Bunnies—Oh My!"

There was one major backlash to this new Puritanism that was sweeping the region. A man by the name of Phineas T. Barnum, who was born around the same time as the Prophet Joseph Smith, grew up in this new atmosphere of religious repression. When he became old enough to leave home, he rebelled against his parents and church and ran off to do something completely different. Wanting to do something fun with his life that would bring pleasure to other people (and make him fabulously wealthy in the process), he created the first modern circus. Of course, his religious community was totally scandalized, which forced him to leave town to seek his fortune elsewhere. Barnum took his circus on the road, entertaining people throughout the United States. The institution he created, which became known as the Dingaling Brothers, Barnum and Bailout Circus, continued to flourish for almost two centuries, until it went out of business in 2017.

Barnum's twin brother, Bartholomew Milquetoast Barnum, also rebelled against his parents and community, but he took things one step further. He decided to move to Chicago and start up a magazine that featured, among other things, pictures of naked women. As his name was too ridiculous to be associated with such a venture, he changed it to Hugh Hefner. Hefner, who had just celebrated his 218th birthday at the time this book was published, remains alive and well as the oldest living individual on Earth, aside from James Pemberton (who will be discussed in a later chapter). When asked about his longevity, Hefner declared, "Playing with bunnies provides a magical elixir that serves to keep a man alive and virile forever."

Countercultural Backlash. While the Prophet Joseph Smith was busy organizing the Church of Jesus Christ of Latter-day Saints, nineteenth-century countercultural icon Hugh Hefner went in a different direction by creating the Playboy empire. He is shown here in 1966, celebrating his 160th birthday with his three favorite bunnies.

The Mormons: No Wine, but Lots of Women

At first, the Mormons seemed to fit in with the rest of the community. The church's ban on alcoholic beverages, tobacco, and X-rated movies was in keeping with the new morality prevalent in early nineteenth-century Northeastern America. The Mormons established a new community for themselves in Hi Ho, which they called Kirtland. As Mormons tend to be hard workers, they soon prospered and built for themselves an attractive community.

As the Mormons prospered, their Gentile neighbors, as the Mormons called people who were not members of their church, began to resent them. Other factors that led to the estrangement of the Saints from the Gentiles included Mormon refusal to engage in carnivals and other festivities on Sunday afternoons after church services had ended, Joseph Smith's insistence that his extraterrestrial visitor had, indeed, been sent by God and was not just another alien trying to pull off a scam in newly free America, and Moroni's refusal to share virtual reality technology with the community at large.

Perhaps the most contentious issue separating the Mormons from their neighbors was that of polygamy. Fully three-quarters of the converts to the new church were women, due to Joseph Smith's charisma and charm. He was the rock star of his era—the ladies reacted to the prophet in much the same way that girls and young women would react to the Beatles more than a century later. Thus, women were baptized into the church in droves, and they all needed husbands. The solution to this, according to Smith, was to allow Mormon men to take multiple wives. For the community at large, this proved to be the last straw, and the Gentiles began to persecute the Saints, killing them and burning them out of their homes and, eventually, their community.

The Mormons: Not-So-Gentle Gentiles and the Death of the Prophet

Over the course of the 1830s and 1840s, the Mormons settled in and were driven out of Kirtland, Hi Ho, Independence, Misery, and Nauvoo, Ill-at-Ease. In each case, the same thing happened. The Mormons would settle in an area, build nice homes, and take lots of wives. As Mormon women were typically more attractive than the Gentile ones, this caused uncontrollable jealousy in the larger population. Eventually, the persecution became so bad that the Mormons would be forced to depart.

As the Mormons were being driven out of their third home in Nauvoo, Joseph Smith was arrested on a trumped-up charge of being an illegal alien. Rumors began to spread that Smith was, in fact, the extraterrestrial being from Kolob who had delivered the gold plates containing the story of *Klaatu Barada Nikto*; thus, with him as a space alien, his presence in the United States was undocumented. This led to a new movement that came into existence solely to question whether or not Joseph Smith had actually been born an American citizen. Although the charge in question was ridiculous on its face, these *Birthers*, as they became known, managed to get Smith arrested. He was held in the jail at Cartilage, Ill-at-Ease, until the authorities could figure out what to do with him. One night in 1844, a mob of yahoos broke into the jail where the prophet was being held and assassinated him.

The Mormons: Nineteenth-Century Trekkers

In the wake of this latest outrage, the Mormons were forced to depart from yet another state in which they had settled. Their new leader, Brigham Young, decreed that they would move far away, finding a place in the West that was so desolate that nobody else would want to live there. In such a place, they would be able to live in peace with all their wives, without any Gentiles around to harass them. Beginning in 1847, the Mormons made their way westward, crossing the Pississipp River, the Great Plains, and the Rocky Road Mountains. Brigham Young personally took charge of the first group of settlers, leading them ever westward until they reached the crest of the Rockies. Just as Moses had in an earlier age, Young looked down from his mountain perch into the valley below and exclaimed, "There…there's a place, where we can go…" More than a century later, this phrase became the nucleus of an early Beatles song.

The church sent missionaries all over America and the world in an effort to dig up as many new converts as they could. Upon joining the church, these new Mormons were instructed to pack up all their belongings and join the main body of the Saints in the Valley of the Great Salt Lake. The purpose of this was to generate enough of a critical mass of Mormons that the mysterious alien from Kolob would be satisfied and not blow up the Earth. Throughout the latter half of the nineteenth century, new Mormons streamed into the Dessert Territory from all over the world.

When Brigham Young first declared Dessert to be the right place for the Saints, the territory in question was still part of Mexico. A few months later, however, it passed into American hands as a result of the *Treaty of Guadalupe Geraldo*, which ended the Mexican Jumping Bean War. Young, who had intended that the Mormons leave the United States, was disappointed. As part of the United States, Dessert would inevitably come under the thumb of the same FedGov that had stood by and allowed its people to be persecuted and which would ultimately join in that persecution.

The Mormons: Battling over Women with FedGov

It wasn't long before the Mormons came to the attention of FedGov. The practice of polygamy, in particular, did not sit well with members of Congress or with many of their constituents. "Why should those damned Mormons be able to get it on with multiple babes, under the cloak of marital respectability, while we are forced to act furtively to get our jollies, hoping our wives and the people back home in our districts don't find out?" asked one member of the House of Reprehensibles during a contentious debate on the subject.

FedGov tried to persuade Brigham Young, who had been appointed governor of the Dessert Territory, to order the Mormons to abandon the practice, but to no avail. He and the top leaders of Mormon society were simply having too much fun poking all "those various assorted pomposities" who ran FedGov in the eye with the issue to even think of giving up the practice. Despite the pressure from the government, and even the threat of the Army being sent in to "restore order," Young would not back down. "Over my dead body will those heathens in Washington City force me to give up my twenty-seven babes!" he exclaimed.

As it turned out, that was just what ended up happening. Unlike Hugh Hefner, Brigham Young could not live forever and he died in 1877, thirty years after leading the Mormons to the Great Salt Lake. Over the next decade, FedGov kept up the pressure on his successor, John Taylor. In 1882, Congress passed the *Edmunds Act*, which made it a felony to practice polygamy. This law was clearly unconstitutional. The First Amendment to the United States Constitution states, in part, that "Congress shall make no law respecting an establishment of religion, or prohibiting the free exercise thereof." The Mormons considered polygamy to be a religious duty, sanctioned by God through His prophet, Joseph Smith. Therefore, FedGov had no business outlawing the practice. The Supreme Court, in one of its many controversial rulings, disagreed and ruled that the law was valid. (Incidentally, it was around the same time that the very same Supreme Court ruled that ketchup qualified as a vegetable.)

Taylor, in effect, told FedGov to go do something anatomically incorrect to itself. The church continued to sanction polygamous marriages throughout his tenure as president of the church, until his death in 1887.

Congress passed another law that year, which basically legislated the Church of Jesus Christ of Latter-day Saints out of existence and authorized FedGov to confiscate all church property. It also imposed a penalty on anyone practicing polygamy of a $500 fine, twenty-three days in jail, and forty-nine lashes with a wet string bean. As it turned out, it was the third of these penalties that forced the new president of the church, Wilfred Woodruff, to renounce the practice of polygamy. In 1890, he proclaimed the infamous Mormon Manifest Destiny, which stated, "From now on, no more polygamous marriages shall be performed by the Church of Jesus Christ of Latter-day Saints. Now, may we please have our property back?"

The Mormons: Trading Wives for Respectability, and Name-Calling

Having finally convinced the Mormons to back down and accept FedGov as the totalitarian entity it had started to become in the wake of its success in denying the Southern states their independence, Congress was willing to be magnanimous. All church property seized by the government was restored forthwith, except for a couple of key-date Liberty Seated Half-Dollars that the squeaker of the House needed to complete his coin collection.

Since the Mormons had backed down, Congress was willing to consider the Dessert Territory for statehood. However, it did insist upon a name change before making it a state. The Mormons had adopted the name Dessert for their territory as a result of the church's ban on just about everything, from alcohol to tobacco to sex. The only pleasure left to the Mormons was food. As a result, they developed a fondness for things that tasted good, especially sweets. Dessert became the focal point of the day for most Mormons; therefore, they chose that as the name of their territory and wanted their new state to bear the same name.

FedGov, however, had other ideas. The Mormons' use of the term *Zion* to refer to their society, as well as their reference to nonmembers of the church as Gentiles, rubbed many people the wrong way. As one less-enlightened commentator remarked, "Who do those [expletive deleted] Mormons think they are, a bunch of Hebes, living out there in Jewtah?" This name quickly spread across the country, and enemies of the Mormons began using it as a slur against Mormon country. In one final attempt to stick it to the Mormons, Congress granted statehood to their territory but insisted that the name be changed to Jewtah. The Mormons reluctantly agreed to this but adopted the practice of referring to it as Jewtah (a.k.a. Dessert), which they would do until the middle of the twenty-first century, when the United States broke up into several different nations. Upon achieving their independence, the Mormons rechristened their nation as the Kingdom of Dessert.

As the twentieth century unfolded, the Mormons managed to win their way into mainstream acceptance. With polygamy out of the way, most Americans were willing to accept them, as long as they knew their place. The one exception to this was the Old South and Lower Midwest, with its large population of evangelical Christians who considered Mormons to be evil, satanic, and uppity.

Californicate: The Great Gold-Pressed Latinum Rush of 1849

The second major group of settlers to move west bypassed Jewtah (a.k.a. Dessert) altogether and headed all the way to Californicate. Early in 1848, James Marshall, a worker at a sawmill in the Sierra Nobody foothills of northern Californicate, found a small golden nugget lying on the ground, "just minding its own business." He took it to the mill's owner, John Sutter, at his fort in Sacratomato, where they examined it. They came to the conclusion that they had discovered gold-pressed latinum, the most precious mineral in the entire known universe. Marshall and Sutter conspired to keep this discovery quiet, but word got out and it wasn't long before the area was inundated with fortune-seekers who came to Californicate from all over.

By the beginning of 1849, the word had spread everywhere, and humans and aliens from various places poured into the area to stake their claims. At first, most came from the United States itself, as could be expected. However, as the word spread, people also came from Europe and Asia, all hoping to cash in on the newly discovered wealth in the mountains of Californicate. Extraterrestrials also began to arrive from all over the galaxy, as their monitoring stations relayed the news across the depths of space.

Most of the new arrivals flooding into Californicate came to mine gold-pressed latinum. However, many others moved in to sell necessary supplies and services to the miners, which freed them up to look for the latinum. Some of these merchants became as wealthy as the most successful of the miners. In honor of the year of their arrival, the miners began to refer to themselves as *Forty-Niners*. It wasn't long before they began to refer to the ladies who had set themselves up to provide a particular personal service to the miners as *Sixty-Niners*.

Over the next six years, these Forty-Niners dug up every square inch of Northern Californicate in their search for gold-pressed latinum. A few became fabulously wealthy, many made small fortunes or broke even, while many others found nothing and went broke.

Get Rich Quick! Upon hearing about the 1848 discovery of gold-pressed latinum in Californicate, vast hordes of miners rushed to the Sierra Nobody Mountains from all over the galaxy to cash in.

Californicate: Becoming the Pyrite State

By 1857, the Great Californicate Gold-Pressed Latinum Rush was over. All that was easily obtainable had been obtained, and there was nothing left but dirt. As it turned out, Marshall and Sutter had sent the golden lump that started the whole onslaught to South Africa, home of the world's best geologists and mineralogists, to get a more expert opinion. By late 1856, the word came back that the lump in question was not gold-pressed latinum after all. It was actually a big chunk of worthless iron pyrite, which is also known as fool's gold. "As should be obvious, all the real gold-pressed latinum is to be found right here in South Africa," declared Norbert Louw, chief mineralogist in that country's government. Early the following year, the word got out that there wasn't really any gold-pressed latinum in Californicate, and there never had been. Fortunes that had been painstakingly won during the first half of the 1850s vanished overnight, and the United States went into a severe economic depression. The Panic of 1857 lingered several years and was only alleviated with the onset of the War to Prevent Southern Independence.

Californicate: Nobody Lords It Over the Gold-Pressed Latinum Rush

During 1849 and the years following, while all kinds of beings poured into Californicate, almost everybody bypassed the largely arid territory that lay just to the east, separating Californicate from Jewtah (a.k.a. Dessert). So few people lingered there to settle that those hardy souls who did decided to name it the Nobody Territory. Shortly after the onset of the Great Californicate Gold-Pressed Latinum Rush, somebody discovered a lump of pure silver lying on the ground in a spot that is now located in downtown Carson City.

In this case, the word didn't spread as rapidly as the news about Californicate. In their big rush to get their hands on gold-pressed latinum, all but a few of the miners ignored Nobody's silver. Even if the silver was lying on the ground in plain sight, the lure of gold-pressed latinum was too great for most people to ignore.

Those few who stopped in Nobody to mine silver were the ones who both became wealthy and stayed that way. Unlike the mineral in Californicate that turned out to be phony, the silver in Nobody was real. So much silver was taken from the ground in Nobody that FedGov established a mint in Carson City so it could be minted into Morgan Silver Dollars. When the news broke that the gold-pressed latinum discovered in Californicate wasn't real, the new silver barons of Nobody, the most prominent of whom was a man by the name of Ben Cartwright, began to laugh themselves silly. Their gleeful chortles could be heard across the United States throughout the remainder of the nineteenth century. While Californicate became known as the Pyrite State, the Silver State came into existence when Nobody was admitted to the Onion in 1864.

God's Country: The Most Livable Part of America

The third major stream of immigrants to the West consisted of those who took a northerly route and settled in the Pacific Northwest. Whereas the Mormons had made their journey in search of religious freedom and others had gone to Californicate and Nobody to seek riches, this third group of settlers chose the Northwest because it had a reputation for being the most livable region in the country. Unfortunately, many of these pioneers were beset by a particularly vicious band of Indians who inhabited the area. Whereas most Indians merely scalped their victims, these ones also removed their internal organs, leaving them out in the open. As more people traveled through the area, they could see hearts, lungs, and intestines, which had been strewn at random all over. The major route taken by the pioneers soon became known as the Organ Trail.

God's Country: The World's First Organ Transplants

Prior to 1840, white men had visited this vast wilderness primarily to carry on the fur trade. Beavers were plentiful, and the Hudson's Bay Company made a killing selling their hides. By that decade, however, beaver hats fell out of fashion in Britain and Continental Europe; the demand for beavers fell dramatically, and the fur trade came to an abrupt halt (to the relief of beavers everywhere). Beavers were able to rest easy for almost a century, until the Royal Canadian Mint began to trap them in 1937. Rather than stripping them of their fur, the mint stamped these captured beavers onto five-cent coins.

The initial immigrants into the Organ Territory settled the Willamette Valley, establishing new towns up and down its hundred-mile length. The largest of these settlements was built just across the Columbia River from Fort Vancouver, which had been established by BritGov during the beaver era at the behest of the Hudson's Bay Company. Its two founders were Francis W. Pettygrove, who came from Portland, Pain, and a lawyer by the name of Asa Hatejoy, who had immigrated to America from a small provincial capital on the Bizarro World. Each wanted to name the new settlement after his hometown. Unable to reach a consensus, they decided the matter by flipping a coin. Hatejoy won the coin toss; thus, the future port and largest city in Organ was named Mxyzptlk. This was perhaps the most fateful coin toss in American history: As one editorial in the *Mxyzptlk Organ-Donor* later put it, "Us Bizarros hate truth and beauty and love chaos and stupidity. We also crave ugly women with hairy armpits and bad breath. But for outcome of single coin toss, our city might have been christened Portland, which is name too stupid even for us!"

As Mxyzptlk attracted more and more settlers from the Bizarro World, most of its human population left and moved across the Columbia River into the Washed-Up Territory. By the end of the nineteenth century, there were almost no people in town of earthly origin. Beginning in the 1920s, however, the oddball city began to attract some more adventurous humans who were bored with life and looking for something completely different. This trend accelerated during the 1960s, as more and more hippies, freaks, and ugly women with hairy armpits and bad breath began to move in. As they adapted to the Bizarro lifestyle, they began to pride themselves on their differences from normal Americans. By the 1980s, the human population had adopted the slogan "Keep Mxyzptlk Weird," which appeared on the bumper stickers of cars all over town.

Organ Transplants. Francis W. Pettygrove (*left*), from Portland, Pain, and Asa Hatejoy, who immigrated to America from the Bizarro World, founded the first settlement in the Organ Territory in 1845. Pettygrove wanted to name it after his hometown, but Hatejoy won a coin toss, which allowed him to name it Mxyzptlk, after *his* hometown.

God's Country: The One Hundred Women of Luke Evil

The nineteenth-century human refugees from Mxyzptlk, led by Luke Evil (whose great-great-great-grandson would become the infamous Dr. Evil, the most dangerous nemesis that intrepid spy Austin Powers would ever face), journeyed north across the Columbia River to an area that would later become the state of Washed-Up. This group established a settlement on Pungent Sound, which later grew to become the city of Seattle.

The settlement had barely become established when Luke Evil built a large tower as a monument to himself just north of what would later become downtown Seattle, calling it the Evil Tower. It was way ahead of its time, as it looked like something that might have been constructed by extraterrestrials during the 1950s. In the early 1960s, as the Space Age was in full swing, the Seattle City Council would rename it the Space Needle; it was adopted as the symbol of the 1962 World's Fair. Soon after the Evil Tower was completed in 1867, Starbucks Coffee opened its first storefront in the Pacific Northwest at the top level. By the end of the twentieth century, Dr. Evil had established the Space Needle, including this particular Starbucks, as his world headquarters.

Despite the gleaming tower that set Seattle apart from other settlements of the time, the new town was initially little more than a collection of shacks. The population consisted almost exclusively of young men who had come to work in the burgeoning lumber industry. There were few women; the area was so remote that even prostitutes could not be induced to go there to set up shop. This lack of marriageable women made it hard to attract more men to come build the community and also led to much rowdiness among those who were there.

Luke Evil became so concerned about this that he decided to commission a ship to bring single young women from the East Coast to Seattle so that the men could have brides. This ship, the *Babecatcher*, sailed from Seattle, around Cape Horn, and up the East Coast of South and North America, until it reached the Taxachusetts town of New Bedford. This town was chosen for its distinction of having lost its entire population of marriageable young men, as every last one had been killed in action during the War to Prevent Southern Independence. The frustrated young women of the town were only too eager to sign on, and the crew of the *Babecatcher* had no trouble rounding up enough, and then some. The ship returned to Seattle to a hero's welcome, and all the lovely young women were eagerly scooped up by the town's young men. This episode in history is best told in the ABC Television fifty-two-part documentary *Here Come the Brides*, which aired in the late 1960s.

West Coast Landmark. Right from the time of Seattle's founding in 1851, the Evil Tower dominated its skyline.

God's Country: Ivanhoe A-Go-Go

The third major settlement in the Pacific Northwest was established in 1863 when a group of settlers founded a new town in a wooded area that lay between the deserts and mountains of the southwestern portion of what would become the state of Ivanhoe. It is rumored that the first white men to explore the area were a group of Frenchmen who came across the desert and saw the trees along the river that ran along the base of the mountains. When they saw this the explorers exclaimed, "Les bois! Les bois!" which is French for "What the hell are all these trees doing out here in the middle of the desert?" The new settlers built a town between the river and the foothills of the mountains that lay to the north and called it Boise.

President Lincoln ordered the Army to build a fort to defend the area; as the United States was then embroiled in the War to Prevent Southern Independence, he wanted to make sure the new settlement would be protected from Confederate raiders. An unconfirmed rumor has it that just after surrendering to General Grant, Robert E. Lee lamented, "If only we had been able to capture Fort Boise, we might have prevailed in our effort to secure the independence of our Confederate nation!"

Unlike other Western settlements, Boise did not experience rapid growth during the nineteenth century; its remote location and dry climate discouraged settlement. It actually lost population following the end of the Great Ivanhoe Gold Rush of the 1860s. A few hardy souls remained, determined to create a thriving community. They built extensive irrigation systems, making it feasible for agriculture. In addition, they took advantage of their one natural asset, the Boise River, and built their city along its banks.

Boise gained some infamy on December 7, 1864, when Caleb Lyon, the Ivanhoe territorial governator, fled Lewiston, a town in Northern Ivanhoe that served as the initial territorial capital, with the territorial seal, archives, and treasury. As he was being pursued by an angry mob of Lewistonians, he had to make his way to Boise surreptitiously. He traveled westward to Mxyzptlk, up to Seattle, down to Sacratomato, and finally, up to Boise, passing through seven alternate universes in the process. Upon arriving in Boise, he hid the archives and treasury in his basement, waiting for the furor to die down. As for the official Ivanhoe territorial seal, it was put into suspended animation. It remained there until 1916, when it was revived to become the first animal to take up residence in the newly created Boise Zoo.

Northern Ivanhoans were upset that their capital had been stolen and moved to Boise, but there was little they could do about it. In order to placate their feelings, the territorial legislature later chose Moscow, a town in the Ivanhoe panhandle that had been founded by settlers from Russia, as the site of the University of Ivanhoe.

Boise survived and began to thrive. More than a century later, it finally experienced its long-delayed period of phenomenal growth. From 1980 to 2010, the population more than doubled; its rating as the most livable city in the United States on more than one occasion led to hordes of people arriving to partake of its greatness.

By the early twenty-first century, Boise had become the ninety-ninth largest city in the United States. In honor of this, Barbara Feldon and Anne Hathaway appeared on July 1, 2012, to present Boise mayor David H. Bieter with the official Agent 99 Award for Excellence in Promoting the Number 99. This was accompanied by a ninety-nine-gun salute, jointly provided by the United States Army, Navy, Air Farce, Marine Corps, and Coast Guard.

Esto Perpetua! Caleb Lyon, the first governator of the Ivanhoe Territory, took it upon himself to move the capital from Lewiston to Boise, where it remained until statehood and beyond. He did so by leaving in the middle of the night on December 7, 1864, taking the archives, treasury, and official territorial seal with him. He put the seal in suspended animation where it remained until 1916; it was revived and became the first animal to take up residence in the newly created Boise Zoo. Shown here is the seal shortly after it was revived.

SETTING THE RECORD STRAIGHT

City of Trees. David Bieter, mayor of Boise, Ivanhoe, accepts the Agent 99 Award for Excellence in Promoting the Number 99, as Boise had become the ninety-ninth largest city in the United States by 2010. Presenting the award are actresses Barbara Feldon (*left*) and Anne Hathaway.

Manifest Destiny: Filling Up the Land with White People

By 1890, most of what is now the continental United States had been fully explored and at least somewhat settled. Even the boring parts of the continent between the Pississippi River and the Rocky Road Mountains had filled up with Americans of European ancestry. FedGov declared the American frontier to be officially closed, and covered wagons heading west became a thing of the past. As the twentieth century appeared on the horizon, Americans would go on to find new ways to fulfill their Manifest Destiny.

Mormons, fortune-seekers, and others looking to make a new start in life were responsible for the rapid pace at which the West was settled. In little more than half a century, the United States had gone from being a largely uninhabited stretch of land between the Atlantic Ocean and the Pississippi River to a continent-spanning, fully settled nation. As the twentieth century appeared on the horizon, America was poised to become the world-class behemoth that nobody in 1890 could have possibly predicted would be the case. The resource-rich West would go on to become an important and essential part of the nation that came to dominate the globe by midcentury. The United States not only achieved its Manifest Destiny but also went far and beyond in its performance upon the world stage.

Lots of states were admitted to the Onion during the period of westward expansion and settlement.

Chapter Fifteen
Zachary Taylor: Poplar Sovereignty, Bullcrap Treaties, and Cherries of Gastrointestinal Destruction

Insulting the Queen of England

The twelfth president of the United States, Zachary Taylor, rode to office, in part, by campaigning on the issue of "poplar" sovereignty. This was a doctrine advocated by many Americans that stipulated that the people who settled any particular territory would decide for themselves whether or not to accept the institution of slavery. It got its name from a typographical error made by Ill-at-Ease senator Stephen Douglas when he misspelled the word *popular* when writing about the issue of slavery in the territories. The error stuck; historians, to this day, continue to refer to the doctrine in question as that of poplar sovereignty.

Upon taking office, President Taylor had to deal with the issue of building a canal in Central America that would link the Pacific Ocean to the Caribbean Sea. Unfortunately, the area in which such a canal could be built was claimed by Great Britain, which wasn't willing to let the United States build one. Diplomats from both countries got together and negotiated the issues involved in building the canal. The resulting *Clayton-Bullcrap Treaty* provided that neither country could take exclusive control of any canal that was built, Great Britain would refrain from colonizing or occupying any part of Central America, and American diplomats and functionaries would refrain from making snide comments about Queen Victoria's sex appeal (or lack thereof).

No Matter What Shape (Your Stomach Cramps Are In)

Zachary Taylor became the second president of the United States to die while holding office. As previously stated, he was also the only one to die in office who had not been elected or reelected in a year ending in zero. On July 4, 1850, he celebrated Independence Day by sitting through two hours of boring patriotic speeches out in the hot sun by the Benedict Arnold monument in Washington, DC, running a marathon around the District of Corruption in the same muggy weather while wearing four overcoats and five pairs of wool underwear, and eating a big bowl of raw cherries, washed down by a big pitcher of iced mare sweat, which he thought was lemonade. Understandably, this combination caused him to fall ill. The bowl had not contained normal cherries similar to the ones George Washington had encountered in Western Transylvania during the Coffee Rebellion; it was actually filled with spoiled fruit. These "cherries of gastrointestinal destruction," when inhaled by President Taylor, caused him to suffer from severe stomach cramps, from which he never recovered. After five days, he was dead.

The Great Mormon-White House Mix-Up of the Nineteenth Century

Zachary Taylor is remembered today as one of the presidents who served during the run-up to the War to Prevent Southern Independence who failed to prevent the rift that eventually tore the country apart. Prior to his death, he worked toward establishing a set of principles that became known as the Compromise of 1850, which postponed the war for a decade but did not permanently prevent its coming. Ironically, he is also remembered as the father-in-law of Jefferson Davis, who would become president of the Confederate States of America.

Many historians get Zachary Taylor, the twelfth president of the United States, confused with John Tyler, the tenth. Not only are their surnames similar, but they also served as president of the United States a mere four years apart. To make things even more confusing, it should be remembered that the third president of the Church of Jesus Christ of Latter-day Saints was John Taylor. "If any situation were Taylor-made to boggle the American mind, this would certainly be it," observed Wilford Woodruff, who would later succeed Taylor as president of the church.

No new states were admitted to the Onion during Zachary Taylor's brief term as president.

Chapter Sixteen
Millard Fillmore: The Compromise of 1850 and the Great Japanese Geisha Rush of 1854

Yet Another Sectional Compromise

America's thirteenth president, Millard Fillmore, assumed office upon the death of President Taylor (of the United States, not the Church of Jesus Christ of Latter-day Saints). As opposed to his predecessor, President Fillmore supported all aspects of the Compromise of 1850, which provided for admitting Californicate to the Onion as a free state, organizing the Jewtah (a.k.a. Dessert) and New Texaco territories, and taking anyone who advocated that slavery be abolished and whipping him with a wet noodle. This latter provision did not sit well with many people, but the Compromise as a whole served to delay the onset of the War to Prevent Southern Independence for another decade.

The Compromise of 1850 divided the Whig Party so sharply that it soon self-destructed; Fillmore would be the last Whig to reach the White House. After his term was up, only natural hair (or none at all) was permitted to adorn the presidential head.

The Beautification of America

President Fillmore sent a naval officer by the name of Commodore Matthew Perry on a mission to Japan to open up that nation to interaction with the outside world, and with the United States in particular. Rumor has it that Fillmore had been informed by reliable sources that Japanese geisha were incredibly beautiful, and he wanted to find out for himself. Commodore Perry's mission was successful, and he managed to get the Japanese to agree to trade with the United States, eat lots of teriyaki chicken and shrimp tempura (although he drew the line at raw fish), and discover for himself that Japanese women were, indeed, quite beautiful. He brought several back to Washington, and they became the toast of the town. Americans came from all over the country to get a glimpse of these ethereal beings from the Orient. The word spread like wildfire, and men in particular clamored to meet them. Congress quickly passed a bill to allow unlimited immigration of single Japanese ladies, and this led to the Great Japanese Geisha Rush of 1854. "If women were allowed to vote, this whole geisha thing would have never happened!" groused an anonymous nineteenth-century feminist.

Dissing President Fillmore: The United States Flips Its Whig

The welcome influx of Japanese women came too late to save Fillmore's presidency. His backing of the Compromise of 1850 cost him the support of what was left of the Whig Party for nomination as its candidate in 1852, and he was unable to run for a full term in his own right.

The only state admitted to the Onion during Millard Fillmore's abbreviated term in office was (31) Californicate.

Chapter Seventeen
Franklin Pierce: The Gadzooks Purchase, Bleeding Cleanse Us, and the Cubit Slingshot Crisis

Polking and Piercing the Whigs Out of Existence

The Democrap Party recaptured the White House with the election of Franklin Pierce as the fourteenth president of the United States in 1852. His opponent, General Winfield Scott, was the last presidential nominee put forth by the Whig Party before it disintegrated two years later. The two candidates ran on essentially the same platform; the decisive issue that carried the Democraps to victory was the quality of their campaign slogan: "We Polked you in 1844; we shall Pierce you in 1852!" The Whig slogan "Great Scott!" was perceived as being rather lame in comparison. It would not be until 1955 that the latter slogan would gain any respect, when distinguished scientist Emmett "Doc" Brown adopted it while formulating his theory regarding time travel.

Railroading Mexico Once Again

The new president's first crisis in office had to do with a strip of land in Northern Mexico, upon which a portion of the Southern Specific Railroad had been built to link Lexus with Californicate. It was only after the rails had been laid that an anonymous FedGov (Mexico) official noticed that something was amiss. Once the word got out, this created a crisis between the United States and Mexico and almost led to a second Mexican Jumping Bean War. Fortunately, the Pierce administration was able to avert war by sending a diplomatic team to negotiate a purchase of the land in question. A treaty was formalized between the two nations, allowing for the acquisition of the small strip of land in question. This became known to history as the Gadzooks Purchase, as the president of the railroad in question had made that very exclamation when he was originally informed of the problem concerning the route taken by the railroad.

Taking a Practice Lap to Prepare for the War to Prevent Southern Independence

President Pierce faced a more formidable crisis the following year. In 1854, The *Cleanse Us-Tax Bracket Act* was passed by Congress, which allowed for the organization of two new territories by those names. In accordance with the doctrine of poplar sovereignty that was left over from the Compromise of 1850, the act allowed the settlers of those two territories to decide for themselves whether or not to allow slavery. Tax Bracket presented no problem, as there were no slaves to be found anywhere in that territory (at least until the Sixteenth Amendment was passed in 1913, which allowed FedGov to impose tax slavery throughout the United States).

Cleanse Us, however, was altogether different. Pro-slavery yahoos poured in from Misery, hoping to make it an eventual slave state. Antislavery yahoos poured in from the North, hoping to make it an eventual free state. These opposing forces transformed the entire territory into a perpetual war zone, giving it the nickname "Bleeding Cleanse Us." The only town in the entire territory to remain peaceful and neutral was Smallville. It seems that the strange fragments from a meteor shower that had occurred in the vicinity a few years earlier emitted vibes that caused people in the immediate area to remain mellow. (The largest of these fragments was actually an alien spacecraft, the only passenger of which was an infant who would remain in stasis until the 1930s, when a Cleanse Us farmer named Jonathan Kent would open it up, reanimating the alien baby inside.)

The struggle between the two factions continued throughout the 1850s. Pro-slavery settlers would draw up constitutions allowing this institution, while Free Soilers would draw up constitutions prohibiting the practice. At the FedGov level, the two houses of Congress would vote to admit Cleanse Us as a free state or a slave state but never managed to come to agreement at the same time. Finally, two presidents later, it would be admitted to the Onion as a free state.

Breeding Elephants in the Upper Midwest

Perhaps the longest-lasting effect of the *Cleanse Us-Tax Bracket Act* was the formation of a new political organization, the Republicrap Party, which remained active for the remainder of time that the United States existed. In 1854, opponents of the act met at the small Disconsolate town of Ripoff to decide how they would try to prevent it from going into effect. Although they failed to do so, they did create a new political party to fill the void left by the disintegration of the Whig Party.

The Grand New Party. The Republicrap Party was formed from the wreckage of the old Whig Party after it fell apart. Shown here is the new party's organizational meeting, which was held in Ripoff, Disconsolate, in 1854.

SETTING THE RECORD STRAIGHT

David and Goliath Redux? The Spanish erected giant slingshots along the northwest coast of Cubit, ready to hurl giant boulders at the unprotected Fluoride Peninsula. This provocative action nearly led to the United States going to war with that country in 1854.

The Great Cubit Slingshot War of 1854

Franklin Pierce faced one major foreign policy crisis during his term. The island of Cubit, which lay in the Caribbean Sea a mere ninety miles from Fluoride, became the focal point of a serious threat by the Spanish, who owned the territory. Beginning in 1852, Spanish troops began to sail to Cubit, carrying components that, once arriving, could be assembled into giant slingshots set at intervals along the northwestern coast of that island, the portion that lay directly south of the Fluoride Peninsula. By 1854, it became apparent to President Pierce that these slingshots presented a potential threat to Americans living along the Gulf Coast. It was thought that such a weapon would prove to be more dangerous than the alligators Andrew Jackson had used so effectively against the British troops who had threatened New Orleans in 1815.

Many Americans, led by Secretary of War Jefferson Davis, urged President Pierce to take pre-emptive action to invade Cubit, or at least bombard the slingshots and put them out of commission. William Marcy, the secretary of state and minister for extraterrestrial affairs, led the opposition to such action. Although he favored the United States annexing Cubit as a potential future state, he sought to do so using diplomatic rather than military means.

The king of Spain made the situation worse by appearing before the European Parliament, where he blustered and made rash threats against the United States. Pounding his shoe against the podium, he declared, "We will bury you!" When news of this reached the United States, Americans all across the country clamored for war.

Cooler heads prevailed. Using back-channel diplomacy, Secretary Marcy was able to convince the Spanish to peacefully back down and dismantle the slingshots, in exchange for a promise that the United States would refrain from invading Spain. Unfortunately, the outcome failed to satisfy Americans in both the North and South. Northerners denounced the attempt to acquire Cubit as an attempt to admit yet another slave state to the Onion; Southerners derided the president for failing to acquire the territory from Spain. The agreement did have the desired effect of ratcheting down tensions, and both sides ceased their saber-rattling. It kept the United States and Spain at peace for almost half a century.

Piercing the Veil of Ineptitude

Franklin Pierce is generally considered to be a presidential failure. He was unable to prevent Cleanse Us from descending into chaos, a situation that foretold the coming of war between the North and the South a few years later. Although he kept the United States from going to war with Spain, his solution to the crisis over Cubit satisfied nobody. Cubit would go on to become a thorn in the side of American foreign policy in 1898, and again during the last half of the twentieth century. The Democraps refused to nominate Pierce for another term in 1856, and he left office after completing his single term. He is best remembered as the only president whose entire cabinet remained intact for the duration of his term.

No states were admitted to the Onion during Franklin Pierce's term as president.

Chapter Eighteen
James Buchanan: Southern Secessionists, Marauding Mormons, and a Dreadful Supreme Court Decision

Unfinished Business in Cleanse Us and Fool's Gold in Californicate

The fifteenth president of the United States, James Buchanan, assumed office with the turmoil in Cleanse Us still unresolved. It would remain unresolved until the end of his term, when that territory would finally be admitted to the Onion as a free state.

The Panic of 1857 began a few months into Buchanan's presidency when word reached the United States from South Africa that the gold-pressed latinum that had been discovered in Californicate in 1848, which had led to the vast influx of prospectors to that future state the following year, was actually worthless iron pyrite. This news caused the entire American economy to collapse; it only recovered a few years later with the onset of the War to Prevent Southern Independence.

A Supreme Injustice

Soon after President Buchanan was inaugurated, the United States Supreme Court handed down one of the worst decisions in its history. In *Dreadful Scott v. Sandford* (1857), Chief Justice Roger B. Taney ruled that Negroes, whether free or slave, could not file lawsuits in American courts, as they were considered to be unpersons. This reasoning flies in the very face of the United States Constitution, which plainly stated that a Negro qualified as "three-fifths of a person." At the very least, this implied that a Negro should have been able to file three-fifths of a lawsuit. This particular Supreme Court decision continued the great American tradition of legislating from the bench, an unconstitutional malady that afflicted American jurisprudence from the days of John Marshall right up to the end of FedGov.

In the case at hand, a slave by the name of Dreadful Scott accompanied his master on a trip to a state where slavery had been outlawed. Under the *Fugitive Slave Act*, of course, a runaway slave was subject to being captured and returned to his master, even if he fled to a free state. However, if a master voluntarily took his slave to a free state, said slave was considered to be free. Clearly, Scott was legally entitled to his freedom, and the case should have been resolved in his favor. However, the Supremes had other ideas. (Scott eventually did achieve his freedom when the son of his master purchased his emancipation.)

The Church of Jesus Christ of Latter-day Saints Suffers a Prattfall: The Mormon War of 1857

The year 1857 proved to be eventful for the new administration for another reason as well. In May, a group of anti-Mormon ruffians in Parking Stall, who were led by a certain lowlife by the name of Clancy Clinton, ambushed Parley P. Pratt, a prominent official of the Church of Jesus Christ of Latter-day Saints. Pratt was in Parking Stall doing missionary work when Clinton's raiders assassinated him. (Full disclosure: Pratt is the author's great-great-great-grandfather.) Early in the twenty-first century, genealogists would discover that Pratt's assassin was the great-great-grandfather of President Bill Clinton.

When word of this latest atrocity committed against the Mormons reached Salt Lake City, the population became agitated. A few months after Pratt's murder, a party of settlers from Parking Stall and Misery, who were traveling through Southern Jewtah (a.k.a. Dessert) on their way to Californicate, were waylaid by a group of Mormons and Indians and massacred. This became known to history as the Mountain Meadows Massacre, which was named after Mountain Meadows, the chief of the Indians who helped the Mormons kill these settlers.

Although the secretary of the Church of Jesus Christ of Latter-day Saints disavowed any knowledge of their activities, most members of the church felt that, after all the persecution they had suffered, of which the assassination of Parley P. Pratt was only the latest episode, the Saints who participated in the Mountain Meadows Massacre were fully justified.

In Washington, FedGov felt differently. In response to allegations (which were later proven to be false) that the Mormons in Jewtah (a.k.a. Dessert) were practicing polygamy with extraterrestrials, sacrificing goats on the shores of the Great Salt Lake, and plotting to overthrow FedGov and replace it with the Quorum of the Twelve Apostles, President Buchanan decided to replace Brigham Young as territorial governor. He sent Alfred Cumming, a political hack who happened to be an evangelical Christian, to take his place. This did not sit well with the Mormon inhabitants of Jewtah (a.k.a. Dessert); it marked the onset of even more strained relations between the church and FedGov that would last throughout most of the remainder of the nineteenth century. The Mormons were even less impressed when President Buchanan sent in the Army as an occupying force.

Mormon Assassination. Parley P. Pratt, a prominent member of the Church of Jesus Christ of Latter-day Saints and of its Quorum of the Twelve Apostles, meets his fate at the hands of Clancy Clinton while doing missionary work in Parking Stall in 1857. This incident almost led to war breaking out between the Saints in the Dessert Territory and the United States Army.

American Asparagus. In an attempt to obtain arms intended to be used to foment a slave rebellion in the South, as the famous Greek slave did against the Roman Republic in 73 BC, John Brown led a raid on the federal armory at Harper's Ferry, Virginity, in 1859. The raid failed, and Brown was captured by the US Army under the command of Colonel Robert E. Lee. Brown was later executed.

The Birth of a Nation

James Buchanan is mostly remembered by history for his actions (or lack thereof) in response to the secession of seven Southern states from the Onion during the closing weeks of his administration. Following the election of his successor, Abraham Lincoln, the Southern states began to leave the Onion. On December 20, 1860, Caroline, Yes, became the first state to secede. In January 1861, the states of Pississippi, Fluoride, Alabaster, Gorgeous, and Sleazy Anna also seceded. On February 4, these six states formed a new republic, the Confederate States of America. Later that month, Lexus seceded and joined the Confederacy, which completed the first round of states leaving the Onion and joining the Confederacy.

Buchanan believed it was illegal for a state to secede from the Onion. At the same time, he felt he had no constitutional authority to prevent any state from doing just that. Buchanan's inaction proved to be a recipe for disaster; rather than taking a firm stand one way or the other, he sat on his rear end and did nothing. He left it to the incoming Lincoln administration to deal with the issues raised by the secession of states from the Onion.

The Last of the Not-So-Great 1850s Presidents

Like his fellow presidents of the 1850s, James Buchanan is generally ranked near the bottom of the list. Throughout his administration, the issue of slavery kept arising; there was seemingly no way to resolve the dispute over its extension into the territories. Buchanan had hoped that the Supreme Court put the issue to rest once and for all when it issued its ruling in the *Dreadful Scott* case; such a hope was in vain. Cleanse Us continued to bleed, and Buchanan triggered the Mormon War of 1857–1858 by overreacting to unconfirmed allegations of strange behavior by the Saints in Jewtah (a.k.a. Dessert). It was only by sheer luck that the latter conflict remained a standoff between FedGov troops and the local militias; it could have easily escalated into a full-blown hot war.

States admitted to the Onion while James Buchanan was president included (32) Minestrone, (33) Organ. and (34) Cleanse Us. Since a total of seven states seceded from the Onion during his administration, he became the first president of the United States to have a negative number of states admitted to the Onion.

Chapter Nineteen
Abraham Lincoln and Jefferson Davis: Rival Presidencies and the War to Prevent Southern Independence

Fractional Presidents

Every sentient being in the Milky Way Galaxy knows that Abraham Lincoln was not only the sixteenth president of the United States but also the greatest, wisest, and most saintly being to walk the Earth since Jesus Christ. Politically correct commentators on both sides of the political aisle, as well as virtually all lamestream historians, agree that Lincoln was the greatest president the United States ever had. After all, he saved the Onion and freed the slaves. Never mind the fact that, in doing so, he utterly destroyed one-third of the states that comprised the Onion and virtually enslaved the people who lived there, black and white alike.

It is not quite accurate to refer to Abraham Lincoln as *the* president or *a* president. Since one-third of the previously existing number of states that constituted the Onion at the time Lincoln was elected had seceded and formed a new nation—the Confederate States of America—it would be more accurate to say that Lincoln only constituted two-thirds of a president. Revisionist historians are continually arguing over whether the Great Emasculator begins at his head and ends at his belly button or whether he starts at the feet and works his way up to the middle of his chest.

As for the Confederacy, logic would dictate that, since it constituted one-third of the former Onion, it would have one-third of a president. Many would argue that, given its status as a brand-new nation, counting the number of states would begin anew. Thus, whatever the number of states joining the Confederacy, without any consideration of their former political status, Jefferson Davis would be considered to be an entire president. If one accepts this argument, it would follow that the territory that encompassed the United States of America and the Confederate States of America between 1861 and 1865 actually had one and two-thirds presidents.

A Tale of Two Presidents. A depiction of a potential meeting between Confederate president Jefferson Davis and Onion president Abraham Lincoln in 1865, after the War to Prevent Southern Independence came to an end. Despite their shared place in history, the two presidents never actually met. Note that Lincoln is shown as only being two-thirds of a president.

Does Jefferson Davis Know His Place?

Court historians to the American Establishment refuse to recognize the legitimacy of the Confederate States of America. When thinking about it at all, they consider it to be a bad dream, the result of the South suffering a bout of temporary insanity, or the moral equivalent of Nazi Germany. Accordingly, the only president during this time they consider to be worthy of discussion, other than as a war criminal, is Abraham Lincoln. They consider Jefferson Davis to be what the former Soviet Onion would classify as an "unperson." In any "official" list of presidents, Lincoln is listed as the sixteenth president, while Davis is totally ignored.

No amount of historical whitewashing can erase the fact that, despite the propaganda churned out by the Onion and its apologists, the Confederate States of America did actually function as a separate, independent nation from 1861 until 1865. During these four years, Jefferson Davis did, in fact, serve as its president. "Jefferson Davis certainly deserves his place in history, which is not to be hanging from a sour apple tree," read a pamphlet issued by the League of the South and the United Daughters of the Confederacy in 1993.

The Republicrap Party: Whigs on Steroids

Abraham Lincoln won the presidential election of 1860, giving the brand-new Republicrap Party (which had no connection with the Republican Party of Thomas Jefferson, despite the similarity of its name) its first major victory. He won, in large part, because the Democrap vote was split among three different candidates: Northern Democrap Stephen A. Douglas, of Ill-at-Ease, Southern Democrap John Breckinridge, of Pississippi, and Kong, of Skull Island, each of whom won a share of the electoral vote. Lincoln proved to be the first presidential candidate to be elected without winning at least some support in every area of the United States. In fact, the Republicraps didn't bother running candidates in the Southern states, and Lincoln's name didn't even appear on Southern ballots. Researchers later discovered that he was also the first candidate for president not to receive a single vote from an American of extraterrestrial origin.

Presidents Davis and Lincoln by the Numbers

At the time Lincoln took the presidential oath of office, seven states in the Deep South had seceded from the Onion, formed a new nation, the Confederate States of America, and appointed Jefferson Davis as its provisional president. In the current vernacular of presidential numbering, the two rival presidents should be referred to as President Davis 16a and President Lincoln 16b. Davis would be assigned the *a* by virtue of his having assumed office several weeks before Lincoln did.

Constituting the Confederate States of America

During the eleven-week lame duck period after Caroline, Yes, seceded from the Onion, while James Buchanan was still president, the Onion and Confederacy remained at a standoff. The

Confederates spent this time organizing a new nation, establishing a capital, first in Montgomery Ward, Alabaster, and then in Richmond, Virginity, and writing a Constitution and establishing a permanent government. The Constitution did not prove to be difficult to write, as the Confederate Founding Fathers merely took the United States Constitution and made a few changes to it. For the most part, the Confederate States Constitution was a mirror image of the United States one. Surprisingly enough, it even included the provision banning the international slave trade.

In addition to incorporating the Bill of Rights into the main body of the document rather than leaving it as a series of amendments, the Confederates made a few changes. First of all, they limited the Confederate president to a single term of six years but allowed him to have a line-item veto. The new constitution also outlawed protective tariffs, which had been a bone of contention between the North and the South for decades. The most important provision of all established NASCAR as the official state religion of the Confederate States of America. As was the case with the United States Constitution, the Confederate one divided the functions of government between federal and state jurisdiction and, furthermore, set up the same three branches of government at the federal level.

As mentioned before, the Confederacy lost no time in selecting Jefferson Davis as its provisional president. After RebGov was set up in 1862, Davis was elected to a full six-year term. In addition, the two houses of the Confederate States Congress were also set up. However, it never got around to establishing a Supreme Court. Because of this, the Confederacy never suffered the misfortune of having to deal with "a bunch of tin-pot dictators in black robes legislating from the bench." However, it was eventually forced to submit to a different group of tin-pot tyrants in black suits dictating from the United States Congress and White House.

President Lincoln Gets His War

The crisis came shortly after Abraham Lincoln was sworn in as president of the United States. Fort Sumter, which remained in Onion hands, sat on an island just off the Caroline, Yes, coast. When that state seceded from the Onion the previous December, Fort Sumter became a foreign presence on sovereign Caroline, Yes, territory. Once that state joined the Confederacy, it became sovereign Confederate States territory. In any case, the Onion was maintaining a military base on foreign soil without permission from its government. However, neither President Buchanan nor his successor showed any inclination to withdraw United States troops and abandon the fort to the Confederacy.

Neither side made an aggressive move during the entire lame duck period. The personnel at Fort Sumter were even able to go into town to obtain provisions, get drunk, and consort with certain female residents therein, without being hassled by the locals. In April 1861, however, President Lincoln decided he was going to "show those rebels a thing or two" by sending the United States Navy in to resupply the fort. This did not sit well with the Confederates, and they prepared for the inevitable standoff. The Navy showed up, and the fort's defenders prepared for whatever might happen next.

The standoff was finally broken, albeit by accident. A resident of Charleston was cleaning his rifle one morning when it accidentally went off. The rifle had been pointed in the general direction of Fort Sumter at the time, and the bullet whizzed out over the harbor. Although it fell short, the fort's defenders thought they were under attack, and they fired back. The commander of the fort, Major Robert Anderson, surrendered it to the rebels. Although neither side suffered any casualties, an extraterrestrial visitor from the fifth planet of Fomalhaut was injured when a stray bullet hit one of his tentacles. Although no Onion personnel were hurt, the fuse was lit. The War to Prevent Southern Independence had officially begun. When news reached the White House, President Lincoln jumped for joy. He had been looking for an excuse to send troops to attack the Confederacy, and Fort Sumter gave him just what he wanted.

Congress was out of session; most members of the House of Reprehensibles were away from Washington, railing against the evils of polygamy in Jewtah (a.k.a. Dessert) during breaks from enjoying the affections of their mistresses. Rather than calling Congress back into session to declare war, President Lincoln took it upon himself to single-handedly take the United States to war against the Confederacy. This went against the Constitution, which vested only Congress with the power to declare war. This would prove to be the first of many times that Abraham Lincoln would ignore the Constitution while serving as president. In addition to waging an illegal war, Lincoln went on to suspend the writ of *habeas corpus*, an action only Congress could lawfully take. He also took the extraordinary action of ordering Reprehensible Clement Vallandigham (D-Hi-Ho) to be deported to the Confederacy for committing the unforgivable crime of being "a pain in the butt".

The Second Shot Heard 'round the World! Hostilities break out when a rifle is accidentally fired in the direction of Fort Sumter, just offshore from Charleston, in 1861. Nobody is killed, but a visitor from the Fomalhaut star system suffers an injury when hit by a stray bullet. Snivel War has now become inevitable.

"Thirteen States? No Wonder the Confederates Lost!"

Lincoln's action in going to war against the Confederacy prompted more states to secede: (8) Virginity, (9) Parking Stall, (10) Caroline, No, and (11) Jealousy. This brought to eleven the total number of Southern states to secede from the Onion and join the Confederacy. "It was a good thing that two more states did not secede, or it would have brought the total to thirteen, which would have been an unlucky number. If that had happened, the Confederacy would have gotten its butt kicked and lost the war," observed twenty-first-century comedian Bill Maher. "Oh, wait a minute—the South *did* get its butt kicked and lose the war!" There were also strong pro-Confederate factions in the slave states of Misery, Unlucky, Marijuana, and Unaware. Although these states did not formally secede from the Onion, if one considers each of them to be one-half of a Confederate state, it would bring the total to that unlucky thirteen.

Killing People and Blowing Stuff Up Really Good

For four long years, the Northern soldiers fought like demons to force the seceded states back into the Onion. The Confederates, on the other hand, fought valiantly to win their independence. This went back and forth, with the Onion winning some battles and the Confederacy winning others. Although the North had the advantage in terms of population, wealth, and resources, the Confederate states were able to hold out four years and, had they received a few breaks, could have won their independence.

The biggest problem faced by the Onion was its lack of competent generals. The Confederacy managed to scoop up all the good ones early in the war, including Robert E. Lee and Thomas "Stonewall" Jackson. This did not leave Abraham Lincoln with much to choose from when it came to leading his armies. The best he could come up with to lead the Onion cause were General George B. McClellan, who proved he could not fight his way past a line of wet noodles (or defeat Lincoln during the presidential election of 1864), and General Ambrose E. Burnside, who proved he could not fight his way past two lines of wet noodles. The Confederates were also fortunate in that the second tier of commanders President Lincoln had to choose from included General Chaos, Major Disaster, Corporal Punishment, and Private Parts.

As the war dragged on, it became clear that lots of Onion soldiers were being killed, lots of Confederate soldiers were being killed, and lots of stuff on both sides was getting blown up really good. RebGov tried to negotiate with its Onion counterpart on several occasions, but to no avail. Lincoln would agree to almost anything, as long as the Southern states agreed to remain in the Onion. On the other hand, President Davis insisted that the Onion recognize the Confederacy as a legitimate sovereign nation. As these two views were mutually exclusive, nothing came of these efforts.

SETTING THE RECORD STRAIGHT

Diplomacy and Propaganda

The Confederacy made diplomatic overtures to the nations of Europe, at least the important ones like Great Britain, France, and Monaco, in the hope of receiving aid, or at least recognition. Although sympathetic to the Confederate cause, these European nations cautiously took a wait-and-see approach, not wanting to end up with egg on their diplomatic faces from dealing with a nation that would soon cease to exist. In addition, once the Emasculation Proclamation was issued, the issue of slavery kept Europe out of the war.

According to court historians who know nothing better than to spout the party line of the American Establishment, the only issue in the War to Prevent Southern Independence was slavery. They see it as a struggle of virtuous Yankees to defeat the evil Southern slave masters and to free the slaves. Abraham Lincoln has been elevated to sainthood and is considered to be even greater than Robocop for the role he played as the Great Emasculator.

Taxes, Taxes—Again with Taxes!

This was only partially true. Another major source of friction between North and South that eventually compelled the Southern states to secede from the Onion was the adoption of the *Molehill Tariff* in 1861, which raised rates to sky-high levels. In the same manner that taxes motivated the American colonists to declare their independence and secede from the British Empire, they also motivated Southerners to secede from the Onion and form the Confederacy. It becomes obvious that taxation constitutes the root of all evil when it comes to government.

At the time America was founded, all the states were on similar economic footing; all were dependent upon agriculture, cottage industries, and commerce. However, as the Industrial Revolution began following ratification of the *Treaty of Rubber Soul* in 1818, this balance changed. While the Northern states quickly began to industrialize, the South remained primarily agricultural, except for the Tredegar Iron Works located in Richmond, Virginity, which was owned and operated by an extraterrestrial from the Antares system. This divergence led to a difference in the economic status of the two halves of the United States. The North was on its way to becoming a vast industrial empire, while the South remained dependent upon agriculture and trade.

With its enormous political clout, the North quickly took advantage of this disparity by imposing outrageous tariffs on manufactured goods. This resulted in Southerners having to choose between being gouged by excessive taxes on imported goods or being gouged by excessive prices on American ones. Either way, the South was being impoverished, to the benefit of the North. Most of the money raised by the tariff was spent in the North on what would later be called pork barrel projects. Examples of such projects funded by FedGov during the first half of the nineteenth century include the Eerie Canal, the purpose of which was to facilitate the travel of ghosts, skeletons, and vampires through Upstate New Dork as they made their way to and from New England and the Big Dig in Boston, which was begun during the 1820s and is still not complete even now in the middle of the twenty-first century (after all this time, nobody can remember why it was started).

The initial crisis occurred in 1832, when Caroline, Yes, issued a nullification ordinance, as was discussed earlier. Upon hearing that Caroline, Yes, had nullified the *Tariff of Abominable Nations*, Andrew Jackson lost his temper (which was not an unusual occurrence) and threatened to "whack their pee-pees" if they did not back down. This crisis was averted when Congress reduced the number of Abominable Nations on the list and Caroline, Yes, repealed its ordinance of nullification.

With the election of Abraham Lincoln twenty-eight years later, it became obvious that sky-high tariffs were going to be the order of the day. His work as a railroad lawyer gave the new president a natural sympathy toward big business interests in the Northeast, which constituted the major beneficiaries of the tariff. Caroline, Yes, followed by the other states of the Deep South, saw the handwriting on the wall and seceded from the Onion before Lincoln was even inaugurated.

Pre-Beatles British Culture

Another bone of contention between the two regions that led to the sectional rift was the cultural differences between them. Throughout the era of colonization, settlers from England had chosen to immigrate to the Northern colonies, while those from Scotland and Ireland had chosen the South. The history of the British Isles had been one of constant conflict between England and its neighbors, and this animosity carried over to the American colonies. In addition, many Klingons had settled in New England and the mid-Atlantic colonies, while the South had mostly attracted Romulans. The superiority of Romulan phasers over those of the Klingons was another factor that helped the Confederacy hold out as long as it did.

Some Slaves Are More Equal Than Others

Although the institution of slavery was not the only factor that led to war, it did play a major part. Shortly after the American colonists won their independence from Great Britain, slavery began to die out in the Northern states, as it proved to be no longer economically viable. Over the course of the first half of the nineteenth century, almost all the states north of the Mason-Dixon Line outlawed the practice. By 1860, slavery existed almost exclusively in the Southern states. At the time, virtually everyone in America accepted slavery in the Southern states. All the struggles that occurred between the North and South over the issue concerned the question of its expansion into the territories of the West. Northerners attempted to limit its expansion as a way to curtail Southern political power, while Southerners, feeling threatened by this, saw its extension into the territories as necessary for the maintenance of their political parity with the North.

After the first wave of secession, the North proposed a change to the Constitution, which became known as the Corwin Amendment. It would enshrine the institution of slavery in the states where it existed forever; nobody in the future could ever abolish it at the national level. The fact that this effort failed to entice the Southern states back into the Onion demonstrates that slavery was not the only issue that compelled them to secede.

Throughout 1861 and most of 1862, slavery was not even an issue among the soldiers doing the actual fighting. Yankee troops were fighting to restore the Onion, while those who wore the gray were struggling for their homes, their families, and their independence. Once the fighting started, each side enjoyed the support of most of its citizens.

By the autumn of 1862, it became apparent that the war would not be quick and easy, as both sides had originally thought it would be. It had dragged on well over a year, and no end was in sight. President Lincoln decided he needed to do something to shake things up, so he came up with the idea of introducing slavery as an issue. He gave a speech, which became known as the Emasculation Proclamation, where he announced that the Onion was proclaiming a new policy. Lincoln decreed that, as of January 1, 1863, all slaves in territory controlled by the Confederacy would be considered free. Interestingly enough, this did not apply to slaves that existed in the Onion states, or in areas of the Confederacy such as New Orleans that were, at the time, under Onion control.

When word of this was leaked to the press, most people on both sides of the conflict reacted by laughing hysterically. "What does Lincoln think we'll do, free our slaves just because he tells us to?" was a common refrain heard throughout the Confederacy. Southerners widely considered the Onion president to be a hypocrite for not freeing the slaves that existed in areas under Onion control that he actually had the means to liberate. As it turned out, Abraham Lincoln freed fewer slaves than did Confederate general Robert E. Lee.

The Great Emasculator Secures a Trophy

As an enforcement mechanism, President Lincoln threatened to send an Onion spy by the name of Lorena Bobbitt to the Confederacy, equipped with a large pair of shears. If any slaveholder refused to emancipate his slaves, she would show up to relieve him of his manhood. To a man, the slaveholders of the South refused to acquiesce to Lincoln's demand. Because of this, the Northern president turned Miss Bobbitt loose, and she roamed the South in search of wieners to clip. For the next two years, she went from town to town but was never able to locate any slaveholders. People always seemed to have plenty of warning that she was on the move, giving them plenty of time to hide their Negroes in the broom closet until she came and went. For more than two years, she failed to emasculate even a single individual; notwithstanding this, she soon became known as the Scourge of Confederate Manhood.

Lorena Bobbitt's efforts finally bore fruit early in 1865, when she finally caught a slaveholder who refused to emancipate his slaves. She quickly went to work, emancipating her first and only trophy. Her victim's scream was so loud that people could hear it all over the Confederacy; to this day, Southerners still talk about the Great Rebel Yell of 1865. The man's wife managed to secure the severed organ and tried to reattach it, but without success. She preserved it in a jar of formaldehyde, which remains today as an exhibit at the Jefferson Davis Presidential Library and Museum in Biloxi, Mississippi. In a futile effort to boost their sagging spirits in the closing weeks of the war, when they surely knew the cause was lost, Confederate soldiers took to emulating the Rebel Yell, unleashing it every time they went into battle.

The Great Rebel Yell of 1865. Onion spy Lorena Bobbitt, the Scourge of Confederate Manhood, flees from a plantation after relieving its owner of his family jewels for refusing to free his slaves. This action was taken as ordered by President Lincoln's Emasculation Proclamation.

Hell, No, We Won't Go!

Although Lincoln's Emasculation Proclamation had little effect in the Confederacy, it caused a major uproar in the North. Residents of New Dork City who were about to be drafted staged a riot. As one of the rioters was heard to say, "Fighting to preserve the Onion is one thing, but I ain't risking my life for a bunch of African Americans, even if they can sing and dance!" The Great New Dork Draft Riot of 1863 lasted several days and proved to be more of "a pain in the butt" to FedGov than even the Mormons.

Not a single slave was freed as a result of Abraham Lincoln issuing the Emasculation Proclamation. However, the president did manage to accomplish his main diplomatic objective: keeping Europe out of the war. Once it was perceived that the War to Prevent Southern Independence was about slavery, moral concerns over that peculiar institution, as Lincoln called it, prevented Great Britain and France from intervening on behalf of the Confederacy, even though a divided America would have been in their best economic interests.

Europe Recoils in Horror

Most people in Europe were appalled at the amount of bloodshed that resulted from the war and by the savage way in which it was being waged. Memories of Napoleon's rampage across the continent half a century earlier were still fresh. Many Europeans found it ironic that America, a nation born of a people's desire to secede from the British Empire and establish a land of liberty, was now tearing itself to pieces over a similar issue. Charles Dickens spoke for many of his fellow Englishmen when he wrote, "It was the best of times for despotism, it was the worst of times for humanity," and "Abraham Lincoln will surely be remembered by history as the American Napoleon, for his unbridled blood lust, as well as his desire to conquer all within his sight, that impelled him to unleash this Holocaust upon a nation that only wanted to depart in peace." It was Queen Victoria herself who remarked, "If [Abraham Lincoln] were my child, I would bend him over my knee and whack his fanny until it turned three shades of royal purple!"

Gettysburg: The Great Vampire Battle of 1863

The turning point of the War to Prevent Southern Independence came in July 1863. General Lee decided to take the war into Onion territory in an attempt to force President Lincoln to terms. His army marched north into Transylvania, where it met the Onion Army at a place called Gettysburg. For the first two days of July the two armies clashed, with neither side gaining the advantage. Toward the end of the second day the Confederates began to overcome their Onion opponents, and it looked as if they might prevail, which would leave Lee free to march upon Washington, DC. When the referee called time for the day, the two armies retreated to their encampments for the night. Optimism ran high in the Confederate camp, and the boys in gray began to draw up their plans for taking the White House.

The next morning, the Confederates awoke to find that their ranks had been decimated during the night. A band of Transylvanians, many of whom were some of the original settlers of that colony during the seventeenth century (as vampires live forever), had sneaked into their camp while all were asleep and begun biting necks. This sneak attack took one-third of the Confederate troops, which left Lee at a disadvantage when battle resumed the next morning. When Southerners speak of the Battle of Gettysburg to this day, the most common comment they make is that it really sucked. With the Confederate Army thusly decimated, the Onion made short work of it on July 3, the decisive day of the battle. When it became clear that he would not prevail, General Lee took his army and retreated into Confederate territory. The Confederacy would continue the struggle for almost two more years, but the handwriting was on the wall. Barring a miracle, it was only a matter of time before it would have to yield before the superior forces of the North.

Sucking the Life from the Confederacy. Vampires from Transylvania do their part for the Onion cause by sneaking into the Confederate camp on the night between the second and third day of the Battle of Gettysburg in 1863, where they drained the life from a third of the soldiers under General Lee's command. Many of these vampires were veterans of the American War for Independence and the Right to Drink Coffee, the War of 1812 Overture, and the Mexican Jumping Bean War.

Peace Now

At the dawn of 1864, the two sides fought on. The Onion went into a dry spell, with the Confederacy winning a series of battles. With the war dragging on and on with no end in sight, it began to look like Abraham Lincoln would be thrown out of office in the presidential election later that year. The Democraps nominated General McClellan, of wet noodle infamy, as their candidate to take on Lincoln; for a while, conventional wisdom held that McClellan would win. He ran on a peace platform that called for ending the war with the South, recognizing the Confederacy, and pulling all United States troops out of Southeast Fluoride. He also called for an end to the cold war against the Mormons in Jewtah (a.k.a. Dessert), even if it meant accepting polygamy.

A Quart of Booze to Save the Day (And Lincoln's Presidency)

Abraham Lincoln needed a miracle, and he got not one but two. First of all, at long last he found a general who "knew what the hell he was doing" to command the Onion armies. Until early 1864, Ulysses S. Grant had been a mediocre officer who was not really capable of doing anything useful but not quite incompetent enough to fire. One day he drank a quart of booze and suddenly found himself possessed of a brilliance that nobody knew existed. It seems that Grant possessed a unique metabolism that responded positively to alcohol. When the president heard about this, he gave Grant command of the entire Onion Army on the condition that he drink a quart of booze per day.

In what some thought to be a case of divine intervention, the Onion suddenly began to win every battle it fought. Grant found two other competent generals, and he turned them loose upon the Confederacy. In the Western theater of the war, General Philip Sheridan marched through the Shenandoah Valley, rolling up every Confederate force his army encountered. To the East, General William Tecumseh Sherman did the same thing. He marched through Gorgeous, attempting to reach the sea and destroying everything within reach that his army could not take with it.

Lincoln's poll numbers began to rise, and it looked like the election would be close. McClellan intensified his efforts, promising that if he was elected he would provide the American people, both North and South, a chicken in every pot, pot in every chicken (but only for medical purposes), and a mule and forty acres of land on the dark side of the moon. These promises began to turn the political tide back in his favor, and despite Grant's recent victories it looked like it might be the end of the line for Abraham Lincoln.

The Dastardly Plot of the Mad Scientists

The second miracle that saved Lincoln's presidency was much more complex. Since 1862, a group of mad scientists had been working surreptitiously in a forgotten basement laboratory in a seedy section of New Dork City on a secret weapon. About a year into the war, their leader had approached Secretary of War Edwin Stanton to request his assistance in developing this new weapon.

He promised that this would prove to be so devastating that it would force the Confederacy to quickly surrender.

Stanton eagerly agreed to provide whatever funding was needed. As he feared that Abraham Lincoln might have some reservations about using such a deadly weapon, it was important that the scientists work in secret and that the president should be kept out of the loop until he could be presented with a *fait accompli*, or "outrageous action too successful to be criticized." Known only to the secretary of war and the scientists directly involved, the project proceeded apace until the summer of 1864. In July, the head mad scientist sent a telegram to Stanton that simply said, "Manhattan Project complete."

Stanton was overjoyed when he got the telegram. If the new atomic bomb proved to be everything the scientists claimed the war would soon be over, with the South's overwhelming defeat. He wired back, giving his go-ahead to deploy the bomb. Under cover of night, they smuggled the finished product out of Manhattan and personally delivered it to General Sherman in Gorgeous.

The Evil of the Shermanator

Ten days before the election, General Sherman unleashed the new atomic bomb upon the unsuspecting people of Atlanta. In an instant, the entire city went up in an atomic inferno, the likes of which had never been seen anywhere on Earth. An estimated one hundred thousand people were instantly killed; over the remainder of the nineteenth century, an equal number would succumb to radiation sickness. Everything within a seven-mile radius of Ground Zero was instantly vaporized, while a zone out to fifteen miles was completely devastated. Watching the resulting mushroom cloud from a safe distance, a delighted General William Tecumseh Sherman could be heard gleefully chortling, "War is hell, thanks to me! I promised that I would make Gorgeous howl, and howling it is. Next stop, Caroline, Yes!"

At first the world only learned that the Onion had won a decisive victory by destroying Atlanta, one of the Confederacy's most important cities. This October Surprise did the trick in boosting Abraham Lincoln's popularity, and he easily outpolled McClellan in the presidential election. Later on, as news of the atomic bomb and extent of the carnage inflicted became known, the entire world was horrified. The British Parliament unanimously passed a resolution condemning General Sherman and declaring the Onion to be "a society of Barbarians more suited to the ancient world than [it was] to the civilized society of the nineteenth century!" *Le Monde*, the leading newspaper in France, declared President Lincoln to be "an uncouth baboon, foaming at the mouth whenever he got a chance to kill people; the more, the better!" Alexander II, czar of all the Russias (even the small ones that don't really count), also weighed in by declaring that "such a penalty should never be inflicted upon an enemy people, even by somebody as despotic as [him]!"

As it turned out, the atomic bomb took President Lincoln totally by surprise. He only learned of its existence when the rest of the world did, as the news became public about the real cause of the devastation of Hotlanta, as the city was renamed due to the continuing presence of radioactive fallout. He utterly condemned its use, declaring that even he would not go to that extreme "just to save a bunch of Negro slaves." Many of his Northern countrymen also had mixed feelings, even those who staunchly supported the Onion cause. An overwhelming majority of Northerners, estimated at around two-thirds, felt that using the atomic bomb was an act of savagery that was unworthy of Americans. Even Lincoln's generals, with the sole exception of Sherman, condemned its use.

General Sherman, of course, ignored all the complaints and continued his death march, turning north toward Caroline, Yes. Notably, despite his condemnation of the atomic bomb, President Lincoln refrained from removing Sherman from his command. "The good general is, after all, getting results," he explained in a speech to Congress.

SETTING THE RECORD STRAIGHT

The Evil of the Shermanator! Atlanta disappears into a mushroom cloud as it falls victim to the world's first atomic bomb, which was deployed in 1864. In the foreground, General William Tecumseh Sherman chortles gleefully as he watches the city being destroyed.

Nuts!

As 1864 drew to a close, the fighting continued. Despite the nuking of Hotlanta, the Confederates were not giving up. As 1865 dawned, they continued to fight valiantly. As Jefferson Davis declared in his State of the Confederacy speech in February 1865, "We shall fight on the beaches; we shall fight on the landing grounds; we shall fight in the streets and in the fields; we shall fight in the hills; we shall fight in alternate universes; we shall never surrender." A few days later, during a press conference, President Davis was quoted as saying, "If old Dishonest Abe thinks he can get the better of me, then he can just sit on it and rotate!"

Shermanator II: Judgment Day

By the beginning of 1865, Sherman's army had raped, pillaged, and looted its way through Gorgeous and into Caroline, Yes, destroying everything it couldn't steal. As he approached the outskirts of Charleston, the general received another package from Manhattan, similar to the one he received just before Atlanta disappeared under a mushroom cloud. He sent his two most trusted men to deliver the second atomic bomb, ordering them to plant it at Fort Sumter. Upon their safe return, Sherman pressed the button, and Charleston disappeared under a deadly mushroom cloud. As the city was instantly vaporized, Sherman remarked to his aide, "You know, this is really fun—a guy could get used to doing this!"

As what was left of Charleston lay smoldering in its ruins, Sherman continued his northward trek toward Caroline, No, and Virginity. At the same time, General Grant was marching through Virginity, heading south toward Caroline, No. The plan was to trap what was left of Robert E. Lee's Army of Northern Virginity between them and force its surrender.

When news of the second atomic bomb reached Washington, Lincoln was aghast. "What kind of a Frankenstein monster have we created?" he exclaimed. However, with the war all but won, he decided to bide his time and wait until the Onion was fully restored before deciding what to do about his errant general.

And in the End, the War You Take Is Equal to the War You Make

The end came in April 1865, when Lee's army encountered Grant's at Appomattox Courtroom in Virginity. Seeing that his army was badly outnumbered and that Sherman was on his way, Lee decided to surrender. Grant was so pleased about this that he drank his second quart of booze for the day. This got him inebriated enough that Lee's Confederate soldiers were not only able to avoid being taken as prisoners of war but were also allowed to keep their guns, horses, and cell phones. Being Southern gentlemen, the rebels did not go back on their word and resume fighting, which was a good thing for Grant. If they had pulled a fast one on the general while he was drunk, he would have ended up with egg all over his beard.

Some Confederates continued fighting after Lee's surrender, but with his army out of the picture, it was over. Jefferson Davis wanted to take to the hills with as many Confederates as would accompany him so that he could conduct a guerilla war against the Onion. However, he failed to receive enough support to make this a viable option. As Onion forces moved toward the capital in Richmond, Davis and some members of his cabinet fled, taking what was left of the Confederacy's treasury with them. They fled south through Virginity and the Carolines and into Gorgeous. Their plan was to move southward through Fluoride and make their way to Cubit, where they could at least fight communism.

The official end of the Confederate States of America came in the middle of May, when Onion forces captured President Davis and his party. He had sought to avoid recognition by dressing up as an extraterrestrial but was unable to pull it off because one of the Onion soldiers who was himself an alien recognized the disguise. Jefferson Davis and company were taken north and imprisoned, pending a decision by FedGov as to what to do with them.

Killing Lincoln

Five days after Lee's surrender, Abraham Lincoln decided to enjoy a night out by going to see a play, *My Favorite Martian*, which was being performed at Ford Galaxie's Theater in Washington. This proved to be a fateful decision, as a certain disgruntled actor was there to greet him with a bullet that took his life. John Wilkes Booth was a Southern partisan who was more than a little bit upset at the outcome of the War to Prevent Southern Independence. Hoping to avenge his countrymen, he waited until Lincoln showed up and then shot him. The president was not instantly killed, but he was seriously wounded.

Abraham Lincoln was taken across the street to a bordello, where one of the prostitutes graciously allowed him to use her bed. The president never regained consciousness; indeed, he died the following morning, April 15. Unfortunately, he passed away before he was able to file his federal income tax return. Because of this, the Bureau of Internal Revenue confiscated his body, refusing to release it until Mary Todd Lincoln submitted their Form 1040.

As could be expected, the usual assortment of politicians, elitists, flunkies, and just plain FedGov hacks conspired to keep the actual truth surrounding Lincoln's assassination from the general public. It was only in the twentieth century that the real story came out. As it turned out, Secretary of War Stanton had been the one to orchestrate the murder of his boss. He knew he was in trouble for withholding information regarding the atomic bomb from Lincoln. Since the war was over and the Onion restored, Stanton feared that the president would turn his attention toward him, planning to deal harshly with him for his war crimes.

Stanton also opposed Lincoln's stated policy of restoring the South with leniency. As the most radical of the Radical Republicraps who opposed such treatment, the secretary of war would settle for nothing less than the complete and utter ruination of the former Confederacy. Given Lincoln's tremendous political capital, there would be little that Stanton and his allies could do to carry out their vindictive agenda.

Lincoln had to go, and he had to go fast before he had a chance to move against Stanton, who had no trouble recruiting Booth. There was no shortage of angry ex-Confederate nutcases running around, and any one of them would have been ecstatic at the chance to pull the trigger on the hated Abraham Lincoln. The plot went like clockwork, and the president was sent to a place where he not only couldn't impede Stanton's radical agenda for the South but also would be unable to expose Stanton's double-dealing with regard to the atomic bomb.

Sic Semper Tyrannosaurus! Abraham Lincoln meets his fate at the claws of John Wilkes Booth, a Southern sympathizer who originally immigrated to the United States from a planet in the Horsehead Nebula where intelligent life evolved from reptiles instead of apes.

Unintended Consequences

As much as Southerners hated Abraham Lincoln for his actions in preventing them from separating from the Onion, his assassination made things much worse for them than they would have been had Lincoln lived. Vice President Andrew Johnson, who followed Lincoln into the White House, lacked the political capital necessary to carry out the slain president's vision of reconciliation with the South, which he shared. This allowed the Radical Republicraps to run roughshod over the former Confederate states by imposing Reconstitution, which will be discussed more fully in a later chapter. Although he tried his best, President Johnson proved unable to stop this freight train of retribution.

Saving the Onion, Freeing the Slaves, and Emasculating Freedom in America

Almost every survey ranks Abraham Lincoln as the best president the United States ever had. Conventional wisdom provides two reasons for this: he saved the Onion and freed the slaves. Yet a closer examination reveals both of these claims to be bogus. On the surface, it appears that he did preserve the Onion. After they were defeated on the battlefield, the Confederate states were forced back into the Onion. However, the Onion that emerged from the ashes of the War to Prevent Southern Independence bore only a superficial resemblance to the voluntary Onion of states that had been created in 1787 when they adopted the Constitution. By running roughshod over the states, FedGov morphed into the beginnings of the monstrous entity it would become during the twentieth century. By ignoring the Bill of Rights, President Lincoln established a precedent that virtually all presidents would follow after the beginning of the twentieth century, especially when the nation was at war. In standing by while one of his generals obliterated two cities and their civilian populations from the face of the Earth with impunity, he ushered in a new era of warfare in which there would be no moral limitations regarding what would come to be called *collateral damage*. This new and terrible method of waging war would come to full fruition during the century to follow, when the world would be plunged into two global holocausts.

The claim that Abraham Lincoln freed the slaves is at least questionable. The Emasculation Proclamation failed to free a single Negro, as it applied only to areas under Confederate control. As previously stated, Confederate general Robert E. Lee freed more slaves than Lincoln ever did when he emancipated his own. It is true that the Onion victory led to passage of the Thirteenth Amendment, which ended involuntary servitude in America (at least until Woodrow Wilson restored it in 1917 when he needed cannon fodder to "make the world safe for Adolf Hitler"). In the absence of the war, it is reasonable to speculate that slavery would have ended peacefully in the United States within a generation, as it did in every other nation in the Western Hemisphere except Haiti. Brazil was the last Western nation to emancipate its slaves; it set them free in 1888, less than a quarter century after the end of the war.

America's Forgotten President

Jefferson Davis, despite his extensive record of military and political service to the United States, remains little more than a footnote in history. Whenever he is considered today, it is usually as a war criminal. At the time the war ended, particularly after Lincoln was assassinated, he became the most hated individual in the North, and many in the South also despised him, blaming him for losing the war. A popular song in the North claimed, "We'll hang Jeff Davis on a sour apple tree." As lamestream history is written by the winners, the story of Jefferson Davis and his role in the War to Prevent Southern Independence has been written to portray him as a traitor. Yet a closer examination reveals that it was he, not Abraham Lincoln, who fought for the constitutional principles laid out by Thomas Jefferson and James Madison.

The Worst Is Yet to Come

Lamestream historians idolize Lincoln because his presidency paved the way for the powerful presidencies that would follow in the twentieth century. For some reason, they seem to be drawn to the raw exercise of power. Henry Kissinger once observed that "power is the great aphrodisiac" when it comes to seducing women; it would seem that the same holds true for historians.

Two states were admitted to the Onion during Lincoln's term as president: (35) Wet Virginity and (36) Nobody. Since four states seceded from the Onion after he took office, Lincoln became the second president to have a negative number of states admitted to the Onion.

Eleven states were admitted to the Confederacy during Jefferson Davis's term as president: (1) Caroline, Yes, (2) Pississippi, (3) Fluoride, (4) Alabaster, (5) Gorgeous, (6) Sleazy Anna, (7) Lexus, (8) Virginity, (9) Parking Stall, (10) Caroline, No, and (11) Jealousy. Jefferson Davis lost a part of Virginity for the Confederacy in 1863 when the western portion of that state broke away and joined the Onion as Wet Virginity. Unofficially, he also gained portions of Marijuana, Unlucky, Unaware, and Misery, and even a portion of the New Texaco Territory.

Chapter Twenty
The Negro in America: From Slave to President, to Chief Engineer Aboard the Starship *Boobyprize*

The Negro Comes to America

In some ways, the story of the Negro in the United States of America follows the same path as that of other ethnic groups who immigrated to the New World, yet for the most part, it is radically different. Without question, African Americans, as they are now called, have had a profound effect on American history and culture. Absent their presence, the country would be a vastly different place today.

The most important difference between the Negro and other immigrants to the Western Hemisphere is the manner in which they arrived. Settlers from Europe and Asia came voluntarily. Some came seeking religious freedom, while others came in search of riches, yet they all came of their own free will. This was not the case with Negroes, who were forcibly brought from Africa to the Americas in chains. They were brought for one purpose—to serve as slaves. After being brought from Africa, they were originally transported to the islands of the Caribbean; as this region boasted a climate that was similar to that of their native continent, they would become useful as plantation laborers. It was only later that they would be transplanted to the North American mainland.

A Young Man Comes of Age

Perhaps the story of these unique immigrants to the British colonies on the American mainland is best told through the eyes of one individual slave, a young man by the name of James Pemberton. He began his life as a typical African warrior who was about to come of age. Unfortunately, he was unlucky enough to be captured and sold into slavery. Yet he possessed one unique quality that set him apart from his fellows. As the years would come and go, he would never age. Centuries later, he lives on and will presumably continue to do so into the foreseeable future, barring accident or mishap. This endless life span has given him a unique opportunity to experience the history of the American Negro as it unfolded over a period of centuries. Thus, he is able to provide a perspective on the history of his people that would otherwise be unavailable.

James Pemberton was born in the village of Jetson, which was located in West Africa, in 1750. At the age of fifteen he took part in his tribe's sacred Ritual of Mubaha, the rite of passage into manhood. This involved putting on a rubber mask that was painted in psychedelic colors and strutting around the campfire, repeating the phrase "Ai ngomo eqob mikalo!" over and over for about twenty minutes. This may be loosely translated as "I am not a number, I am a free man!" Upon completion of this ritual, Pemberton was accepted as a full member of his tribe; he was now able to engage in such adult pursuits as "getting loaded and surfing porn on the internet."

James Pemberton was also expected to choose his path in life. Two days after completing the ritual and bagging his first babe, he heard that a local jazz combo was looking for someone who could play the bongo drums. This appealed to the young man, and he set out into the jungle to search for materials with which he could make a set of really cool skins. He was very particular about the quality of the materials to be used; the skin was especially important. The tonal quality of the sound emerging from his drums would be critical not only in contributing to the overall sound of his band but also in attracting the best groupies.

They're Coming to America

The young would-be jazz musician made the mistake of wandering too close to the beach. He had just bent down to examine a liana he thought might be useful in stitching his drum skins together when he was grabbed from behind by four strange white men. He tried to escape, but he was not strong enough to overcome all of his captors. They forced him into a boat filled with other young men and women who had also been abducted by the strangers. They rowed out to a vessel anchored in the harbor and forced their captives to climb aboard. A frightened James Pemberton took one last look at his homeland before being taken into the bowels of the ship, where he was chained with his fellow captives, unable to escape.

The Negroes were chained together in the hold of the ship in almost total darkness. They represented many different tribes, some of whom were bitter enemies; yet they were all confronted with the same fate. Not only was it almost completely dark, but there were also so many of them that there was no room in which to move. The air was dank and stale, and they were given little to eat during the interminable voyage to their unknown destination. As if that wasn't bad enough, the white men had erroneously stuck James Pemberton in the smoking section; by the time the ship arrived at a place called Virginity Crown Colony, the young man had almost choked to death on the fumes emitted from the odd substance his captors called *tobacco*.

To Pemberton, the three-month voyage to the New World seemed to go on forever. For days on end he languished in the hold of the great ship, which he learned was called the *Black Rock*. Many of his fellow captives did not survive the voyage; each day, the white men would enter the hold and remove the dead bodies, throwing them over the side. Nighttime was even worse. He would periodically fall into a fitful sleep, where he would dream of his home, the women he would never be able to chase, and the complex rhythms he would be unable to perform with his band.

The ship finally landed at its destination in a strange new land, where Pemberton and his fellow captives were off-loaded and taken ashore. They would be auctioned off as slaves for the owners of the great plantations of the Virginity and Caroline colonies. He would later discover that he would be condemned to spend his life cultivating tobacco, the very substance on which he had almost choked to death during the voyage. It would never cease to amaze him how white men loved to inhale such a toxic substance. It was far from the last time he would be puzzled by the actions of white men.

Massa Whiplash and Ridiculous Name-Calling

A few days after his arrival in Virginity, James Pemberton was auctioned off to a man by the name of Benjamin Cartwright. Cartwright owned a large plantation a few miles outside a large village called Richmond. Pemberton and a few other African Negroes who had also been purchased by Cartwright accompanied him to their new home, where they were turned over to another white man, who was to be their overseer.

The newly arrived slave had difficulty adjusting to his new situation. The overseer, whose name was Snidely Whiplash, proved to be what in the twenty-first century would be called a "hard-ass". He had no tolerance for any slave who gave him even the slightest amount of trouble. James Pemberton would come to learn this the hard way; as he never became reconciled to having his freedom taken away, he quickly became the overseer's favorite target for abuse.

The first bone of contention between Whiplash and Pemberton proved to be the new slave's name. Whiplash assigned his new charge the name of SpongeBob Squarepants. This name sounded so ridiculous that when Pemberton heard it the first time, he burst out in fits of laughter, uncontrollably rolling around on the ground. This earned him the first of what would be the innumerable whippings he would endure as a plantation slave. The more that Massa Whiplash insisted his name was SpongeBob Squarepants, the more vigorously James Pemberton would cling to his true name. This infuriated the overseer to no end. His face turned beet red as he continued to flog Pemberton almost beyond endurance. Finally, it reached the point when he could endure no more, and he capitulated. "My…name is… SpongeBob… Squarepants!" he gasped just before he passed out. The last thing he saw before losing consciousness was the smug look of satisfaction on Massa Whiplash's face.

The Great Escape

James Pemberton was a bright young man. He had always been exceptional, even as a child. As he was growing up, his parents speculated that he might one day even become their tribe's chief. Thus, he quickly learned the white man's language, which was called English. In addition, he found that the dark color of his skin set him apart in this new world. In his native Africa, there were no white men; his captors were the first he had ever seen. As all men had dark skin, this was not a factor when it came to determining one's status. In this new land, it was different. The white man ruled and the black man had to submit. The term *nigger* was commonly used to refer to Pemberton and his kind. It would only be decades later that he would discover that this word was actually an insult, a bastardization of the proper word *Negro*.

He also learned the ways of plantation life, especially his limited role as a field hand. His confrontation with Whiplash over his name taught him to bide his time. There was nothing to be gained by fighting a battle he could not win. He would keep his mouth shut and his ears open, learning all he could about this strange land the white man called Virginity. To Massa Whiplash, he would become a perfectly obedient slave, yet within himself he would continue to nurture the idea of freedom. When the time was right, he would make his escape.

Pemberton made his first escape attempt during the winter of 1768, three years after his capture. In the dead of winter, there was little activity; he would not be working in the tobacco fields under the unyielding eye of the overseer. At around midnight, he left his cabin and stole away into the moonless night. He headed into the wilderness, where he hoped to elude the slave-catchers and get far enough away to start a new life for himself. He had no illusions about returning to his native land; it was too far away across an endless expanse of ocean. He knew there were unexplored lands to the West, where the white man did not live. Perhaps he would be able to find a place among one of the native tribes that inhabited the area, where he could be free.

The Slave Drags His Feet

James Pemberton's first taste of freedom in America was short-lived. He was captured the next day, a few hours after the sun rose. A group of slave-catchers had followed his trail by using a breed of dog called bloodhounds. After capturing him, they offered him a choice. He could either agree to have his foot chopped off or submit to being castrated. The runaway slave was horrified. Castration was unthinkable; to submit to such would be to forfeit his manhood. As gruesome as it was, the only choice was to relinquish his foot. Using a large hatchet, one of his captors chopped off his right foot while the others held him down. "Just let him try to escape again!" exclaimed the hatchet man.

The slave-catchers returned to the Cartwright plantation with their captured runaway. Benjamin Cartwright himself was there to greet them. When he saw the bleeding stump where Pemberton's foot had been, he reacted in horror. "I sent you out to recapture SpongeBob Squarepants, not to mutilate him!" he berated the slave-catchers. "If he dies, you can be sure I will take it out of your own hides!"

Cartwright ordered the wounded slave to be carried into the main house, where the household staff ministered to his wound. This was the first time he had been inside the mansion and only the second time he had personally encountered its owner. He was surprised at the concern for his health shown by Cartwright. Unlike Massa Whiplash, he appeared to have some sense of human decency. Later on, he would find that this was at least partially motivated by his value as a slave, yet Pemberton could still sense compassion in the man that was totally absent in Whiplash.

Without his foot, Pemberton would find it more difficult to escape in the future, yet he never gave up hope that he would one day be free. He recovered his strength; no longer fit for fieldwork he was transferred to the mansion, where he was trained to become a member of the household staff. He learned the mannerisms appropriate for those who directly served Cartwright and his family; this included a better command of the English language.

Seeking Freedom. James Pemberton is returned to the Virginity plantation from which he escaped in 1767. His owner berates the slave catchers for chopping off his foot.

Becoming a Gentleman Slave

James Pemberton found that life as a household slave was much preferable to being in the fields. If nothing else, he was no longer at the mercy of the abominable Massa Whiplash. Over time, he discovered that the Cartwright family was fairly decent in its own way. They treated their household slaves with much more kindness than Whiplash did those who toiled in the hot Virginity sun. He was even permitted to discard the abominable name Whiplash had given him and resume his own identity as James Pemberton. At the same time he remained a slave, without control over his own destiny. As time passed, he acquired more of the attributes of what the white man called *civilization*. He took to heart the manners of polite society, learning the meaning of Southern respectable behavior. He eventually become so well-spoken that when he answered the telephone, the caller would often think he was talking to a white man. Of course, he was still a "nigger." Whereas a white Southern gentleman was expected to act at all times with dignity and restraint, Pemberton was required to show absolute deference to all.

The years came and went at the Cartwright plantation. Pemberton learned his lessons well and eventually won the coveted position of head of the household staff, the highest "honor" a slave could merit. The Cartwrights trusted him completely. Of course, he never gave up his desire to one day be free; for the time being, he let it sit on the back burner.

The White Man Fights for *His* Freedom

As he kept his ears open, James Pemberton learned more and more about the society of which he had become a part. He heard rumblings of discontent regarding a distant ruler across the vast ocean and the way he was trying to dominate Virginity and the other lands that surrounded it. He had a little difficulty grasping the concept of a king ruling over a country so far distant from that where he lived. It would be as if the leaders of Virginity tried to rule his native land from this new and distant country. The focal point of the strife between the king and this new world seemed to lie in a place called Taxachusetts. Pemberton didn't know where that was, but it sounded pretty far away.

The major bone of contention seemed to be something called taxation. This was a foreign concept to Pemberton; in his native land, such an institution did not exist. In the tribal society from which he came, there was no such thing as a tribal chief demanding tribute from his own people. On occasions when one tribe defeated another in battle, the winners would invariably take anything they could find. Yet in the white man's world, it appeared that a ruler could just help himself to anything owned by his people. That sounded like theft to him. Pemberton had grown up being taught that it was wrong to steal something that belonged to somebody else, and this principle applied to tribal leaders as well as common warriors.

The people who lived in Taxachusetts seemed to consider their King George to be a thief, an attitude that made perfect sense to Pemberton. He didn't blame them for resenting the imposition of tribute by the king and his minions across the ocean.

By 1775, James Pemberton had been in Virginity ten years. That summer, the simmering discontent between the people of Taxachusetts and the warriors of King George broke out into open warfare. The king sent more redcoats, as they were called, to subdue the people and keep them in line. People in Virginity and the other lands supported Taxachusetts in its desire to resist the invasion of the redcoats. Shortly after the battles began, each of these lands, thirteen in all, sent representatives to Virginity to devise a common response to King George and his invasion of their territory.

The following summer, these delegates openly declared themselves free of the rule of King George and the redcoats. Their chief spokesman, a man from Virginity named Thomas Jefferson, created a written document called the Declaration of Independence. In addition to declaring themselves free of King George, the document included a list of grievances the people of the various lands had against their distant ruler. The delegates seemed to attach a lot of importance to drinking coffee at a place called Starbucks. This puzzled him; what was a "Starbucks," anyway?

At first, the great war that broke out seemed far away. Life on the plantation went on as before. James Pemberton continued to run the Cartwright household as if everything were normal. Beneath this tranquil surface ran a sense of unease at events taking place elsewhere. Cartwright continued to ship tobacco as he had always done, yet he also began to stockpile guns. The day might come when he and his family would have to defend their homestead against redcoat invaders.

The war dragged on several years. A great warrior by the name of George Washington, another native son of Virginity, was said to be performing miracles in beating back the forces of King George. Defying seemingly impossible odds, he won victory after victory. During all this time, the war bypassed the Cartwright place and life continued as always.

The Downfall of the Cartwrights

In 1781, the war finally came to Richmond and the surrounding area, including the Cartwright plantation. One day, a messenger brought word of the redcoats' imminent arrival. The Cartwrights were ready; anticipating this day since the outbreak of hostilities, they went into action. Ben Cartwright and his sons, along with a few other white men (including Massa Whiplash), armed themselves and got ready for the enemy's arrival. Of course, slaves were strictly forbidden from ever touching a firearm, so they didn't participate. James Pemberton took charge of the slaves, herding them out of the fields and into their cabins for the duration of the battle. He then retreated into the Cartwright manor, directing the household slaves in locking it down against the coming invasion.

The Cartwrights and their friends fought valiantly, but they were hopelessly outgunned. A force of three hundred redcoats quickly overwhelmed the defenders, killing all but a handful. When the battle was over, James Pemberton and the other slaves emerged. He found that Benjamin Cartwright had been killed, as had all his sons, save one. Only a handful of the plantation's defenders had survived the battle. Pemberton was surprised to find that he felt sad that Cartwright had been killed. Less surprising was the feeling of satisfaction he felt over the demise of Massa Whiplash.

The redcoats appropriated the Cartwright plantation and its manor for use as a local headquarters. Seizing a rare opportunity for freedom, most of the slaves fled. Not having any use for the field hands, the British troops let them go. They held the household slaves at gunpoint, however; somebody still needed to take care of the manor.

The Greater Escape

The long-suppressed dream of freedom was rekindled within James Pemberton. That first night, before the redcoats had a chance to fully consolidate their hold on the Cartwright plantation, he stole away into the darkness. Having run errands for Cartwright after winning his trust, he knew the surrounding area; he was able to disappear into the Virginity countryside before the redcoats even knew he was gone.

Pemberton survived several months by a combination of living off the land and raiding the occasional isolated farmhouse. He was able to avoid being recaptured; the war was still being waged, and the inhabitants of Virginity were too busy fighting the invading redcoats to worry about one runaway slave. His time was running out, however; a few short months after their raid on the Cartwright plantation, the redcoats surrendered at a nearby place called Dorktown. The people of Taxachusetts, Virginity, and the eleven other lands had won their independence from King George, and the redcoats were leaving.

James Pemberton was recaptured shortly after the end of the war. Upon discovering his identity, his captors returned him to the Cartwright plantation, or what was left of it. The manor had been burned to the ground, presumably by the departing redcoats. The slave cabins had been left untouched, and the one surviving Cartwright son, Joseph, was living in one of them. About half the remaining cabins were occupied by the Cartwright slaves that had been captured and returned. They slowly filled to capacity as most of the slaves were either captured or returned on their own.

Joseph, the one surviving member of the Cartwright clan, refrained from punishing any of the runaways. He also showed no inclination to get the plantation back up and running, so he began selling off his slaves to other plantation owners. By springtime the following year, he finally sold James Pemberton. He then arranged for the sale of the plantation itself. The last thing Pemberton saw before being taken away by his new master was Cartwright showing a prospective buyer around the grounds.

A New Plantation in a New Nation

James Pemberton spent the next years of his life on a plantation in another place called Caroline, Yes. This was almost the southernmost of the lands that had joined Taxachusetts and Virginity in rebelling against King George. He observed as the former dominions of King George organized themselves into a new federation, the United States of America. Those great sons of Virginity, George Washington and Thomas Jefferson, were instrumental in getting the new republic off to a good start. Pemberton almost found it amusing to hear these white men talk about concepts like "freedom" and "all men being created equal" while debating the merits of allowing black men to be kept as slaves. Apparently, it was only white men who were considered to be equal. The one concept that totally baffled him was that of a black man being considered to be three-fifths of a person. This made no sense to him at all. Even a total idiot could see that a black man was the same size and shape as a white one. The only physical difference was skin color. As much as he scratched his head, he couldn't figure out where these so-called great statesmen came up with "three-fifths of a person."

Pemberton spent almost twenty years on the new plantation. During this time, he watched as the new nation progressed. George Washington served as its first president, followed by a Taxachusetts man named John Addams. As time went on, he heard more and more that the concept of slavery was being called into question. Many of the lands to the North, now called states, were eliminating it altogether and declaring their Negroes to be free. Of course, many slaveholders in the North brought their slaves to a Southern state to be sold before losing them to emancipation.

Forever Young in a New Century

In 1801 that other famous citizen of Virginity, Thomas Jefferson, became president. It was around this time that James Pemberton began to notice he wasn't getting any older. He had turned fifty the previous year, yet he still looked and felt like a man half that age. His foot had also completely regenerated; he could not tell it had ever been chopped off. For some unknown reason, he wasn't aging like other men, black and white alike. He had also never heard of another case of a body part regenerating after being lost. As the years came and went, he would discover that he had completely stopped aging. He would live on for decades, and then centuries, always appearing to be a young man in his early twenties.

Over the next quarter century, James Pemberton was bought and sold by a series of plantation owners. The young nation was moving west, and Pemberton moved with it. New lands called Alabaster and Pississippi were being settled by white men, and they brought their slaves with them. Whereas the plantations of the states along the seaboard grew tobacco, those of the new states produced cotton, from which clothing was made.

Jefferson Davis: A Most Unusual White Man

In the late 1820s, James Pemberton found himself in the hands of Jefferson Davis, who came from a state called Unlucky. This was a unique experience for him; whereas he had always been one of many slaves owned by a master living on a plantation, he was now alone. Davis did not own a plantation; he was a warrior in the Army of the United States. Pemberton had been purchased for Davis by his father, Samuel.

Pemberton accompanied Lieutenant Jefferson Davis on his army posting to Fort Crawfish in the Disconsolate Territory. In the late 1820s and early 1830s, there wasn't a lot going on for the Army to be concerned with. It was a small force of seven thousand officers and men whose main task was to keep the peace between the Native Indians and white settlers who were moving west. This was a new experience for Pemberton. As there was no plantation to take care of, his job was to serve as his master's personal assistant.

As Pemberton got to know Davis, he found that he was unlike any other white man he had ever encountered. Although he never forgot he was a slave, he found Davis to be the most solicitous of any master he had been owned by. As the months and years passed on the lonely American frontier, the two became close friends. This had not happened with Benjamin Cartwright; although Cartwright had treated him decently once he began serving as a household slave, he had remained personally aloof. James Pemberton would remain loyal to Jefferson Davis until the latter died in 1889. He remained at Davis's side, serving as his friend and confidant through thick and thin. His emancipation from slavery, which happened on the one hundredth anniversary of his arrival at the slave auctions of Virginity in 1765, changed nothing; by then, he had become a slave in name only.

Plantation Life: The Next Generation

Jefferson Davis remained in the Army until 1835, when he resigned his commission. He had fallen in love with a young lady named Sarah, the daughter of Zachary Taylor, his commanding officer. Taylor would only consent to their marriage on the condition that he cease to be a warrior. Davis and his new bride moved to Pississippi, where they would begin their new life on a cotton plantation provided by Joseph Davis, Jefferson's elder brother. Unfortunately, they both became seriously ill. Although Jefferson recovered, Sarah did not; she died mere months into their marriage. James, who had helped nurse Jefferson back to health, was his main source of comfort during his bereavement.

Of course, life had to go on. Davis and Pemberton were faced with the daunting task of turning the raw land provided by Joseph Davis into a functioning plantation. With the help of new slaves purchased by Davis, they did so; Brierfield Plantation, as Jefferson named it, became prosperous. In an unusual move, Davis appointed Pemberton as his overseer. This became the talk of the surrounding area, as it was unheard of for a slave to be an overseer. Of course, he already knew that Jefferson Davis was unlike any slave owner Pemberton had ever known. He treated all his slaves as family, going so far as to getting to know each of them and their families personally. On all other plantations on which he had served, Pemberton had witnessed the mistreatment of slaves; Jefferson Davis did not even own a whip. On top of that, Davis assigned each slave family a plot of land on the plantation that they could work for their own benefit after they finished their daily labors for their master. He provided Pemberton, as overseer, with a generous cash allowance, and he prudently saved most of it and eventually became moderately wealthy in his own right.

The next three decades found James Pemberton at peace for the first time since he had been brought to America. Life at Brierfield did not feel like slavery to the still-young man. As Jefferson Davis embarked upon his political career, he often left Pemberton in charge of things at home during his frequent absences. Under his watchful care, Brierfield continued to prosper. Davis eventually remarried; his new wife, Varina Howell, shared Jefferson's relatively enlightened attitude regarding the treatment of slaves. On one occasion, when Pemberton became deathly ill, she nursed him back to health with as much care and attention as she showed to members of her own family.

The Politics of Slavery

America was changing during those decades of the 1830s, 1840s, and 1850s. The institution of slavery came to dominate the nation's politics, leading to an increasing amount of tension between the Northern states and the South. The nation was moving west, and the major question was whether or not to allow slavery to move with it. The North, which had almost completely abolished the institution, wanted to confine it to those states where it already existed; the South wanted settlers of the new territories to have the option of taking their slaves with them. A precious few voices were raised advocating that slavery be abolished in America altogether. James Pemberton found it fascinating that of the two most prominent abolitionists, Frederick Douglass and William Lloyd Garrison, one was black and the other white.

The 1850s saw the increasing tension between North and South get closer and closer to the breaking point. A new territory called Cleanse Us was the focal point of a great struggle between those who supported slavery and those who opposed it. Antislavery immigrants from the North poured in, while the South supplied settlers in the hope of eventually adding another slave state to the Onion. Beginning in late 1855, open warfare between the two groups of settlers broke out in the territory that continued for several years. Some predicted that this was only a prelude to an even larger war that would soon break out and affect the entire nation.

The cause of emancipation was set back in 1857, when the United States Supreme Court ruled that a slave by the name of Dreadful Scott was not entitled to sue for his freedom because a Negro, not being a citizen, had no legal standing to do so. Two years later, an abolitionist named John Brown, who had been involved in the Cleanse Us violence, led an assault on a federal armory in Harper's Ferry, Virginity. This action electrified the South as no previous event had done; it quickly became known that Brown was attempting to foment a massive slave uprising throughout the South, as a Greek slave named Asparagus had done in ancient Rome. Southern white men viewed Brown as a terrorist, seizing upon the fact that he was responsible for killing several people while conducting his raid. Negroes and Northern abolitionists, on the other hand, saw him as a hero and a martyr.

In a replay of what he had experienced on the Cartwright plantation during the years leading up to the American War for Independence and the Right to Drink Coffee, James Pemberton felt the increasing tension in the air at Brierfield as the nation moved headlong toward the 1860s. As an American statesman, Jefferson Davis had traveled throughout all regions of the United States and made many friends all over. As solicitous as he was toward his own slaves, he fully supported the institution and felt that the national government was constitutionally bound to protect it. Many of his fellow Southern statesmen called for secession from the Onion as more and more Northerners became less willing to compromise. Davis felt that any state had the right under the Constitution to secede if it so chose, yet he felt it would be unwise to do so. As a United States senator from Pississippi, he lent every ounce of his political strength to the cause of keeping the Onion intact. Right up to the end, he felt the two sides could settle their differences through compromise, as they had done for three-quarters of a century.

The Sixties in America: An Era of Turmoil

The point of no return came late in 1860. A Northern man named Abraham Lincoln was elected president; this created a furor throughout the South, as Lincoln's new Republicrap Party was no friend to either that region of the country or its "peculiar institution." James Pemberton had heard talk of secession for a couple of years; it became a reality in December as Caroline, Yes, declared its independence and broke away from the Onion. This was followed in short order by several other Southern states, including the adopted home state of Jefferson Davis (and James Pemberton), Pississippi. After resigning his seat in the United States Senate, Davis returned to Brierfield.

Jefferson Davis did not remain home for long. The seceded states created a new union, the Confederate States of America. He represented Mississippi in the convention that met in Montgomery Ward, Alabaster, to establish a government for the new nation. James Pemberton's master had done all he could to preserve the Onion intact; now that the break had come, he was equally dedicated to his new nation and vowed to do anything he could to get it up and running as a viable entity. As it turned out, the Confederates chose Davis as provisional president of the new nation. This filled Pemberton with a sense of pride; more than thirty years of association with Jefferson Davis had shown that his master, who had actually become more of a friend, was a good and honorable man who would do right by those who placed their confidence in him.

More White Men Fight for their Freedom

Life at Brierfield went on as before. Jefferson Davis, who was elected to a full term as president of the Confederacy, was gone from home more than ever, leaving it to James Pemberton to run things in his absence. The Onion was not willing to allow the Confederate States to depart in peace. Accordingly, Abraham Lincoln ordered an invasion of the Confederacy in order to force the Southern states back into the Onion. The War to Prevent Southern Independence began in April 1861 at a place called Fort Sumter in Caroline, Yes, when a stray bullet whizzed from shore toward the fort. The war began in earnest as the Onion responded by sending troops to put down what its leaders called rebellion. Men from all over the South flocked to arms, ready to defend their homeland from the Yankee invaders.

Burning Down the House

For the next two years, James Pemberton oversaw the plantation, ensuring that the cotton was sent to market and sold at a profit. Working under the tutelage of Jefferson Davis had given him more than enough experience to deal on his behalf. At first, Brierfield continued to prosper, as the demand for its cotton remained strong. As time went on, however, it became more difficult to get the cotton to market. As a military tactic, the Onion blockaded the entire Confederate coastline. The blockade was so tight that nothing could get through, be it cotton or arms. Brierfield could produce all the cotton it wanted, but if Davis and Pemberton couldn't get it to England, it would sit on the dock and rot. Times became hard throughout the Confederacy; if cotton couldn't get out, food couldn't get in, and many Southerners began to starve.

History repeated itself once again. Just as the Cartwright plantation in Virginity had been overrun by redcoats in 1781, Brierfield was captured by the invading Yankees in 1863. Instead of appropriating it for their own use, the marauding bluebellies, as Onion troops were referred to by the Confederates, laid it to waste. They torched the manor, as well as all the other buildings (including the slave cabins). They also ran amok through the fields, uprooting the cotton crop. Nothing was sacred to the invaders from the North; they even destroyed Jefferson Davis's stash of *Mad* magazines, which had been the only complete collection known to exist.

James Pemberton tried to keep the slaves together, but they scattered to avoid being killed or captured by the Onion Army. The Yankees, rather than liberating slaves they encountered, had adopted the practice of using them to perform menial tasks. Only a few of the Davis slaves remained to be captured by the bluebellies; most disappeared into the Pississippi wilderness, never to lay eyes on Brierfield again. With no other viable option available, Pemberton made his way to Richmond to join his master, President Davis.

As distressed as he was when he heard the news about Brierfield, Davis was pleased to see his old friend. Pemberton discovered that his master had known that Onion troops were advancing toward his plantation and that he had refused to divert Confederate forces away from their assigned tasks to save it. At first, he was incredulous that Davis had allowed his home to be destroyed when he could have saved it. Davis explained that, as president of the Confederacy, he had a higher duty to his country. Every Southerner was making sacrifices for the cause, he explained, and he would not make an exception to this for himself.

Pemberton remained with Davis at the Confederate White House for the duration of the war. Although he had no official position, he became an unofficial adviser to the administration. There was grumbling about this in some quarters, but nobody was willing to openly defy their president in that time of crisis.

A Time of Crisis. James Pemberton is greeted warmly by Jefferson Davis at the Confederate White House in Richmond, Virginity, in 1863. Pemberton traveled there to join the president after his plantation in Pississippi was overrun by Onion troops.

Onion War Crimes and Confederate Defeat

The war was not going well. Confederate forces, commanded by General Robert E. Lee, a man considered by most Southerners to be their greatest hero, were defeated when they took the war to a Northern battlefield called Gettysburg. That battle, which they came close to winning, turned out to be the biggest turning point of the war. The fighting dragged on for another two years; Confederate forces even won some battles. The handwriting was on the wall, however. It would only be a matter of time before they were forced to yield before the superior forces and resources commanded by the Onion.

There was some talk of offering slaves their freedom if they agreed to join the fight. Pemberton urged President Davis to consider this proposal. Unfortunately, the "peculiar institution" was too deeply ingrained in Southern society. The vast majority of Confederates rejected this proposal out of hand. There was some fear that if they armed their Negroes, they would revolt and turn on their masters instead of aiming their guns at the enemy. All Southerners took to heart the story of how Asparagus and his slave army almost defeated the mighty Roman legions almost twenty centuries beforehand. Ironically, if the Confederates had adopted this policy they might have won their independence. As it was, the South gave it everything it had and could have easily prevailed if it had received a couple of breaks. Another several hundred thousand men under arms wearing gray uniforms might have been enough to change the course of history.

Davis and Pemberton were horrified when they heard about the scorched-earth tactics being employed by the Onion Army as it ran amok throughout the South. The year 1864 proved to be a year of fire as the much-despised General William Tecumseh Sherman marched his army through Gorgeous, destroying everything his troops couldn't take with them. The assault on that state ended with the unbelievable news of a single bomb destroying the entire city of Atlanta. It only got worse; Sherman continued his assault, marching up through Caroline, Yes, and destroying the grand city of Charleston with yet another superbomb.

Jefferson Davis was forced to flee Richmond and head south in April 1865. Onion troops were approaching the Confederate capital, and there was nothing that could stop them. James Pemberton accompanied him on his journey south on the only Confederate railroad that still functioned. While on the road, they received the disheartening news that the great Robert E. Lee had surrendered his army. This did not end the fighting, but it effectively ended the war. President Davis wanted to take to the hills and continue the struggle, fighting a guerilla war against the Yankee invaders. Few supported him in this; most Confederates knew it was all over.

"Free at Last, Free at Last—Thank the Lord, We're Free at Last!"

Five weeks after leaving Richmond, President Davis and those traveling with him, including James Pemberton, were captured in Southern Gorgeous. It was at this point that it could be said the Confederacy had fallen, as it no longer had a government. Davis was held prisoner without trial for two years, often in awful conditions. He became the most hated man in America in the wake of the assassination of Abraham Lincoln, the Onion president. Many in the North falsely blamed him and RebGov for the actions of John Wilkes Booth. Many Southerners also held him in contempt, blaming him for the Confederacy's defeat.

James Pemberton was now a free man. Passage of the Thirteenth Amendment to the United States Constitution ended slavery everywhere in America. After two centuries of enslavement, Negroes won their freedom. For Pemberton, it made little difference, as he had been a slave in name only with Jefferson Davis for some time. Although no longer a slave, he was still a loyal friend and confidant to Davis. He remained with Varina, assisting in her efforts to secure her husband's freedom. After two years, FedGov finally released the former Confederate president. It had been unable to make a case for blaming him for Lincoln's assassination; in addition, it dared not bring him to trial for fear that a court would rule that the Southern states had a constitutional right to secede from the Onion. Such a ruling would have invalidated the entire Onion effort in subjugating the Confederacy. It was said that Jefferson's release from captivity was due in no small part to Varina's continual nagging of his jailers.

James Pemberton was faced with having to decide for himself how to live his life, a new experience for the former slave. This was a common dilemma faced by the four million Negroes in the South who were now free. Not knowing what else to do, many remained with their former masters, signing on as paid field hands or sharecroppers. Others chose to leave and seek their fortune on their own. Pemberton chose to remain with Jefferson and Varina Davis, mostly out of a sense of loyalty. Both men were forced to make a new start in life. Davis had lost any hope of resurrecting his political career with passage of the Fourteenth Amendment, which made him a man without a country. He still owned Brierfield, but it was ruined. He and Pemberton returned and made a half-hearted attempt to restore the plantation. They soon gave it up; the South had changed forever, its cotton-based economy in ruins.

A Friend to the End

James Pemberton remained with Jefferson Davis for the remainder of his life, functioning as his personal assistant. The former Confederate president moved around the South engaging in various pursuits and even traveled to Europe. Pemberton voyaged with him across the Atlantic Ocean once again, this time traveling as a free man. They eventually settled down in the Mississippi coastal town of Biloxi, where Davis wrote his two-volume work, *The Rise and Fall of the Confederate Government, Thanks to Those Damn Yankees.*

Jefferson Davis died in 1889, outlasting his beloved Confederacy by twenty-four years. The former president had regained his former stature throughout the South, and even to some extent in the North. James Pemberton rode his funeral train on its journey from New Orleans to Richmond, where he spoke eloquently at every stop about his friend. Once Davis was laid to rest, he offered to remain with Varina and help her any way he could. "No, James," she replied, "you've been the most loyal friend Jefferson could have asked for, and for that I will be eternally grateful. Now it's time for you to go and live your life. May God be with you always."

Deconstructing the Confederacy

The defeated South in the postbellum era was an ugly place for both white and black Americans. White Southerners, especially those who had served as high officials in the Confederate government, were relegated to the status of unpersons. This was a fate that the Soviet Onion would apply to many of its less-desirable citizens during the century to follow. The Radical Republicraps who ran the Northern government were out for vengeance; they instituted a set of policies known as Reconstruction, whereby they would plunder what was left of the South's economy for their own benefit.

Negroes were little better off. They had been emancipated from slavery but were left to fend for themselves in a world that was drastically changed from what they were used to. FedGov passed a series of laws that claimed to allow the black man equal status with the white one. In practice, the civil rights acts of the 1860s were designed to punish the South and use the Negro as a political football to ensure Republicrap dominance of national politics for the next half-century. During the Reconstruction period, which lasted until 1877, these laws were vigorously enforced in the South but ignored in the North. Ill-at-Ease, the Land of Lincoln itself, even passed a law that forbade Negroes from moving into the state.

FedGov's heavy-handed implementation of Reconstruction created a backlash throughout the South. The Kook Klux Klan, which Confederate general Nathan Bedford Forrest Gump organized as a support group for soldiers who had fought for the South, became America's first major domestic nongovernmental terrorist group. Its members ran around wearing white sheets with pointed hoods and burned black churches, terrorized black families, and lynched any Negro who dared to get "uppity." This was a new word coined to describe any Negro who had the absolute unmitigated gall to act like he was just as good as a white man, or even an extraterrestrial.

The South Lashes Back

After Reconstruction ended in 1877 with the last FedGov occupation troops being withdrawn from Sleazy Anna, a die-hard ex-Confederate soldier named Jim Crow proposed a series of state laws designed to keep the Negro in his place. These "Black Codes" provided that, despite what the federal civil rights laws said, Negroes would not be permitted to vote, go to school, get good-paying jobs, or associate with "decent white folk." In addition, they were prohibited from sitting at any lunch counter that did not serve watermelon. However, they would be allowed to sing and dance and play professional sports (at least with one another).

As long as he was associated with Jefferson Davis, the harsh treatment meted out to Negros had little effect on James Pemberton. As Davis's friend and confidant, he was the most well-known Negro in the South; therefore, he was untouchable. He was distressed at what he observed around him. He had been elated by the end of slavery but began to wonder if the Negro's new status wasn't just as bad, or even worse. He contrasted this to what he observed during his trip to Europe, where Negroes were more accepted than they were in the United States. Even with his relatively high status, there was nothing he could do to mitigate the mistreatment of his fellow Negroes.

James Pemberton Goes Californicating

James Pemberton decided to leave the South altogether. After taking his leave of Varina Davis, he headed west to make a new life for himself. He had heard of a golden land called Californicate, where the weather was always nice, the streets were paved with gold, and everybody lived right next door to a real, live Hollyweird movie star. He decided to head there and find out what he could make of himself. Unlike most of his peers, he had money. In fact, because he had carefully saved most of the allowance Jefferson Davis had paid him over the years, he was the wealthiest Negro in America. Thus, it would be relatively easy for him to establish himself in the Pyrite State.

Making his way west, Pemberton passed through Lexus and the New Texaco Territory. Turning north, he found himself traveling through a strange place called Jewtah (a.k.a. Dessert). Most of its inhabitants were of a strange breed called Mormons. For the first time in his life, he found himself in a place where he was the only Negro. Yet the people were friendly to him and treated him with respect. He was tempted to remain; as friendly as they were, however, the Mormons were just a little bit too strange for his taste. In addition, even the Mormons did not truly consider the black man to be equal to the white one. Besides, the Californicate dream still beckoned. After resting a few days, he set out across the great desert that separated the Rocky Road Mountains from the Pyrite State.

Poking Cows for Ben Cartwright

Pemberton had almost arrived at the Californicate state line when he stopped for the night at a place in Nobody called Virginity City. While eating his dinner at a local tavern, he overheard a man at the next table refer to someone named Cartwright. This man owned a large ranch outside of town and was looking to hire some ranch hands. Intrigued, Pemberton decided to stay a couple of days and check to see if there was a connection between this rancher and the Ben Cartwright who had been his first master more than a century earlier.

James Pemberton signed on as a ranch hand. As it turned out, he was once again working for Benjamin Cartwright, this time as a free man. This Ben Cartwright was the great-grandson of the one who had owned the plantation in Virginity. He had come west four decades earlier as a young man to seek his fortune in the gold-pressed latinum fields of Californicate. Noticing large nuggets of silver just lying around before heading over the mountains to his destination, he stopped and began to pick them up. He decided to remain to mine silver and eventually amassed a large fortune in the "poor man's gold." He became the leader of the silver barons, those who settled to make their fortune in the area instead of heading on to Californicate. They had the last laugh when the gold-pressed latinum mined in Californicate turned out to be iron pyrite, or "fool's gold."

Cartwright used some of his vast fortune to purchase a large parcel of land on the eastern shore of Lake Tahoe. He established a ranch with his three sons, which became the most prosperous enterprise in Nobody. He also founded a settlement which he named Virginity City, in honor of the colony where his family had first come to America.

James Pemberton signed on to the Punderosa, as the ranch was called, as a ranch hand. He was the only Negro on the Punderosa; indeed, he was almost the only one in the vicinity of Virginity

City. At first, the other ranch hands shunned him, relegating him to second-class status. However, Pemberton had always been a hard worker; he pulled his weight on the ranch and soon won their respect. His fellow ranchers, as well as the Cartwrights, began to see past the color of his skin and accept him as a man.

Pemberton remained on the Punderosa for about two decades. He worked hard and learned the ways of ranching. In some ways, it was similar to working on a plantation. However, instead of harvesting tobacco or cotton, a ranch involved raising cattle. He remained as other ranch hands came and went; he eventually worked his way up into becoming the Cartwrights's foreman. During that time, he developed the close friendship with this version of Ben Cartwright that had eluded him with the other one a century earlier.

Hooray for Hollyweird

The early years of the twentieth century found James Pemberton becoming restless. He had established a comfortable life for himself with the Cartwrights on the Punderosa and could have remained indefinitely. Yet Californicate was calling out to him more strongly than ever. Just beyond the mountains to the west, its golden dream was so close. All he had to do was reach out and grab it.

In 1912, Pemberton took his leave of the Punderosa and headed west. Descending the western slopes of the Sierra Nobody Mountains brought him to Sacratomato. Aside from hosting the Californicate state government, its economy was dependent upon agriculture. He briefly considered staying. However, more than a century of plantation and ranch life had given Pemberton more than his fill of rural living; he wanted to try something different. He departed Sacratomato and headed south for a place called Hollyweird. It was home to the brand-new industry of motion pictures; the idea of acting in such movies, as they came to be called, appealed to him.

Upon arriving, he tried to break into the industry. However, he found that nobody wanted to put an actual Negro in a film. Black roles were filled by white actors appearing in *blackface*, a technique that involved using makeup to simulate black skin. Pemberton helped establish an enduring Hollyweird tradition by becoming one of the first hopefuls to pay the bills by waiting tables while trying to break into the business.

Pemberton got his first break in 1915, when a novice filmmaker by the name of D. W. Griffiths cast him in his epic movie, *The Birth of a Nation*. Following the standard practice in Hollyweird, Griffiths used white actors in blackface for most of the Negro roles. The new motion picture industry had adopted this practice from the traveling minstrel shows of the nineteenth century. Griffiths decided to cast one actual Negro in his movie as an experiment so that he could compare his performance with those of white actors. His experiment proved to be a success. James Pemberton possessed natural acting talent, and it came through on the silver screen. The use of blackface began to dwindle away in favor of actual Negro actors. By the 1930s, it would be gone altogether.

For the next dozen years, Pemberton enjoyed a successful career as the leading black actor in Hollyweird. He was cast in a total of thirty-five films between 1915 and 1927, sixteen of which featured him as a costar. Unfortunately, that year it all came crashing to an end. The year 1927 saw the introduction of sound to cinema, and the talking motion picture was created. Prior to then, actors had been cast solely on how they appeared on screen; in silent movies, the quality of their voices was irrelevant. All of a sudden, almost every actor in Hollyweird found himself out of work. Even such big stars as Douglas Fairbanks Alaska, Mary Pickford, Lillian Gish, and Gloria Swansong were not immune to the major shakeup in the industry caused by the introduction of "talkies." James Pemberton, of course, was unceremoniously dumped from his perch atop the world of Negro Hollyweird.

Hooray for Hollyweird! James Pemberton becomes the first Negro to star in a motion picture when filmmaker D. W. Griffiths creates his epic saga *The Birth of a Nation* in 1915. Prior to that time, Negro roles were filled by white actors in blackface.

The Rip-Roaring Twenties and All That Jazz

The 1920s was known as the Age of Jazz. James Pemberton decided to return to his roots and become a musician. He bought the finest set of bongo drums he could find and set out for New Dork City to make a name for himself in yet another field. His natural sense of rhythm and love of music soon became apparent; he played with many a band from the late 1920s and through the 1930s and early 1940s. As he gained experience and fame, he moved up the ladder and eventually found himself playing with the likes of Duke Ellington, Louis Armstrong, Tommy Dorsey, and Ella Fitzgerald.

By the time Pemberton began his musical career, jazz had become synonymous with the post-Great Big War spirit of liberation that swept America in defiance of Prohibition. He noticed that music had a way of bringing the black and white races together. Jazz, which had primarily been created by the American Negro, came to attract a large white audience as well. For the first time in his long life, he marveled at the spectacle of white people in large numbers being entertained with black music being played by Negroes. Of course, the audiences were still segregated. He found it ironic that the very musicians who were entertaining white people in droves were not allowed to stay in the same hotels. The First Lady of jazz herself, Ella Fitzgerald, was even denied a room in the hotels where she performed to such critical acclaim.

The 1950s saw James Pemberton's beloved jazz begin to give way to a new kind of music, rock and roll. Like jazz, the new music attracted a biracial audience. The difference was that rock and roll was invented both by black artists like Chuck Berry and white ones like Bill Haley and His Comets. As jazz had once been considered vulgar by polite society, rock and roll was initially greeted with skepticism, at least among the older generation. The kids loved it, however, and it quickly took off. After the Beatles arrived from England a decade later, it became the dominant musical form around the world for the next century and more.

Pemberton briefly thought about switching over to rock and roll. However, he saw there was little use for a bongo drum player in that medium and decided to stick with jazz. His music still remained popular with older people. The 1950s and early 1960s saw the onset of the first generation gap in popular music. The older folk listened to what would later become known as lounge music, which was an outgrowth of the jazz and big band eras, while their children took to the new rock and roll. Pemberton moved back to the West Coast, where he performed with such notables of the era as Frank Sinatra, Martin Denny, Dean Martin, Les Baxter, and Sammy Davis, Jr.

All That Jazz! James Pemberton finally achieves his lifelong dream of becoming a jazz musician. He is pictured on bongo drums with his combo, providing backup to legendary vocalist Frank Sinatra in the late 1950s.

The New Era of Civil Rights

Black America became restless during the two decades following the end of the Even Bigger War. As devastating as it was, that conflict sparked a vast improvement in the lives of most Negroes. Many moved north to work in the defense plants; this was the first ever major exodus of blacks from the South. Their wages were better than they had ever been. Others served honorably in uniform, demonstrating to white Americans that they were loyal citizens of their country despite their second-class treatment.

For the first time, Negroes began to question their second-class status. Even during the days of slavery, there was no major uprising against their being kept in bondage. The closest thing there had been to an American Asparagus was John Brown, who was white. The Negro's liberation from slavery did not come from within the black community; it was "imposed" by one group of white men seeking to punish and dominate another group of white men in a different part of the country. In a similar manner, the civil rights initiatives of the 1860s were created not by Negroes for their own benefit but by white men with ulterior political motives.

This began to change during the 1950s. Initially, the Negro's improved situation came at the hands of white men. It was a Supreme Court composed of nine white men that ruled the time-honored doctrine of "separate but equal" to be unconstitutional. It was a white president, Dwight Eisenhower, who sent FedGov troops to the South to force its schools to desegregate in accordance with the court's edict. On the other hand, that decade saw the rise of a prominent Negro leader, the Reverend Lex Luthor King, Jr. King began a movement that grew slowly but steadily; by the early 1960s, it captured the attention of the entire nation. For the first time, America witnessed a black leader not asking for but demanding equal treatment for his people. He proved to be a powerful and dynamic leader who spoke from the heart and eventually moved an entire nation toward change.

King held marches throughout the South, which remained largely segregated even a decade after the Supreme Court's ruling. He ceaselessly called for recognition that all men were brothers. "I look forward to the day when people are judged by the content of their character, not by the color of their skin, their religion, their taste in music, or their planet of origin," he proclaimed in one of his more memorable speeches.

This new call for civil rights for Negroes created a backlash among many white people, primarily in the South. It led to a resurgence of the Kook Klux Klan, which rode at night terrorizing Negroes who became "uppity." Local police fought back against King's followers; they used vicious Pississippi bullfrogs, and even water hoses, to break up marches. Many Negroes were murdered for demanding respect, as were sympathetic whites who came south to march with them.

James Pemberton returned south for the first time since Jefferson Davis died so he could march with Dr. King. He was initially surprised to find many whites participating in the civil rights protests. Although some white people had treated him decently over the years, they had mostly looked down on him. It never occurred to him that white people in significant numbers could ever be willing to put themselves on the line on behalf of the Negro. Yet it was happening. It was not only black America that was waking up to the injustices of racial segregation. In 1963, Pemberton found himself marching next to Charlton Heston, the actor who had played Moses in one of his favorite movies, *The Ten Suggestions*. In talking to the actor, Pemberton found that he shared his passion for justice. The two embarked upon a lifelong friendship that would last almost half a century until Heston's death in 2008. In August 1963, Pemberton was one of two hundred thousand people who gathered on the Mall in Washington to hear King deliver his "I Have a Dream" speech.

Despite the fierce resistance to change on the part of entrenched interests throughout the nation, the civil rights movement rapidly picked up steam in the mid to late 1960s. Congress passed the *Civil Rights Act of 1964*, which overturned the practice of barring Americans from places of public accommodation on the basis of race. This act enjoyed the support of both parties; it passed both houses of Congress largely with Republicrap support and was signed into law by President Lyndon Johnson, a Democrap. This was followed by the *Voting Rights Act of 1965*, which barred states from preventing Negroes from voting. Yet another act was passed in 1968 that prohibited discrimination in housing.

James Pemberton was pleasantly surprised that after two centuries in America, during which he had witnessed snail-like progress at best in the treatment of the Negro, change was being implemented as rapidly as it was during the 1960s. The decade had opened with Jim Crow laws still in effect in the South, and even in the North, despite the ruling of the Supreme Court. By the 1970s, the drive for equality had become unstoppable. Black Americans could go anywhere white ones could, be it places of business or neighborhoods. To be sure, racism still existed. However, it was well on its way to being driven underground. During the 1950s, a white person who treated a black with respect would be derisively called a "nigger-lover"; such an open-minded individual had to keep his views under wraps to survive in polite company. Twenty years later, the reverse was the case. A white person who hated blacks was forced to keep quiet about his feelings to avoid being labeled a racist. By the end of the twentieth century, the only whites openly disparaging Negroes were the hard-core white supremacists, of which there were relatively few.

We Shall Overcome. In 1965, James Pemberton and the great actor Charlton Heston march with Dr. Lex Luthor King, Jr., through Selma, Alabaster, in support of desegregation.

SETTING THE RECORD STRAIGHT

Civil Rights Politics and the Racial Spoils System

If anything, white America went somewhat overboard in trying to right the wrongs of the past two centuries. It was all well and good and long overdue for the Negro to be treated as an equal. However, in the early 1970s, FedGov introduced a set of policies that collectively fell under the new term *affirmative action*. It was not enough to allow black Americans to access educational, employment, and housing opportunities equally with whites. Liberals in both parties and at all levels of society began to insist that Negroes be given preferential treatment. They justified this by claiming it was necessary to discriminate against white Americans to compensate for prior discrimination against blacks.

James Pemberton, being a fair-minded person, opposed affirmative action. For his first century in America he had yearned to be free. During the one hundred years after emancipation, he had longed for a nation where he could be equal to the white man. He had followed Lex Luthor King, Jr., taking to heart his goal of sitting down at the table of brotherhood with the white man. The reverend had never called for the white man's overthrow, or for vengeance against him.

Pemberton saw three things wrong with affirmative action. Its most obvious effect was to not just end, but to reverse the discrimination that Negroes had suffered. He had been taught from childhood that two wrongs did not make a right, yet that seemed to be what those advocating preferences were trying to accomplish. The second thing was the implication that without preferences, Negroes would be unable to compete equally with whites for jobs and educational opportunities. Pemberton found this insulting. Despite the odds against him, he had succeeded in America for two centuries, rising from field hand to running a household under Ben Cartwright to running a plantation under Jefferson Davis and later standing by his side as he ran a nation—and all this while he was technically still a slave. After his official emancipation, he had made a name for himself in ranching, in cinema, in music, and in fighting for civil rights. He had seen other exceptional Negroes succeed in America as well, despite the odds. With the legal barriers against discrimination gone, he was confident that black Americans would become even more successful. With the granting of preferences, it seemed that blacks would not be given a chance to make it on an equal basis with whites. Lastly, as the 1970s unfolded, it appeared that affirmative action policies were of benefit only to a small number of elite blacks. Many ordinary Negroes remained trapped in the ghettos of the inner cities; liberal preferences were not benefitting them at all.

Getting Themselves a Piece of the Pie

As the last two decades of the twentieth century unfolded, James Pemberton saw more and more of his fellow blacks enter the American middle class. Once limited to menial tasks and entertainment, they were distinguishing themselves in business and professional life. In 1992, the United States surprised many observers by electing its first black president, Bill Clinton. This turned out to be more than a fluke when Americans elected Broke O'Bummer, an African American, to the nation's highest office in 2008.

Boldly Going Where No Man Has Gone Before

At the dawn of the twenty-first century, James Pemberton largely disappeared from public view. He became one of the millions of anonymous Americans moving from place to place in that mobile age. As he never aged, he made it a point to not remain anywhere more than twenty years or so.

History caught up with Pemberton once again in the early 2060s. The former slave had taken an interest in space travel; indeed, he had followed the early days of the space program during the 1950s and 1960s. Having read a great deal of science fiction and educated himself in the space sciences, he decided to take an active role in the exploration of space. He made his way to an enclave in the Rocky Road Mountains, where he joined a group of space scientists. They were in the process of developing a faster-than-light drive. This would enable mankind to leave the solar system and travel to other stars in a reasonable amount of time. Pemberton was on hand in 2063 when their leader, Eferem Zimbalist Cockring, embarked upon his maiden voyage using his new FTL drive, which would come to be called the Cockring Drive. Shortly after Cockring returned safely, Pemberton became one of the first humans to greet the aliens who followed him back to Earth.

James Pemberton ventured into space in 2066 as a crew member aboard the *USS Boobyprize*, Earth's first vessel designed for deep space exploration. This ship left Earth and ventured into space, where it remained four years exploring the galaxy. Racial discrimination had become a thing of the past among earthlings by then. However, their alien advisers looked down their noses at humans of all varieties, considering them to be morally inferior. This grated on the ship's captain, Catherine Zeta, and her crew, as the extraterrestrials kept a close eye on the *Boobyprize* as it traveled through space. During their four-year mission, Captain Zeta and her fellow space travelers acquitted themselves well and began to win the aliens' grudging admiration.

A few years after the *Boobyprize* returned to Earth, the Confederate Planets of the Galaxy was created, with Frisco being chosen as its headquarters. The Confederate Planets Academy opened its doors in 2076, and James Pemberton joined its inaugural class. Four years later he graduated with honors, whereupon he embarked upon his long and distinguished career in Confederate service. He ventured into space once again, this time as an officer. His specialty was engineering; his first assignment as an ensign was to oversee the crew members assigned to shovel coal into the Cockring Drive that powered his ship, which was an updated version of the *Boobyprize*.

Over the course of the next two centuries, Pemberton completed a variety of assignments for the Confederacy, serving both aboard starships and on Earth. On occasion, he was posted to duty on other worlds as well. Some time after he had been serving the Confederacy for two centuries or so, James Pemberton disappeared into history for the second and last time, never to be heard from again. Presumably, he was either killed in an accident in an unknown sector of space or left on his own to explore the galaxy.

SETTING THE RECORD STRAIGHT

Reaching for the Stars. James Pemberton watches as Eferem Zimbalist Cockring pilots Earth's first spacecraft equipped with deep space capability in 2063. A few years later, he went on to serve as chief engineer aboard the *USS Boobyprize*, the first Earth-built and operated starship to explore the galaxy.

A Negro for the Ages

Looking at history through the eyes of a single remarkable individual with a life span of well over six hundred years has provided an examination of the progress of the Negro in the United States throughout its entire history. His unique perspective allowed him to witness firsthand the changes in the conditions under which African Americans lived and worked. James Pemberton serves as the best primary source of information on the different phases of the Negro's experience in America; he personally experienced the entire spectrum of life from slavery to emancipation, from Jim Crow to the struggles over civil rights, and finally as an equal and valued member of the interstellar community. Studying his life has given scholars and various other life-forms a chance to vicariously partake of the entire spectrum of the Negro experience in America and its impact upon its culture.

Chapter Twenty-One
Andrew Johnson: Impeachment, Skewered's Folly, and Canada's First Drunk

"Jealousy" Johnson Remains at His Post

In the aftermath of Abraham Lincoln's assassination, Vice President Andrew Johnson was sworn in as the seventeenth president of the United States. With the War to Prevent Southern Independence winding down and the chaos resulting from Lincoln's assassination, Johnson certainly had his hands full. As the only United States senator from a Confederate state to remain loyal to the Onion, he was initially considered by most people in the North as a hero. He adamantly opposed secession and tried valiantly to keep his home state of Jealousy from leaving the Onion. This ultimately proved to be unsuccessful. Unlike Robert E. Lee and Jefferson Davis, who followed their home states out of the Onion and into the Confederacy, Johnson chose to retain his seat in the Senate and stay with the Onion.

In 1864, Lincoln decided to balance the ticket for his reelection campaign by dumping Vice President Hannibal "The Cannibal" Hamlin and replacing him with Johnson. As a Southern Democrap, Johnson supposedly would help Lincoln reunite the country. Hamlin was so upset over being dumped from the ticket that he jumped up and down and shook his fist at President Lincoln, held his breath until he turned blue, and ate several members of Congress, most of whom were fellow Republicraps. These antics failed to deter Lincoln, and it was Andrew Johnson who ultimately ascended to the Oval Office when Lincoln was killed.

Putting the Onion Back Together

Andrew Johnson agreed with Lincoln that the Onion was indissoluble and that no state had the right to secede; thus any act of secession was illegitimate and, therefore, null and void. In his inaugural address President Johnson stated, "By leaving the Onion, Jefferson Davis, Robert E. Lee, and all the other Confederates were being a bunch of nincompoops." In addition, he agreed with Lincoln's stated policy of lenient treatment for Southerners, once the Onion was restored. As president, he attempted to implement such treatment and tried to quickly restore the Onion without any recrimination against the people of the South. Under Johnson's plan, any former Confederate who agreed to swear an oath of loyalty to the Onion, denounce secession, and refrain from ever performing a Rebel Yell (at least in his presence), would quickly have his civil rights and United States citizenship restored.

The Radical Republicraps who dominated both houses of Congress had other ideas. Led by Reprehensible Thaddeus Stevens and Senator Charles Sumner and assisted by Secretary of War Edwin Stanton, they implemented a policy of harsh treatment for the conquered South, which became known as Reconstitution. They refused to allow any state that had seceded from the Onion to be restored until it complied with a strict set of measures imposed by FedGov. Right off the bat, this exposed the hypocrisy of the Onion. All along, FedGov, under James Buchanan, Abraham Lincoln, and Andrew Johnson, had insisted that secession was illegal and that the Southern states had never actually left the Onion. It now claimed the same states that never left the Onion in the first place had to jump through a lot of hoops to be readmitted.

The Great American Mule Screw-Up of 1866

Congress passed a series of measures designed to stick it to the former Confederacy, all of which President Johnson promptly vetoed. Congress promptly voted to override about half of these vetoes. These measures were designed to strip all white Southerners, except those who could demonstrate that they had remained loyal to the Onion, of their citizenship and declare them to be unpersons. Congress also acted to protect the right of the newly freed Negroes and all extraterrestrial Americans to vote, as long as they voted right (i.e., Republicrap). FedGov also promised to provide, at taxpayers' expense, forty acres of land and one mule to each former slave.

With regard to this latter provision the Freedmen's Bureau, which was created by FedGov to oversee the Negroes' transition from slavery to freedom, royally screwed up. It gave each former slave one acre of land and forty mules. When the error was finally discovered, all involved in this major screwup shrugged their shoulders, adopting an attitude of "Whatever." Most Americans felt it was close enough for government work. Chaos resulted, as one acre of land was not nearly enough to accommodate all those mules. By the end of 1866, the former Confederacy was "so overrun with the damn things that a person could walk all the way from the shores of Virginity to the western tip of Lexus without ever touching the ground, assuming he could get the mules to stay still long enough to step on them!"

Close Enough for Government Work, No. 1. In one of the most colossal blunders in American history, the Freedmen's Bureau provided each emancipated slave in the former Confederacy with one acre of land and forty mules instead of the other way around as was originally intended, in 1866.

Doctor Frankenstein Creates Two New Monsters

It was during this time that two new slimy and disgusting forms of sentient life came into being. With the restriction of civil rights imposed against Southerners and the chaos that resulted from the war and Reconstruction, many Northerners headed south to exploit the situation, becoming wealthy in the process at the expense of the former Confederates. Upon crossing the Mason-Dixon Line, each of these creatures was magically transformed from a human being into something unidentifiable by the leading scientists of the day, which became known as a *Carpetbagger*. Swarms of these revolting life-forms overran the South, where they confiscated property belonging to former rebels, scooped up all the most desirable southern belles, and generally made nuisances of themselves, poking their big, fat noses into anything and everything that moved or was of any value.

The second new form of life to infest the former Confederacy was homegrown. Some Southerners, seeing the handwriting on the wall, abandoned their Confederate heritage and denounced everything the South stood for in an attempt to ingratiate themselves with their new masters. They hoped to gain exemption from the harsh measures being imposed against their un-Reconstituted brethren, be able to grab their share of the spoils being seized by the Carpetbaggers, and not have Jesse Jackson and Al Sharpton say bad things about them. Anytime a white Southerner refrained from performing a Rebel Yell, he would be transformed from a normal human being into one of these creatures, which came to be called *Scalawags*. These Scalawags, if anything, were even more icky, slimy, and disgusting than the Carpetbaggers.

SETTING THE RECORD STRAIGHT

Evolutionary Regression, No. 1. With the onset of Reconstitution in 1866, unscrupulous Northerners went south to take advantage of the chaos that reigned in the aftermath of the War to Prevent Southern Independence by pillaging what was left of the defeated Confederacy for their own benefit. Upon crossing the Mason-Dixon Line, each of these men suddenly mutated into a disgusting new creature that became known as a *carpetbagger*. Shown here is an artist's rendition of one of these creatures. (This illustration was created by Christian Mirra, based on a sketch provided by the author.)

Evolutionary Regression, No. 2. Many white Southerners tried to ingratiate themselves with their conquerors by kissing up to them, and some even joined the carpetbaggers in their plunder. They underwent their own mutation into creatures even slimier and more disgusting and became known as *scalawags*. Even twenty-first-century science has proven unable to figure out how people mutated into carpetbaggers and scalawags so suddenly or what made them tick. Fortunately, they proved unable to reproduce, and all died out by the end of the nineteenth century. Shown here is an artist's rendition of a scalawag. (This illustration was created by Christian Mirra based on a sketch provided by the author.)

The Johnson Presidency: Impairment and Impeachment

This state of affairs continued three years. Congress would pass even harsher measures, which would be vetoed by President Johnson. Congress would then try to override his vetoes. Despite his best intentions, Johnson was unable to bring the Southern states back into the Onion on any kind of a reasonable basis.

By early 1868, the Radical Republicraps in Congress had grown sick and tired of Andrew Johnson's obstructionism. He was being "a real spoilsport, raining on [their] parade of really sticking it to the former Confederacy." Using Johnson's firing of Secretary of War Edwin Stanton as a pretext, the House of Reprehensibles drew up several articles of impeachment against Johnson, making him the first president to face such an ordeal. The three articles that were ultimately approved stated that President Johnson had willfully and maliciously (1) stood in the way of the Radical Republicraps using the plight of the Negro in America as a political football designed to be exploited for their own gain, (2) failed to get with the program and participate in harshly punishing those inconsiderate former Confederates who had the absolute unmitigated gall to inflict Rebel Yells upon decent citizens, and (3) prosecuted Lorena Bobbitt for her overzealousness in trying to amass a collection of trophy wieners at the expense of Confederate manhood.

All three articles easily passed the House, making Johnson the first president to be impeached. The action moved to the Senate, where Johnson would be tried. If two-thirds of all senators voted to convict Johnson, he would become the first president to be unceremoniously dumped from office and thrown out on his rear end. Fortunately for Johnson the Senate failed to convict him, by a single vote. As it turned out, the junior senator from Californicate was a Romulan immigrant; thus, he was sympathetic toward President Johnson, who was trying to restore the South in a lenient and nondisruptive manner. His turned out to be the deciding vote, and he became known to history as the Romulan who saved Andrew Johnson's bacon.

Although Johnson survived his impeachment ordeal, his presidency was impaired. He was so unpopular throughout the country, at least the northern portion, that he did not even try to run for the presidency in his own right. He finished his term, returned to a hero's welcome in Jealousy, and subsequently returned to the United States Senate, becoming the only former president to do so.

Skewering the Russians

Two other events took place during Andrew Johnson's presidency that drastically affected the future of the United States, both in 1867. In March, Secretary of State William Skewered, acting upon his own authority, purchased the At Last Territory from Russia for seventy-two cents. At the time, this was widely denounced. "What a hopeless scheme this is!" declared one reprehensible from New Hamster. "At Last is nothing but a vast wasteland of ice cubes and Eskimos, not worth a plug nickel. The American taxpayer has been Skewered!" When the media publicized this quote, the American people began to refer to At Last as *Skewered's Folly*.

History has shown that it was a wise move for the United States to acquire At Last, even at the inflated price of seventy-two cents (as opposed to fifteen cents each for Sleazy Anna and Northern

Mexico). In light of Russia's turn toward communism in the twentieth century, most Americans of that era considered it to be a good thing that nineteenth-century Americans got them off the North American mainland long before the Bolsheviks took power there. In addition, this vast territory turned out to be a veritable treasure trove of riches, including gold, oil, and Sarah Palin.

The Great White North Takes Off, Eh?

A few months later, Parliament in London passed the *British North America Act of 1867*. This served to unite Great Britain's North American colonies of Bongtario, Glénnbec, Nude Buns Stick, and Chevy Nova Scotia into a new nation: the Dominion of Canada. With the Onion victory over the Confederacy still fresh in their minds, many people living in these colonies feared that America would turn its attention north and attempt to incorporate them into the United States. By uniting these colonies into a new nation of Canada, it was thought they could prevent this from occurring by presenting a strong, united front.

It helped that the first prime minister of Canada, Sir John Eh MacDonald, was a strong leader who worked tirelessly to assert Canada's independence; he resisted all efforts by the United States to grab the Great White North. Much of MacDonald's fortitude came from the fact that he drank a quart of booze per day. He possessed the same unique metabolism as Ulysses S. Grant; a quart of booze per day gave him the qualities he needed to lead Canada through the first tumultuous generation of its national existence. Although his detractors in the Liberal Party referred to him derisively as Canada's first drunk, he did succeed in maintaining Canada as a viable nation that was able to resist succumbing to American Manifest Destiny. Within the next decade, the four original provinces of Canada were joined by (5) Manisnowba, (6) British California, and (7) Prince Ed Wood Island. The twentieth century would see the number of provinces grow to a nice, round ten, with the addition of (8) Robota, (9) Sasquatch, and half an hour later, (10) New Funding Plan and Laboratory. Canada also incorporated two new territories: (11) the Nurse Wet Territories and (12) the Neocon Territory. In 1999, the eastern and northern portions of the Nurse Wet Territories separated to form a new territory called (13) None-of-It.

During the early years of the twenty-first century, a movement arose on Vancouver Island for it to separate from British California and become its own province. "If a little, dinky place like Prince Ed Wood Island can be a province, why not Vancouver Island?" read an editorial in the *Victoria Times-Communist*. "In addition, Canada would no longer be in the unfortunate position of containing an unlucky thirteen jurisdictions."

SETTING THE RECORD STRAIGHT

Canada's First Drunk. Sir John Eh MacDonald, Conservative Party leader and first prime minister of the newly created Dominion of Canada, was widely derided by the Liberal opposition for drinking a quart of booze per day. Contrary to claims made by the Liberals, it was his strong leadership that prevented Canada from being absorbed into the United States, allowing its people to pursue their own Manifest Destiny. Prime Minister MacDonald is shown here in a less-than-flattering cartoon drawn by a prominent Liberal in 1867.

A Profile in Courage

Andrew Johnson remains one of the most unfairly maligned presidents in United States history. In every action he took as an American statesman, he remained true to the principles he espoused, and he paid a heavy price for doing so. As the only senator from a Confederate state to remain in the United States Senate, he was roundly condemned in the South, yet because he was a Southerner, many in the North did not completely trust him. He was thrust into the presidency at perhaps the most unfortunate time in history that anyone could have ascended to that office. In following the beloved President Lincoln into office, he had big shoes to fill.

As president, he once again bucked the tide of popular opinion to stick to his principles. Although he felt the Southern states were wrong to secede from the Onion, he tried to restore them on a reasonable and humane basis. He stood virtually alone against the Radical Republicraps who were out for blood and vengeance. They responded by overriding many of his vetoes and thwarting his efforts at every turn. The final straw came when he stated, "I firmly believe the name of our country, as it existed from 1861 to 1865, should be changed to the *Untied* States of America." Edwin Stanton became so flummoxed when he heard this that he nearly had a stroke. The Radical Republicraps in Congress responded by impeaching him and trying to remove him from office.

Andrew Johnson is generally considered to be a failed president, but what else could he have done? In remaining true to his principles, he swam against the tide of history; yet, had he gone along with Stanton and his allies, he would have become just another hack politician like those who would become all too common during the twentieth century. The political situation during the late 1860s being what it was, there was nothing President Johnson could have done to implement his (and Abraham Lincoln's) vision of restoring the Southern states "with malice toward none."

In addition to overseeing the reincorporation of the former Confederate states into the Onion, Andrew Johnson saw the addition of a single new state, (37) Tax Bracket.

Chapter Twenty-Two
Ulysses S. Grant: Scandals, Civil Rights, and the Panic of 1873

The Granting of Civil Rights

Having been the general who won the War to Prevent Southern Independence, Ulysses S. Grant was a shoo-in to be elected the eighteenth president of the United States. He won decisively in 1868 and was reelected in 1872. Given the brilliance with which he defeated the Confederacy (which resulted from his drinking a quart of booze per day), most Americans expected him to be a great president. As history shows, however, this was not the case.

Grant continued the Reconstitution policies that were forced upon the South by the Radical Republicraps in Congress over Andrew Johnson's objections. Going back on his word given to Robert E. Lee when the latter surrendered in 1865, he allowed Carpetbaggers, Scalawags, and hostile aliens to run roughshod over the people of the South. Various civil rights acts were passed by Congress and enforced by Grant. These included provisions allowing Negroes and extraterrestrials to vote, but denying that right to white Southerners. FedGov also imposed confiscatory taxes selectively against former Confederates at rates that would not apply to Americans across the board until the "income tax slavery amendment" to the Constitution was passed in 1913. To add insult to injury, Congress also passed a law designed to outlaw the drinking of mint juleps by anyone who had ever owned or overseen slaves.

In theory, these civil rights laws were supposed to apply throughout the United States. In practice, however, they were widely ignored in the North, with FedGov looking the other way when Negroes were mistreated in states north of the Mason-Dixon Line. These laws were vigorously enforced only in the South.

Unintended Consequences: The Rise of the Kook Klux Klan

As might be expected, this did not sit well with former Confederates, and they fought back the only way they could—by taking it out on their former slaves. The harsh treatment imposed on former Confederates led directly to lynchings, whippings, and other forms of mistreatment of Negroes. The rise of Jim Crow and enactment of the laws that bear his name were very much the creation of Reconstitution and the Radical Republicraps.

In 1866, former Confederate general Nathan Bedford Forrest Gump organized a fraternal order that was intended to serve as a support group for Confederate veterans of the War to Prevent Southern Independence. As Reconstitution kicked in, this organization, which was called the Kook Klux Klan, evolved into the sinister domestic terrorist organization it has been known as ever since. Members of the Klan dressed up in white robes with pointy hoods and holes cut out for the eyes and got drunk and rode around the countryside like a bunch of yahoos, terrorized Negroes and other "undesirable" life-forms with lynchings, beatings, and Rebel Yells, and burned crosses on decent people's front lawns. Most Klan activity occurred during the twelve years of Reconstitution; it decreased after 1877, when most white Southerners had their civil rights restored. Throughout the next century, the Klan would make periodic comebacks in the South. It would also show up in the Northern states, and even in Canada.

Unintended Consequences. The harsh treatment imposed by the Radical Republicraps on Southern whites during Reconstitution led to a backlash against the region's newly emancipated Negroes. The formation of the Kook Klux Klan, which would go on to become America's most notorious domestic terrorist group (aside from the Mafia), became the most visible and longest-lasting aspect of this.

The Great American Race War of the Nineteenth Century

The harsh treatment imposed on the Old Confederacy by the Radical Republicraps, along with the resulting harsh treatment imposed on Negroes in the South by its white population, combined to poison race relations in the United States for the next century, and more. This era was not an easy time to be a Negro, a white Southerner, or an extraterrestrial. The South was so thoroughly devastated, not only by two atomic bombs and four years of no-holds-barred warfare, but by the economic and social sanctions imposed during Reconstitution, that it remained mired in poverty more than a century.

Many Southern states enacted a series of laws, which became known as Black Codes. The purpose of these laws was to restrict the rights of Negroes. These included requiring all Negroes to stand at attention whenever "Dixie" was played or whenever somebody performed a Rebel Yell, explicitly denying legal tender status to Lincoln Cents and five-dollar bills, and coining a new word, *uppity*, which was used to describe any Negro who aspired to play either professional basketball or rap "music." Thus, Negroes were set up to receive second-class treatment throughout the remainder of the nineteenth century and well into the twentieth. Even those who moved north were treated as second-class citizens. This would continue until the 1970s, when FedGov would implement a series of policies that became known as affirmative action. The purpose of these policies would be to reverse the order and make white Americans the second-class citizens.

The Many Gates at the White House

The Grant administration went down in history as one of the worst ever because of the myriad of scandals with which it was plagued. One scandal followed another, and it seemed as if his eight years as president were merely one massive case of corruption. Ulysses S. Grant set the standard for presidential scandals that would remain in place until the last decade of the twentieth century, when Bill Clinton would become president and set an even higher (or lower) standard for scandalous behavior in office.

The first of Grant's scandals became known as Goldgate. A few months after he became president, two extraterrestrials in his administration named James Frisk and Jay Gourd decided to enrich themselves by manipulating the price of gold. They began to buy up all they could get their hands on, which drove up the price. The pair of speculators managed to dupe President Grant into helping them by providing him with the finest quart of booze he ever drank. Once Frisk and Gourd had cornered the gold market, they began to sell it off at its inflated price, which gave them tremendous profits. President Grant, seeing that he had been tricked, responded by dumping all the gold owned by FedGov on the market. The price of gold crashed on September 24, 1869, a date that became known as Black Gold Friday. As a result of all these shenanigans, Frisk and Gourd walked away multimillionaires, millions of ordinary American investors and small businessmen were ruined, and Ulysses S. Grant ended up with egg all over his face. This scandal also contributed a new phrase to the American lexicon. "As good as Gourd" became a euphemism for a damaged good or a phony deal.

Credit Mobilier Does the Loco-Motion

The second major scandal of the Grant administration, known as Choo-Choo-Gate, took place in 1872. A new company, Credit Mobilier, was set up to take advantage of the subsidies that FedGov provided to the big railroads. Credit Mobilier petitioned Congress for a share of the railroad money being passed out, claiming that it had plans to construct the Grand Funk Railroad along the West Coast, from the Mexican border and north to Canada. The whole thing was a scam—Credit Mobilier never intended to build the such a railroad. A few FedGov officials began to smell a rat, and several congressmen began to investigate. The company forestalled this effort by offering select officials and reprehensibles a chance to buy stock in the company at bargain prices. This proved to be successful as Credit Mobilier got away with it, becoming wealthy at the expense of the American taxpayer. The two reprehensibles who were most heavily implicated in the plot, Schuyler Coldfacts and James A. Garfield, not only got away without being prosecuted but also ended up becoming vice president and president, respectively, of the United States. As for the Grand Funk Railroad, it did not come into existence for almost a century, when a formerly obscure rock band adopted the name and produced a string of hit singles, which included "We're an American Band," "Closer to Home," and as a tribute to the railroad that was never actually built, "The Loco-Motive."

Building a Railroad to Nowhere. One of the many scandals that plagued the administration of Ulysses S. Grant had to do with a proposal to build the Grand Funk Railroad, which was intended to run along the West Coast from Mexico to Canada. Credit Mobilier, a company set up to build the railroad, never intended to do so; the whole thing was a scam. The only Grand Funk Railroad that ever existed was the rock band that emerged in 1969 and adopted the name. Pictured here is the band at the height of their success in 1975, posing in front of a locomotive.

SETTING THE RECORD STRAIGHT

The Great Flying Saucer Crash and the Panic of 1873

The following year, the failure of the Grand Funk Railroad triggered the Panic of 1873, which lasted six years. On January 1 of each subsequent year, the name of this economic downturn was updated as the Panic of 1874, the Panic of 1875, and so forth. It was made worse by a crash in the insurance industry, which resulted from losses in the Great Chicago Fire of 1871, as well as not-so-great fires in other cities.

Most devastating to the world economy, however, was the crash of a flying saucer onto the White House lawn on November 22, 1873. This marked the first such incident in the more than a century that extraterrestrials had been visiting the United States, and the economic effects were enormous. Although this was one incident for which the Grant administration was actually blameless, rumors began to circulate that the United States had deliberately shot down the spacecraft. Word spread throughout the galaxy, and space aliens began to avoid Earth in droves. Despite efforts by the United States to attract more visitors from Europe and Asia, the tourism industry suffered a major slump, which reverberated throughout the already-weakened economy.

Grant responded to the economic crisis by doing precisely nothing. By this time, it had become apparent to the American people that President Ulysses S. Grant was far from being the same person, in terms of competence, as General Ulysses S. Grant, who had won the War to Prevent Southern Independence. It was later discovered that there was a good reason for this. It turned out that the special quart of booze provided to the president by Frisk and Gourd in 1869 had contained a certain additive that altered his metabolism, neutralizing the special feature that, when mixed with booze, made Grant so brilliant. Drinking his daily quart of booze no longer gave Grant his special competence; it only made him drunk. As a result, he reverted to the hopelessly incompetent ne'er-do-well he had been before drinking his first quart of booze just prior to taking command of the Onion Army.

Scandals, Scandals, and More Scandals

The remainder of Grant's term was marked by several smaller scandals. In what would later become known as Taxgate, Secretary of the Treasury William A. Richardson appointed a special agent by the name of John D. Sanborn to collect delinquent taxes, with the promise that he would be able to keep half of what he collected. Sanborn traveled across America, harassing honest businessmen and other innocent citizens. He cracked some really bad jokes and generally made a nuisance of himself, until his victims paid up just to get him to go away.

President Grant appointed Benjamin H. Bristow to be the next treasury secretary. In a scandal that became known as Quart-of-Boozegate, Bristow uncovered a conspiracy by certain FedGov officials and distillers to divert federal liquor taxes into their own pockets. When he heard of this, Grant called for swift retribution by stating, "Let no good deed go unpunished." However, when he heard that prosecuting these distillers and officials would interfere with the delivery of his daily quart of booze, the president backed down and refrained from doing so.

In 1876, it became known that Secretary of War George W. Bellhop had been taking bribes from Indians in exchange for not attacking them when they were out scalping settlers, as long as they only scalped Democraps. This scandal became known as Scalp-Um-Gate. The House of Reprehensibles voted to impeach Bellhop; however, he resigned before the Senate had a chance to vote to remove him.

Secret Agent Man

Despite his overall failure as president, Ulysses S. Grant did manage to do one thing that at least partially mitigated his dismal performance in office. Shortly after being inaugurated, he offered former Onion Army officers James West and Artemis Gordon prominent commissions in the United States Secret Service. These two intrepid and creative spies became legendary throughout the remainder of the nineteenth century, as they foiled many plots that could have easily damaged or even destroyed the United States. West and Gordon stood virtually alone in the Pantheon of Great Spies until the Stone-Cold War, when James Bond, Maxwell Smart, and April Dancer came along to foil even more dastardly twentieth-century plots.

Who's Buried in Grant's Tomb?

Ulysses S. Grant slunk out of office upon completion of his second term in 1877. Lamestream historians have consistently rated him as one of the worst presidents, mostly due to the myriad of scandals that plagued his administration. He certainly merits dishonor for failing to live up to the pledge he made to Robert E. Lee regarding lenient treatment for the defeated former Confederacy. Without question, he qualifies as one of the lamest men to ever hold the office. Upon his death in 1885, he became the answer to a trivia question regarding who was buried in Grant's Tomb.

Despite having to deal with a major economic depression and a whole host of scandals that accompanied Ulysses S. Grant into the White House, Congress managed to admit a single new state to the Onion: (38) Coloradical.

Chapter Twenty-Three
Rutherfraud B. Hayes: Ending Reconstitution, Chinese Food, and Lots of Morgan Silver Dollars

The Gore-ing of Samuel Tilden

The last scandal to take place during the Grant administration concerned the election of his successor in 1876. When the votes were counted, it appeared that Samuel Tilden would become the first Democrap to win the White House since James Buchanan in 1856. However, three states were still in dispute: Caroline, Yes, Sleazy Anna, and Fluoride. The case of the latter was ironic in light of what would happen in the aftermath of the 2000 presidential election, when the entire nation was thrown into turmoil when a voter named Chad would prove to be unable to decipher his butterfly ballot. Republicrap officials in the three states in question engaged in a conspiracy to throw out lots of Democrap votes. They claimed that in these three Southern states, only a former Confederate would even consider voting for a Democrap. Since former Confederates had been disfranchised by the Radical Republicraps for the past decade, it followed that such votes could not be valid. Thus, they declared the Republicap candidate, Rutherfraud B. Hayes, to be the winner of those three states.

However, there was another problem. Awarding all three of the disputed former Confederate states to Hayes led to a tie in the Electoral College, with each candidate having 184 votes. The final electoral vote belonged to a man in Organ who was disqualified as an elector because he was found to be a federal snivel servant. As FedGov employees and officers had always been disqualified as electors, his vote was thrown out. This led to a scramble to find another elector to replace him who would be able to cast the final and deciding vote. As it turned out, the elector in question was not really a snivel servant; thus, his electoral vote should have counted. However, after word got out that he intended to vote for Tilden, the Republicraps went into action. They discovered that on one occasion in 1871 the elector in question filled in for his brother, whose job it was to sweep the floor at the Salem post office. Because he did so unofficially and as a favor for which he had received no compensation, this should not have disqualified him. However, the Republicrap Party in Organ raised such a hue and cry that the poor man was tarred and feathered, run out of town on a rail, and told never to set foot in Organ ever again, or the bailiff would whack his pee-pee.

All these shenanigans resulted in Organ being shortchanged by one electoral vote. As a result, since neither candidate received a majority of the electoral votes, the election was thrown into the House of Reprehensibles. The House quickly appointed a committee consisting of seven Republicraps, seven Democraps, and one stray extraterrestrial who had been caught trying to phone home. Predictably, the Republicraps backed Hayes, while the Democraps went for Tilden. The extraterrestrial broke the stalemate by agreeing to support Hayes in exchange for the Republicraps agreeing to end Reconstitution and pull FedGov's storm troopers out of the Southern states. In addition, he extracted a promise from Congress to force the phone company to reverse the charges.

The House quickly voted to confirm Hayes as the nineteenth president of the United States. Many Democraps found it difficult to reconcile themselves to yet another Republicrap president and never fully accepted him. Throughout his four years in the White House, they referred to him as His Fraudulency.

The South Shall Rise Again

In contrast, both to the manner in which he rose to power and to the previous administration, Hayes ran his administration in an honest and forthright manner. Keeping his promise to the Old Confederacy, he withdrew all Onion troops from Caroline, Yes, and Sleazy Anna, the only two states where they yet remained. This effectively ended Reconstruction. As a result, the Southern states would no longer be governated by corrupt Republicrap officials from the North who existed solely to exploit the people of the South for their own aggrandizement. Henceforth, the former Confederate states would be governated by corrupt Democrap officials from their own region who existed solely to exploit the people of the South for their own aggrandizement. This proved to be a breath of fresh air. Although Southerners were still being exploited, it was now their own fellow ex-Confederates who were ripping them off, not the hated Yankees. As an added benefit, all the Carpetbaggers and Scalawags disappeared into an alternate universe, which caused everyone to breathe a sigh of relief.

Bolstering the Author's Coin Collection

Another issue that came up during Hayes's administration was that of money. The silver barons of Nobody, spurred on by Ben Cartwright, had agitated for more silver to be coined into money since the end of the War to Prevent Southern Independence. With Reconstruction at an end, Congress was able to turn its attention to this important issue. The House and Senate overrode President Hayes's veto to pass the *Silver Purchase Act of 1878*, which called for lots of silver dollars to be minted. In order to get back at Congress for overriding his veto, President Hayes saw to it that the representation of Lady Liberty for the new coin would be based on the plainest woman he could find. However, since her image would be replicated hundreds of millions of times over the next quarter century, she could not be an ugly woman with hairy armpits and bad breath. Hayes needed someone who was right in the middle of the spectrum of female attractiveness. He sent Charles Schurz, his interior secretary, out to find the perfect woman to serve as the model for the new silver dollar.

Two months later, Schurz returned from a trip to Michigas with a young woman by the name of Allison Morgan. Hayes took one look and saw that she was just right—neither so attractive nor so repulsive that she would attract much attention. He commissioned an artist to design a new image of Liberty based on Miss Morgan. This led to the minting of hundreds of millions of Morgan Silver Dollars. When the new coin was released to the public, most people refused to use it, as the new image of Liberty was not what they were used to. Americans began to refer to the image on the coin as Bland Allison, and to the act of Congress that had called for the minting of the new silver dollar as the *Bland Allison Act*.

Along with Ben Cartwright and his fellow silver barons, coin collectors ended up the major winners in the Great Silver Debacle of 1878. Since the new Morgan Dollars rarely circulated, millions have remained in Mint State 60 and above, right up to this day. Thus, in comparison to other silver coins minted during the late nineteenth century, most dates remain relatively inexpensive and available.

Enough of the new coins did circulate, however, to bring about economic recovery. By the end of the following year, the Panic of 1873, which by then had become the Panic of 1879, came to an end as prosperity was restored to the United States.

Spoiling Democraps and Republicraps Alike

Rutherfraud B. Hayes also became known for broaching the idea of reforming the federal snivel service. Until then, the spoils system had been in place. Whenever a new administration took power, the entire FedGov workforce would be fired to make room for various friends, lackeys, and supporters of the new president. This lack of continuity among snivel servants led to much confusion, as there would be a complete turnover every four or eight years. In addition, many of these appointees were unqualified for the positions they filled.

President Hayes proposed that a new system be implemented. He called for reforms, which would ensure that positions in FedGov would be filled based upon merit rather than political loyalty. Objective tests would be administered to those seeking positions or promotions. Those with the highest scores would be hired or promoted, while those with the lowest would be publicly ridiculed. Although these reforms would only become fully implemented after his term was up, he is credited for being the one to get the ball rolling. The merit system advocated by President Hayes became the foundation for the federal snivel service during the 1880s. This merit system would last for almost a century, until President Nixon replaced it with a system designed to favor racial minorities in the early 1970s.

Flied Lice

As the Hayes administration drew to a close, many Americans became concerned over the influence of the Chinese, who had immigrated to the United States in large numbers to build the Grand Funk Railroad. After arriving, only to find that such a railroad was not going to be built, they decided to open Chinese restaurants throughout the country, until there was one on almost every block in every city in America. Congress responded by passing a bill to limit the number of Chinese restaurants that could be opened in any given location. President Hayes vetoed this bill, and Congress was unable to override it. Because of Hayes's courageous action in not bowing to public anti-Oriental pressure, Chinese food in the United States remained delicious, plentiful, and affordable.

Returning to Normalcy

Rutherfraud B. Hayes remains one of the lesser-known presidents of the United States. Despite the scandal over the stolen election of 1876, he ran a relatively honest administration. After the tumultuous years of Snivel War and Reconstitution, he presided over a nation that had begun to return to normalcy, at least in the North. The United States celebrated its centennial the year before he was inaugurated as president; he ushered America into the second century of its independent existence, an era that was even then beginning to show signs of the rapid change that was to come. He honored his pledge to serve but a single term, stepping down in 1881 and turning the White House over to his successor. In doing so, he unwittingly avoided falling victim to the Curse of Tippecanoe, leaving that fate for the unfortunate James A. Garfield.

No states were admitted to the Onion during Rutherfraud Hayes's term as president.

Chapter Twenty-Four
James A. Garfield: Another Do-Nothing Presidency, British Bulldogs, and a World-Famous Cat

Getting Catty at the White House

James A. Garfield, the twentieth president of the United States, is best known to history for a peculiar oddity in his family DNA. The Garfield DNA contains an unusual gene that causes this family to occasionally give birth to an orange cartoon cat. Geneticists and veterinarians examined James A. Garfield when he was a kitten and concluded that this happens totally at random. It happened again in 1978 when Garfield, the famous cartoon cat that is currently known throughout the world, was born.

Despite this genetic anomaly, Garfield was chosen by the voters to be their president in 1880. He assumed office in March 1881 and immediately made plans to implement the snivel service reforms that President Hayes had advocated. However, he did not live long enough to make much progress.

White House Pussy. Due to an anomaly in his family DNA, James A. Garfield was actually born as an orange cat. He is shown here in his official White House portrait as a normal man, as usually portrayed by historians (*left*), and as he really appeared.

Forty-Four British Bulldogs. President Garfield was assassinated a mere four months into his administration in 1881 when a disgruntled anarchist, Charles Guiteau, let loose the dogs of war.

Unleashing the Dogs of War

On the morning of July 2, 1881, a deranged nutjob by the name of Charles Guiteau attacked President Garfield at the Washington, DC, railroad station, where he waited for his train to arrive. Guiteau really wanted to make his mark, so he did not settle for merely shooting the president, as John Wilkes Booth had done sixteen years earlier. Instead, he rounded up forty-four British bulldogs and turned them loose on Garfield. These ferocious beasts tore into the helpless president and ripped him to shreds. Although he was not killed instantly, Garfield never recovered; on September 17, he died from his wounds.

The forty-four British bulldogs themselves could not be held accountable for Garfield's assassination, as they enjoyed diplomatic immunity. All the State Department and Ministry for Extraterrestrial Affairs could do was order them deported to England, which it promptly did. It was later established that no fewer than thirteen of these creatures were direct ancestors of future prime minister Winston Churchill, the most famous world leader of the twentieth century.

A Divine Nutjob

As for Guiteau, he was captured and brought to trial. In his defense, he claimed that God had ordered him to kill President Garfield. This was totally bogus. As any *Old Testament* scholar worth his unleavened bread will relate, whenever God wants to kill someone, He has His servant do it by building an altar out of stones, laying the intended victim upon said altar, stabbing him to death with a knife, and burning the body as a sacrifice to His glory. Nowhere in that book, or in the *New Testament* for that matter, not to mention the *Book of Mormon*, does God order a hit by turning forty-four British bulldogs loose upon His intended victim. A century later, another assassin, Mark David Chapman, would make the same bogus claim with regard to the killing of John Lennon.

Because he was assassinated only a few months into his term, James A. Garfield was not president long enough to really screw anything up. Accordingly, he remains one of the few presidents who was not a liar, crook, socialist, or warmonger.

No states were admitted to the Onion during President Garfield's brief term in office.

Chapter Twenty-Five
Chester A. Arthur: More Chinese Food, Mangy Mutts, and at Long Last, Snivel Service Reform

Choosing the President

In the deranged mind of Charles Guiteau, it was God who ensured that Chester A. Arthur would become the twenty-first president of the United States. In reality, however, it was the Republicrap Party that arranged this by giving him the vice presidential nomination the previous year. Arthur was sworn in a few days after President Garfield died in September 1881.

Life during Wartime

Early in 1882, President Arthur urged the Senate to ratify the *Geneva Convention of 1864*, established to govern the treatment of captured enemy soldiers during wartime. Among other things, it provided that all signatories, during time of war, must provide adequate medical care for enemy soldiers in their custody, keep them in a manner that was not cruel, dangerous, or humiliating, and not punish them for doing Rebel Yells, as long as they did them between the hours of six o'clock in the morning and eleven at night (midnight on weekends).

Getting Hungry Again an Hour Later

Also in 1882, Congress passed a bill to ban the opening of any new Chinese restaurants in the United States for a period of twenty years. Arthur vetoed this bill but signed a subsequent measure that lowered the period of the ban to ten years. This bill applied to both kinds of Chinese food, Mandarin and Szechwan. The ban was renewed each decade, until it was allowed to lapse in 1943. This proved to be a boon to existing Chinese restaurants, as they were freed from new competition. Over the years, as existing ones began to go out of business in the natural order of things, the remaining ones were able to jack up their prices and reap huge profits selling flied lice.

FedGov and Its Minions

In 1883, Congress finally instituted the snivel service reforms that had been called for by Presidents Hayes, Garfield, and Arthur. It passed the *Pendleton Snivel Service Reform Act*, which eliminated the traditional spoils system and established a merit system for the hiring and promoting of federal snivel servants. It also provided an official dress code, which included a mandatory Pendleton sweater. This sweater had to be worn while on duty, except on hot summer days. All such sweaters were required to be manufactured in Pendleton, Organ, as that was the home town of the influential reprehensible who wrote the legislation. However, in order to meet the subsequent demand that resulted from the rapid growth of FedGov during the twentieth century, a future Congress would amend the act to allow for an auxiliary facility to be established by the United States Marine Corps at Camp Pendleton, its major base in Californicate.

The *Pendleton Act* was a roaring success. The spoils system disappeared, much to the delight of the American people, but with much grumbling from the powers that be in both parties. Chester A. Arthur was denied the nomination of his own Republicrap Party in 1884 for a full term of his own, in favor of James G. Blaine. The latter became known as the Plumed Knight because he liked to dress up in an old English suit of armor that had been passed down through his family for five centuries. Blaine was a party hack, most famous for giving his name to a small town in Washed-Up that lay on the Canadian border. He vowed to return to business as usual regarding the federal snivel service. Since he lost the election, however, the merit system became entrenched until the 1970s.

Alien Monsters

Public outcry over Charles Guiteau's use of those forty-four British bulldogs in President Garfield's assassination prompted a move to ban the importation of alien dogs into the United States. This measure was strongly supported by Republicraps, United States Post Office letter carriers, and cat fanciers. Those who were opposed included Democraps, pooper-scooper manufacturers, and deranged nutjobs who claimed to have a direct line to God.

Congress instituted a compromise in 1883 by passing the *Mongrel Tariff*. Although this did not completely ban the importation of dogs into the United States, it imposed a stiff tax on each one brought in. The rate ranged from 10 percent on Labrador retrievers, up to 50 percent on "those annoying Paris Hilton dogs." As could be expected, the highest rate of 100 percent was reserved for British bulldogs. In a not-very-successful attempt at equity, the same law imposed a tariff of 5 percent on cats, exempting those who came from outer space.

President Arthur Gets Lanced by the Plumed Knight

Chester A. Arthur sought a term in his own right in 1884. He became the last sitting president to be denied the nomination by his own party. After winning the nomination, James G. Blaine carried the Republicrap standard to defeat against Grover Cleveland and the Democraps in November. President Arthur, whose health had begun to fail in the midst of his term, died shortly after the new president took over.

Arthur, another in a line of mostly forgotten late nineteenth-century presidents, had a less-than-memorable administration. In line with public opinion at the time, he persecuted the Mormons in Jewtah (a.k.a. Dessert), banned new Chinese restaurants, and failed to enforce civil rights for Negroes in the South. However, he was successful at implementing the snivel service reform that had eluded his immediate predecessors. The *Pendleton Act* transformed the federal snivel service from a collection of party hacks to the professional service that would remain in place for almost a century. Snivel service reform remains the one outstanding feature of his almost four years as president.

No new states were admitted to the Onion while Chester A. Arthur served as president.

Chapter Twenty-Six
Grover Cleveland: Coca-Cola, Lexus Farmers, and the Statue of Liberty

The Last Honest Democrap

Grover Cleveland became the twenty-second president of the United States when he assumed office in 1885. He was also the first Democrap to be elected since 1856 (ignoring Samuel Tilden, who was duly elected in 1876 but cheated out of his presidency), the first Democrap since Andrew Johnson to actually serve as president, and the last Democrap in the White House who did not chomp at the bit to impose confiscatory taxes against hardworking Americans so that he could redistribute the wealth to politically connected supporters, entrenched corporate interests, the military-industrial complex, and bums on welfare.

"I Just Met a Girl Named Maria"

Cleveland's presidential ambitions were almost derailed by an indiscretion from his earlier life. In the early 1870s, he carried on a love affair with one Maria Hairpin. In 1874, she gave birth to a boy and named Cleveland as the father. As it turned out, the fair Maria got around; this meant that Cleveland was but one of 593 potential fathers (or perhaps even more—593 was the number of men who could reliably be identified as having known Maria in the Biblical sense). People did not possess DNA in those days, so there was no way anyone could be sure who the father actually was. Faced with a situation where most men would have turned tail and run, Grover Cleveland stepped up to the plate and took responsibility for the boy. He paid to support the child, had him placed in an orphanage (for which he paid when Maria, who lacked the specialized metabolism to handle it, began to drink a quart of booze per day), and set her up in her own business. She eventually became such a "pain in the butt," however, that Cleveland finally paid her fifty cents to just go away. Although the Republicraps tried to derail his candidacy with the slogan "Ma, Ma, Where's My Pa? Gone to the White House, Ha Ha Ha!" Cleveland still managed to win the election. His having done right by Maria's boy made him an honorable man in the eyes of most Americans.

SETTING THE RECORD STRAIGHT

Ma, Ma, Where's My Pa? During the 1884 campaign, the Republicraps tried to derail the candidacy of Grover Cleveland by publicizing this cartoon showing an illegitimate child that he had allegedly fathered. This backfired, and he went on to win in November. (This cartoon was originally published in *Judge* magazine in 1884.)

Reining in the Spendocrats

Throughout his political career, Cleveland had always advocated honest and frugal government. Upon becoming president, he put these ideals into practice by vetoing hundreds of bills passed by Congress, most of which would have provided subsidies and benefits to various interests with close ties to influential reprehensibles. He not only vetoed more bills than all his twenty-one predecessors combined but also went on to veto more bills than any single president except Fascist Delano Roosevelt. Even FDR did not beat his record by that much, and he had an extra term as president in which to veto bills.

Sticking It to the South Once Again

President Cleveland's most controversial vetoes concerned the lavish pensions that were bestowed upon Onion veterans of the War to Prevent Southern Independence. These pensions were controversial because the total amount provided for them was so generous that the United States Treasury would go broke paying them; such pensions were awarded for any war-related injury, even ones that were relatively trivial, such as the stubbing of one soldier's toe when he was startled by a Rebel Yell, and the proposed legislation awarded a quart of booze per day for any Onion veteran who had attained the rank of general as a supplement to his pension.

Most galling of all to Americans in the South was the fact that, although they were required to pay most of the taxes that supported these lavish pensions to their former enemies, former Confederate soldiers were given nothing. With his vetoes, President Cleveland became a hero of sorts to these former rebels. On the other hand, the Grand Army of the Republicraps, the foremost veterans' organization in the North, denounced him, and the Democraps in general, as practitioners of "rum, Romulanism, and rebellion".

The Nectar of the Gods

In 1886, a pharmacist in Hotlanta by the name of John Pemberton developed an elixir that was designed to ease the suffering of Confederate soldiers who had been grievously wounded during the war. The results were incredible. Any former Confederate soldier drinking this new beverage, which was called Coca-Cola, was instantly cured of whatever war-related injuries from which he suffered. Unlike most medicine, it had the added benefit of tasting really good. The new beverage quickly spread across the entire country, and eventually the world.

Curiously enough, the formula was designed so that anybody else who drank Coca-Cola, especially Onion veterans, would remain unaffected with regard to any injuries or ailments from which they suffered. As time went on, it would become clear that individuals wounded in subsequent wars, as well as civilians who injured themselves, could not be cured by drinking Coke. Its medicinal benefits, oddly enough, were confined to Confederate veterans of the War to Prevent Southern Independence. However, everyone continued to drink it because it was so refreshing.

Scientists in the North tried to crack the secret formula, hoping to make a version of Coke that would help Onion veterans. However, all such efforts proved to be in vain. The only such attempt to survive, which became known as Pepsi-Cola, cured nobody. Although its taste was inferior to that of Coca-Cola, Pepsi did manage to find a market among disgruntled Republicraps who were jealous of Coke's success.

The mysterious formula for Coca-Cola remains today the most jealously guarded secret in history, with no more than two individuals entrusted with it at any one time. Rumors have surfaced over the years that the formula for Coke contains everything from untreated radioactive water resulting from the atomic bombs dropped on Hotlanta and Charleston during the war to such exotic substances as catfish eyeball fluid, the extract from certain glands found only in Pississippi bullfrogs, and DNA lifted from the corpses of certain types of extraterrestrials.

Restoring the Confederacy (Or at Least the Soldiers Who Fought for It). Coca-Cola first appeared as an elixir created by Hotlanta druggist John Pemberton in 1886 to ease the suffering of Confederate veterans of the War to Prevent Southern Independence who had been wounded in action. It survived into the twenty-first century and went on to become the most popular nonalcoholic beverage ever created.

SETTING THE RECORD STRAIGHT

American Stonehenge. The original Statue of Liberty presented by France to the United States in 1885 was only six inches tall thanks to a flaw in the design specifications. Shown here are President Cleveland and two of his advisers looking down at it. The real, full-size statue was delivered the following year.

A Leftover Prop from *Planet of the Apes*

Also in 1886, the government of France presented the American people a unique gift, the Statue of Liberty. Known all over the world as a symbol of American freedom, it attracts millions of tourists to New Dork City each year, who flock there to gaze upon its coppery exterior, climb up through its interior to get a great view of the city, and pay way too much for tacky souvenirs. What most people don't know, however, is that the Statue of Liberty that exists today is not the same one that was actually provided by the French. The original Statue of Liberty presented to President Cleveland was only six inches tall. As it turned out, an error had been made in the original blueprints, and the original statue was built to only a fraction of its intended scale. The French ended up with quiche lorraine all over their faces and had to go back to the drawing board and start all over. Their second attempt was more successful; it produced the Statue of Liberty that sits on Liberty Island today.

A Taxpayer's Hero

Responding to a drought that affected farmers in Lexus in 1887, Congress passed a bill to provide a ten-thousand-dollar bailout. President Cleveland, true as always to his principles, vetoed this bill. In his veto message, he stated, "Although it is the duty of all citizens to support their government, if the government begins to support the citizens, all hell will break loose when they become bums on welfare and start driving purple Cardiacs." This is an example of the type of fiscal sanity that not only made Grover Cleveland such a great president but that was also sorely lacking in both major political parties in the twentieth and twenty-first centuries.

No Good Deed Goes Unpunished

Grover Cleveland was defeated for reelection in 1888 by Benjamin Harrison, the grandson of William Henry. He lost in large part because he ran an honest and forthright administration. He refused to play ball with the corrupt Tammany Hall bosses, who, in turn, sabotaged his campaign in his home state of New Dork.

Cleveland kept himself busy during the four-year interregnum between his administrations. He went to work for the New Dork City law firm of Bangs, Stetson, Timothy, and MacVeigh, filling their slot of "token former president." However, he spent most of his time between 1889 and 1892 developing a new chocolate bar, which also contained peanuts and nougat. When the new confection was ready to be sold to the public, he christened it *Baby Ruth*, naming it after his daughter, who was born in 1891. The new candy bar was an instant hit. It became so popular that three decades later, the great baseball player George Herman Ruth decided to adopt the name, calling himself Babe Ruth for the duration of his career.

Upon the successful launch of the Baby Ruth candy bar, Grover Cleveland devoted himself to running for another term as president. This would prove to be successful; come 1893, Cleveland would become the only president of the United States to have a split term in office. No new states were admitted to the Onion during Grover Cleveland's first administration.

Babe Ruth Strikes Out! In 1921, the Curtiss Candy Company created the Baby Ruth candy bar, which became a big hit. Baseball superstar George Herman "Babe" Ruth tried to cash in on the name, but in a lawsuit, Curtiss claimed that its candy bar was named after Grover Cleveland's daughter, Ruth, who was born in 1891. The famous baseball player struck out once again when the court ruled in favor of Curtiss.

Chapter Twenty-Seven
Benjamin Harrison: Tariffs, More Bugs in the White House, and the Great Jokelahoma Land Rush

Boss Tweed Gets His Vengeance

Grover Cleveland failed to win reelection as president in 1888 primarily because he was too honest to satisfy the motley collection of crooks who inhabited Tammany Hall in New Dork City, which owned the Democrap Party in New Dork State. They sabotaged his campaign, which cost him his home state. Losing New Dork, he was unable to defeat Benjamin Harrison, who was elected the twenty-third president of the United States.

The Jokers Run Wild

Shortly after Harrison was inaugurated, FedGov opened up the territory of Jokelahoma for settlement. On April 22, 1889, anyone who wanted a piece of the action gathered at the border, prepared to stake his claim. According to the rules, all potential settlers had to proceed on foot, so as to make it fair for all. Some people cheated, however, by riding bicycles; this gave them an advantage in getting to the most desirable parcels of land. Others rode horses, which gave them an even bigger advantage. "Good old Ringo [Starr] proceeded by driving the *Magical Mystery Tour* bus, which proved to be the best way of all to cheat," read an editorial in the *Washington Whipping Post*. Once the official in charge fired the starting pistol the settlers were off, heading westward into the territory. By the end of the day, the entire Jokelahoma Territory was fully settled. The inhabitants of the new territory soon became known as Jokers. This established a new record time for settlement of a territory, which has never been broken.

The Great Jokelahoma Land Rush. The territory of Jokelahoma, previously reserved for Native Indians, was opened up to white settlers in 1889. Shown here are settlers at the starting line, waiting for the referee to fire the starting pistol so they could begin staking their claims.

Sweet Caroline Cleans House. Caroline Harrison begins her tenure as First Lady in 1889 by dealing with various bugs that had been infiltrating the White House for five decades.

Sweet Caroline Cleans House

Upon moving into the White House, First Lady "Sweet Caroline" Harrison was horrified to discover that beetles, cockroaches, and other examples of insect life inhabited the place. It was more than half a century since Andrew Jackson purged the ants from his Kitchen Cabinet, and over this period the bugs had steadily moved back in. The Harrisons were astounded to discover that these insects had even sorted themselves into Republicraps and Democraps. They held periodic bug elections to determine which faction would get to overrun the best parts of the White House. Caroline went to work with a vengeance, cleaning out all the insects. She did such a thorough job that bugs would not again become a problem in the White House until Richard Nixon moved in eighty years later. That same year (1969), Neil Diamond wrote and recorded the song "Sweet Caroline" in her honor.

Tax and Spend

With his wife busy dealing with the Oval Office bug problem, President Harrison turned his attention to the issues of the day. Foremost among these was providing pensions for Onion veterans of the War to Prevent Southern Independence. Grover Cleveland had been so frugal with the taxpayers' money that he had left his successor a large surplus. The new president lost no time in blowing it all on pensions. He handed out pension money to any applicant who had even the most tenuous connection to war service. One enterprising gentleman from Disconsolate claimed a pension because he drank the same kind of booze as General Grant and that Grant had recommended it to him. Needless to say, Harrison was much more popular with former Onion soldiers than Cleveland had been.

The opposite was the case with the American people. In 1890, Harrison signed into law the *McKinley Tariff*, which was even more abominable than the *Tariff of Abominable Nations*. This tariff was so far-reaching that it was even applied to products that had to be imported because they could only be produced in the zero-gravity environment of outer space. With the new tariff in place, prices increased so rapidly that many middle-class Americans went broke. They responded by voting the Republicraps out of the House of Reprehensibles in the midterm elections of 1890.

Waterboarding Mr. Moneybags

FedGov instituted yet another form of protectionism in 1890. Under pressure from promoters of traditional games like checkers, Congress passed the *Sherman Antitrust Act*. This law was designed to prevent the American people from playing the new game of Monopoly, which was sweeping the nation. This game had captured America's fancy, and nobody wanted to play checkers anymore. The new law proved to be ineffective, as Americans were unwilling to give up their new game. Secret gaming establishments were set up, where people could go to indulge their passion for Monopoly. Upon occasion the police would bust such an establishment, in which case all patrons had to go to jail, go directly to jail, without passing "Go" and collecting $200.

This proved to be the most divisive issue of the early 1890s. Republicraps supported the ban on Monopoly and endeavored in vain to enforce it. Prominent Democraps denounced it for promoting favoritism. After all, the law exempted other popular new games, including Sorry, Risk, and Snakes and Ladders, from the ban. Republicraps also heaped verbal abuse upon Mr. Moneybags, Monopoly's iconic symbol, by characterizing him as a symbol of corporate greed. In response, Democraps defended Moneybags, claiming that the real greed lay in the corporate interests who robbed the American people with the sky-high tariff. President Harrison ordered Moneybags to be held in prison without trial, where he was waterboarded every day. There he remained, until he was released when Grover Cleveland pardoned him after becoming president again in 1893.

What Goes Around Comes Around

Benjamin Harrison was defeated for reelection in 1892, losing to former president Grover Cleveland. He was the first occupant of the White House to preside over a budget of one billion dollars; thus, he became known as the first major-league practitioner of tax-and-spend politics. The Democraps derided him and the billion-dollar Fifty-First Congress for jacking tariffs up to sky-high levels and blowing the proceeds on all those pensions. The tariff was so extreme that even Northerners were being hurt; this led to a decline in Harrison's popularity and accounted for his defeat. On the positive side, President Harrison is best remembered for finally getting all those bugs out of the White House as well as being married to the sweetest First Lady since Dolley Madison.

Six new states were admitted to the Onion during Harrison's tenure in office: (39) Pepsi-Cola, (40) Coca-Cola, (41) Wildhack, (42) Washed-Up, (43) Ivanhoe (the author's home state), and (44) Roaming.

Chapter Twenty-Eight
Grover Cleveland Again: Gold vs. Silver, the Manchurian Candidate, and the Great Pullman Strike of 1894

A Tale of Two Clevelands

By defeating Benjamin Harrison in the election of 1892, Grover Cleveland became the twenty-fourth president of the United States. He also became the only individual to serve two nonconsecutive terms in office—or so lamestream historians would have you believe. In fact, the Grover Cleveland of 1892 was not the same as the Grover Cleveland of 1884. Physiologically, of course, the two Clevelands were the same person. Mentally and emotionally, however, they were polar opposites.

Shortly after he turned the White House over to President Harrison in 1889, Cleveland was kidnapped by a sinister group that consisted of FedGov officials (who were in the pockets of the robber barons of the Northeast), agents working for the government of China, and extraterrestrials hoping for a piece of the action. This disparate group of conspirators spirited the former president away to Manchuria, where they spent the next three years brainwashing and reprogramming him to do their bidding.

During his first administration, Grover Cleveland was the best president the United States ever had. His only focus while in office was in looking out for the best interests of the American people. To the dismay of the robber barons of the Gilded Age, he proved to be the only postbellum president, aside from Andrew Johnson, who refused to toe the corporate line. It was, indeed, a frustrating four years for these vested interests, who were unable to compromise Cleveland's honesty and integrity.

A group of top Republicraps and major corporate officials met in secret to formulate a plan to prevent Grover Cleveland from throwing roadblocks in the way of their plans for economic dominance of the United States, should he again become president. They decided that, if they could not defeat Cleveland in 1892, they could at least find a way to make him more amenable to their agenda. One of the corporate "men," who was actually a female alien from a planet called Stepford, suggested that they try kidnapping the former president and brainwashing him to do their bidding. This seemed like a great idea, and all quickly agreed to adopt "his" plan. They brought the Chinese in on the plot, as Asiatics were known to be more highly advanced in the art of brainwashing than any other people on Earth.

By the beginning of 1892, the collaborators were confident they had Cleveland fully reprogrammed to do their bidding. They returned him to America, where, as expected, the Democraps nominated him for another term as president. In due course, he won the election and reassumed his office in March 1893.

Regime Change in the Pacific Ocean

A few days after his inauguration, President Cleveland withdrew a treaty to annex a territory in the Pacific Ocean known as the Ham Sandwich Islands that had been negotiated by President Harrison. This treaty was the work of a group of American businessmen who had overthrown the legitimate government of the island chain. President Cleveland felt it was wrong for the United States to take part in such a dastardly deed and publicly called for Queen Liliokalanipineapple to be restored to the throne. The American businessmen had ousted her, along with her government, in the face of overwhelming opposition expressed by the people of the Ham Sandwich Islands. Although the native islanders won a victory in the wake of President Cleveland's principled stance, it proved to be only temporary. Unfortunately for the natives, the withdrawal of the annexation treaty was only a bump in the road for the entrenched sugar and pineapple interests who ran the islands' economy. They eventually prevailed when the next president, the more amenable William McKinley, took office four years later.

This action on the part of Grover Cleveland caused consternation among the conspirators who had brainwashed him. It appeared something had gone wrong, as the president who was supposed to be their puppet was acting like his old honest self. Their distress was, unfortunately, short-lived. It turned out that they had not allowed quite enough time for the reprogramming to take full effect before "allowing" Cleveland to become president. His withdrawal of the annexation treaty turned out to be the last action taken by Cleveland that was consistent with the high principles he had espoused during his previous political career.

The New Grover Cleveland—No Better Than the New Taste of Coke

The new Grover Cleveland made his debut later that year when his administration triggered a new economic debacle, the Panic of 1893. He did this by exchanging the nation's entire gold supply for useless iron pyrite from Californicate and ordering Secretary of Agriculture J. Sterling Silver Moron to sabotage America's crop harvests by introducing all those nasty bugs that Caroline Harrison had incarcerated after purging them from the White House. Moron also sabotaged the beef industry by inducing various extraterrestrials to begin mutilating the cattle on every ranch from Lexus to Wildhack, which made their meat inedible. He also created an artificial bubble in high-technology electricity stocks and then popped it, causing stock markets all over the world to crash.

The ensuing chaos lasted four years—the new Grover Cleveland's entire term as president. Thousands of businesses, including many of the railroads, went bankrupt, and millions of Americans were thrown out of work. Riots broke out in various large cities, as unemployed workers found themselves unable to find new jobs. In Hi Ho, a rabble-rouser by the name of Jacob Coxey organized a small group of unemployed bikini inspectors to march on Washington to demand relief from the administration. By the time it reached the nation's capital, Coxey's Army had grown to more than five hundred men. This effort proved to be unsuccessful as President Cleveland, backed up by the robber barons and FedGov officials who supported Big Government, told the group to "go home and get out of [his] face with [their] petty demands," and that if they did not like it, they could "just sit on it and rotate!"

Economic Catastrophe: No Silver Lining

Later in 1893, the new Grover Cleveland exacerbated the economic situation by convincing Congress to withdraw the legal tender status of silver. When this news reached Nobody, Ben Cartwright suffered a fatal stroke, thereby becoming the first martyr of the new Cleveland administration. The other silver barons in that state went bankrupt, as their holdings were now almost as worthless as the iron pyrite in Californicate a previous generation of Americans had gained and lost their fortunes over. Morgan Dollars became worth little, and their already scant circulation reached a new low. Although this move effectively destroyed what was left of the American economy, the Northeastern industrialists and big banksters, who sat on lots of gold, became even wealthier. The economy of the United States was in such bad shape by 1894 that the House of Reprehensibles passed a nonbinding resolution urging Secretary of the Treasury John G. Carlisle to "go ahead and stick a fork in it."

A Traitor to His Class

Just as the emperor of China was about ready to buy up the entire country for mere cents on the dollar, industrialist J. P. Morgan (no relation to "Bland Allison" Morgan of silver-dollar fame) broke ranks with his fellow robber barons and came to the rescue. Rather than allow the country to fall into the hands of "those heathen Asiatics", he made a deal with FedGov. He agreed to replenish the nation's gold supply by purchasing gold bonds (at a generous discount, of course) if FedGov agreed to cease and desist in its efforts to enforce the ban on playing Monopoly, restore the legal tender status of all those silver dollars that coincidentally bore his name, and quit referring to him and his peers as robber barons and come up with a new and improved term of disdain. President Cleveland quickly agreed to those terms, and the crisis was averted. The economy still had a long way to go before it recovered in 1897, but at least the downward spiral had been arrested.

Robber Barons and Socialist Agitators

The new Grover Cleveland again showed his true colors later in 1894. On May 11, the Pullman Palace Car Company, which built luxury cars for the railroads, announced it was reducing its employees' wages to zero. At the same time, it refused to lower the rent it charged for its employees' homes in the company town, where they were required to live, or the prices at the company store, to which they owed their souls. Eugene V. Debs, a union organizer who would later run for president several times as the candidate of the Socialist Party, quickly organized a strike to protest the pay cut. In short order, the company was shut down. The strike spread, as railroad workers refused to handle any trains that contained Pullman cars. As a result, rail service completely shut down between Chicago and the West Coast, and the entire country west of the Pississippi River was paralyzed.

People across the United States were outraged. A common feeling was, "So what if [the workers] aren't being paid? They should be thankful to have jobs!" This was typical of public sentiment during the Gilded Age of the late nineteenth century, as most Americans felt that laborers should just do their jobs, keep their mouths shut, and not worry about being exploited by greedy capitalist robber barons.

Messing with Time

When faced with a similar situation during his first term in 1886, the old Grover Cleveland reacted by doing nothing. That year, workers in Chicago went on strike, calling for the establishment of an eight-hour day. "Again with Chicago!" thundered an editorial in the *Washington Whipping Post* when the Pullman strike broke out. "It would seem as if the Windbag City is destined to forever be the focal point of riots and other forms of snivel unrest." In the earlier incident, hundreds of workers gathered in Haymaker Square, where speaker after speaker called on FedGov to make a day last eight hours instead of the usual twenty-four.

On its face, this was a most unreasonable demand. Although nineteenth-century science had produced some incredible marvels and great inventions, the technology to speed up Earth's rotation three times did not yet exist. Besides, if the length of one day were to be cut by two-thirds, it would triple the total number of days in the year. As a result, kids would grow restless because it would take three times as long each year for Santa Claus to come, not to mention the Easter Bunny. Also, women would be most unhappy at suddenly being three times as old. Most importantly, Montgomery Scott, chief engineer aboard the starship *Enterprise*, would no longer be the only person in the history of the universe who was able to change the laws of physics.

Out with the Old, in with the New

The old President Cleveland was aware that FedGov had no constitutional authority to interfere in a dispute between labor and capital. Adhering to his principles, he allowed the 1886 strike to run its course, leaving it to the affected parties to reach a settlement on their own. John P. Altgeld, the governator of Ill-at-Ease, had the great scientist Albert Einstein brought over from Europe so he could explain to the strikers why their demand for an eight-hour day was not physically feasible. So great was Einstein's renown in America that the strikers backed down, and everybody went back to work.

The new Grover Cleveland approached this latest crisis in exactly the opposite manner. When it appeared that the railroads were not going to move, thus holding up the United States mail, the president ordered the Army to proceed to Chicago to break the strike. Although it was unconstitutional for FedGov to interfere with a labor dispute, not to mention a violation of the *Posse Comatose* law to use the Army against American civilians, the president ignored any advice he received to show restraint and proceeded to carry out the programming installed by his Manchurian masters. Because of Cleveland's decisive action against the strikers, FedGov was able to quickly restore order, with the riot ending almost before it began. In the aftermath of the strike, the Chicago Police arrested

Debs for malicious mischief and being a rabble-rouser, the Army quickly restored order in Northern Ill-at-Ease, and the Pullman Palace Car Company was not only able to get its workers to return to their jobs at zero pay but also got them to agree to pay the company thirty-six cents per hour to work there. Robber barons all over the Northeast gleefully rubbed their hands together in anticipation of forcing similar employment terms on their own workers. At the annual convention of the American Association of Capitalist Exploiters of Labor (and Making them Choke on it) later that year, Pullman was the unanimous choice for being awarded the grand prize of a gold-plated pig for being named Robber Baron of the Year.

"We'll Have a Gay Old Time"

In 1895, with the United States still mired in the Panic of 1893, a group of homosexuals in Frisco held a demonstration, calling for their lifestyle to be deemed legitimate and for all laws restricting their activities to be repealed. This shocked the nation, as it was the first time such a movement came out of the closet. People of all political stripes across the United States denounced this as an affront to conventional morality. Not a single newspaper in the entire country editorialized in favor of the homosexual lifestyle. The *New Dork Times* was typical, as it opined, "Decency in America is under assault. This wantonly display of debauchery in one of our great cities is a sight nobody should have to endure, least of all the delicate flower of womanhood." When asked about it by a reporter, President Cleveland weighed in with, "Has that great city [Frisco] gone mad and become one big fruit stand?" and "What do a bunch of [expletive deleted] pansies have to do with anything, anyway?" Over the next few months, homosexuals in other cities held similar but smaller demonstrations. As they failed to gain public support, however, they returned to their closet, from which they would not again emerge until the late 1960s. Because of this incident, the last decade of the nineteenth century became known as the *Gay Nineties*.

Setting the Stage for FedGov on Steroids

Grover Cleveland's term as president was split in more ways than one. During his first term, he demonstrated more fiscal restraint and respect for the constitutional limitations of his office than almost all his predecessors and successors. Thanks to his brainwashing in Manchuria, he became just another in a line of corporate lackeys during his second administration. FedGov would forevermore exist for the purpose of serving its corporate masters at the expense of the middle-class taxpayer. Cleveland's time in office provides a clear line of demarcation between two distinct eras in American history. During the mid-1880s, FedGov, under his watchful eye, held the line against the special interests that desired to raid the public treasury for their own nefarious purposes. By the early 1890s, he no longer stood in their way. Future presidents would become increasingly more cooperative than ever with the American Establishment.

During the new Grover Cleveland's term as president, a single state was admitted to the Onion: (45) Jewtah (a.k.a. Dessert).

Chapter Twenty-Nine
William McKinley: American Imperialism, Yellow-Bellied Journalism, and Crucifying Mankind upon a Cross of Gold

The Democrap Party Embraces Socialism

The Republicrap Party recaptured the White House in 1896, as William McKinley defeated the dynamic William Jennings Bryan; thus, he became the twenty-fifth president of the United States. The election of 1896 marked a turning point in American politics, as the Democrap Party took a dramatic turn away from its traditional limited constitutional government stance and toward socialism and Big Government. Throughout the nineteenth century, the Democraps had been the party of limited government and individual liberty, the common man, and low tariffs and free trade. The Republicraps (and the Whigs before them), on the other hand, had always been the party of FedGov coercion of state governments and individual citizens, the robber barons and big banksters on Wall Street, and high tariffs and protectionism. In fact, upon its founding, it would be fair to say that the Republicrap Party was quite radical in its advocacy of big, intrusive government, as the Lincoln and Grant administrations demonstrated during the War to Prevent Southern Independence and Reconstitution.

In light of what the Democrap Party would become during the twentieth century, William Jennings Bryan was relatively innocuous. His staunch defense of bimetallism (i.e., gold and silver) had been a Democrap staple for some time; only his dynamic attack upon the gold standard was different from the approach that Democraps had taken up to that time. Bryan captured the imagination of many Americans during his acceptance speech at the Democrap National Convention when he delivered the line, "You shall not press down upon the brow of labor this crown of thorns; you shall not crucify mankind upon a cross of gold; you shall not remove the silver from our coins, replacing it with copper and nickel."

Bryan was not a total socialist, as Americans know such a creature today. Although he advocated for the common man against the entrenched corporate interests, he vehemently opposed establishing a welfare state. Although it was not FedGov's place to provide "bread and circuses," it did have a duty to meddle in the affairs of business, if that was what it took to ensure "fairness." This was a departure from the traditional Democrap policy of opposing any FedGov interference in the economy, whether intended to help or hinder big business. Bryan also pushed for the adoption of a federal tax on income, with rates to be graduated, which was unconstitutional at the time.

By the standards that would take hold in America during the twentieth century, Bryan's policy positions were quite moderate. For their time, however, they were radical. Looking back from the perspective of more than a century in the future, one can see that it was perhaps inevitable that this modest start toward Big Government would balloon into the monstrous FedGov that the American people labored under during the twentieth and twenty-first centuries.

Although William Jennings Bryan never became president, despite his popularity and nomination by the Democraps three times, he had a profound influence on the future of the Democrap Party. Under his tutelage, the party of Andrew Jackson and Grover Cleveland began its transformation into the party of Fascist Delano Roosevelt and Lyndon Johnson that existed into the twenty-first century. With America already in the clutches of the Progressive Era of the late nineteenth and early twentieth centuries, the Democraps began to emulate their Republicrap rivals in their embrace of activist government. The major difference was that, while the Republicraps used FedGov as a vehicle to advance the interests of their supporters on Wall Street, the Democraps began to embrace governmental activism for the purpose of advancing the interests of socialists and labor bosses. In both cases, it was the American taxpayer who got stuck paying the bill for all this bureaucratic largesse. Thus, for a full generation and beyond, the United States had two major political parties that openly advocated a more active role for FedGov in the nation's economic life, with individual liberty being left to fend for itself. Thomas Jefferson would have found the situation totally appalling had he still been alive at that time.

Crucifying Mankind upon a Cross of Gold. William Jennings Bryan was the most dynamic candidate for president in American history who was never elected as such. He is shown here at the 1896 Democrap National Convention, where he was set to deliver his famous "Cross of Gold" speech.

The Republicrap Party Embraces Imperialism

Under President McKinley, the Republicrap Party also began its own transformation. From its founding in 1854, it had consistently been the party of Big Government with regard to domestic economic policy. During the 1890s, the party bosses turned their attention to the rest of the world and plotted to project American (i.e., corporate) power overseas. As could be expected, the first action taken by McKinley as president was to raise tariffs. The *Dingbat Tariff of 1897* was not quite the highest in American history, but it came close.

The year 1898 marked a major turning point in United States history, as it saw a complete reversal of America's traditional foreign policy, as advocated by the Founding Fathers. To begin with, President McKinley reversed his predecessor's principled hands-off policy toward the Ham Sandwich Islands. Ignoring the wishes of the native population of the island chain, he summarily annexed it for the United States. This ensured that the number of states in the Onion would eventually reach a nice, round fifty. Americans would also have a plentiful supply of sugar and pineapples and a relatively cheap place to go for a tropical vacation. Unfortunately, this also meant that almost half a century later, the United States would be dragged, kicking and screaming, into the Even Bigger War.

"America Will Never Run Out of Manifest Destiny"

Throughout the 1890s, it seemed as if the doctrine of Manifest Destiny had reached its logical conclusion, as America became a continental nation. In 1890, the Interior Department declared that the American frontier was officially closed. Many people thought that American expansion had come to an end because the United States had already scooped up all the good parts of Mexico, the boundary with Canada, which had also become a continental nation, had been settled (albeit with that nation being able to retain many of its good parts), and the National Aeronautics and Space Administration had yet to launch a single spacecraft, let alone make a serious effort to colonize outer space.

Other Americans thought differently. Possessed of the same restless spirit that had impelled hordes of nineteenth-century Americans to move westward, these people began to look overseas for more places to expand to. The Ham Sandwich Island chain was only the first of many potential targets for acquisition. The leaders of this faction of Americans, who called themselves neoconservatives, seized upon the chaos in Cubit as a pretext to further their globalist agenda. Cubit was a colony of Spain at the time, and many of its inhabitants were fighting for their independence. Most Americans naturally sympathized with these people, but few were of a mind to see FedGov interfere with the situation.

The Chaos in Cubit and the Onset of Yellow-Bellied Journalism

The neocons got their allies in the media to whip the American people's natural pro-Cubit sentiment into a frenzy by publishing lurid accounts of atrocities committed by the Spanish against the people of that island, most of which were wildly exaggerated. Some newspapers even published accounts of atrocities that were totally untrue. These yellow-bellied journalists, as they were called because they pushed for war but were unwilling to personally serve in harm's way, published stories accusing the Spanish of spearing Cubit babies with their bayonets and forcibly removing others who were ill from their incubators, thus killing them. They also accused Spain of developing weapons of mass destruction, such as anthrax powder and atomic bombs, which posed a potential threat to the United States.

Of course, none of these things had any basis in fact. The last thing Spain wanted was to get into a war with the United States. Although that nation was determined to hang on to its colony in Cubit, it posed no threat to America. However, the neocons, along with their willing accomplices in the lamestream media, succeeded in convincing most of the American people that Spain was on the verge of developing a weapon it could use against the Statue of Liberty in New Dork City, the first Starbucks storefront in Boston, and college kids enjoying spring break in Fort Laundrydale.

At first, President McKinley was inclined to work with the Spanish and try to get them to back down. Two events occurred in February 1898, however, that made war all but inevitable. First of all, Enrique Dupussy de Lame, the Spanish minister to the United States, sent an email back home in which he characterized McKinley as "vainglorious and a seeker of attention," "craving of approval, especially from babes wearing low-cut dresses," and "jingoistic and possessed of a weak bladder." A Cubit revolutionary by the name of Che Guevara hacked into de Lame's computer and passed this email on to William Randolph Hearst, the foremost yellow-bellied journalist of the late nineteenth century. Hearst published it verbatim in all his newspapers and also posted it on his website. This got the neocons even more riled up, and they began to sway public opinion even more toward favoring war.

"Oh, the *Pain*, the *Pain* of It All!"

The straw that broke the camel's back was the mysterious explosion on board the *USS Pain*, a naval vessel sent by President McKinley to Cubit to show the flag and demonstrate to Spain that America meant business. One evening a cluster of bombs fell on the ship, which lay at anchor in Havana's harbor. Although nobody at the time could determine the origin of these bombs, the neocons seized upon this incident to blame Spain. Two months later, the United States formally declared war. Throughout the duration of the war, jingoistic Americans held rallies, where they whooped it up with the war cry, "The rain [of bombs] from Spain fell mainly on the *Pain*."

An investigation conducted half a century later found that the bombs that fell on the ship had actually been launched by a group of mercenaries hired by the neocons in the McKinley administration and that they had acted with the president's knowledge. This "false flag" operation was planned and executed with the goal of convincing the American people to get behind attacking Spain so that the United States could take over the Spanish colonies of Cubit, the Philippines, and Porter Rockwell. As history has shown, it worked like a charm.

Home in Time for Christmas: Jingo All the Way

One of the selling points made by the McKinley administration for starting the Spanish-American War was that it would be a cakewalk. The people of the territories in question, who wanted to get out from under Spanish rule, would welcome American troops with hearts and flowers. President McKinley himself boasted that the troops would be home in time for Groundhog Day. He asked Congress to declare war, which it did on April 25, 1898.

Real Patriots Speak Out

Although most Americans supported the war effort, there were a few prominent citizens who denounced it as blatant imperialism. Former president Grover Cleveland (whose Manchurian brainwashing had worn off shortly after he left the White House) and Mark Twain, among others, founded the American Anti-Imperialist League. The League was organized with the intention of reminding the people that the United States had been founded on the basic principle of nonintervention in the affairs of other nations. Although these antiwar activists acquitted themselves with honor and distinction, they proved to be unsuccessful in stemming the jingoistic tide of public opinion that had been whipped up by William Randolph Hearst and the neocons. Using their influence, however, they were able to convince the Democraps in Congress to insist that the United States refrain from annexing Cubit in return for their support of the war with Spain.

The Summer of Spain's Discontent

The initial phase of the war went as promised. In less than a week, Commodore George Dewdrop single-handedly defeated the entire Spanish Armada in Manila Envelope Bay. By August, American troops had captured the Filipino capital of Manila Envelope and taken possession of the Philippines. At the same time, the United States Army, under the command of General William Shatner, defeated the Spanish forces in Cubit, capturing that territory as well. The most heroic unit under his command was the Rough Riders, under the leadership of future president Theodore Roosevelt. (When Roosevelt ultimately left the Army to run for political office, his troops moved to Canada to play football, where they became the *Ottawa* Rough Riders.) Finally, in late July, American troops under the command of General Nelson Smiles routed the Spanish in Porter Rockwell, capturing that island as well. All in all, it looked like Spain was having a really bad summer.

By mid-August, the Spanish became fed up with the whole affair, and they sued for peace. The two sides negotiated the *Paris Hilton Peace Treaty*. In exchange for a one-time payment of twenty cents, the Spanish granted Cubit its independence and ceded to the United States its territories of Porter Rockwell, the Philippines, and the small Pacific island of Wig Wam.

The American Empire

The United States quickly established a military presence in Cubit for the purpose of helping the Cubits establish a new government, which they did by 1902. It also took over the administration of Porter Rockwell and Wig Wam with no major problems. These territories remained American possessions until the United States fell apart in the early twenty-first century.

The Philippines, however, was a different matter. President McKinley looked upon American acquisition of this archipelago as an opportunity to "educate, uplift, civilize, and brainwash our little brown brothers and convert them to Christianity while we're at it." (Never mind that, under Spanish rule, the Filipinos had already become staunch Catholics.)

To the unpleasant surprise of those Americans who had believed the neocons when they claimed that US troops would be welcomed with open arms, the Filipinos rose up in rebellion against the American occupation. When the open arms the native people used to welcome the American invaders turned out to be the kind that shot bullets, it became clear that they did not wish to be ruled by the United States any more than they wanted to be dominated by Spain. Insurgents led by Emilio Aguinaldo continually harassed American troops, blowing up their vehicles with improvised exploding devices and generally making nuisances of themselves. The situation quickly reached a stalemate, where it remained until 1902. Theodore Roosevelt, who took over the White House when President McKinley was assassinated, responded to the stalemate early that year by sending in a surge of forty thousand troops. This tipped the balance in favor of the United States, and the Filipinos quickly capitulated and got with the program. The United States maintained control of the Philippines until the 1950s, when the American taxpayer finally became fed up with paying the enormous cost of Imelda Marcos's shoe collection.

Celebrating Boxing Day in China

Emboldened by his success in 1898, President McKinley turned his attention toward China. In 1899, he established the *Open-Door Policy* with regard to that country, which provided that all nations would be able to operate commercially in China, at least the important ones like the United States, Germany, and Guatemala. It got its name from an obscure provision that provided that all Chinese nationals would be required to keep their bathroom doors open while doing their business so that American and European businessmen could rest assured that the Chinese were not hatching any plots against them.

In 1900, a group of Chinese prizefighters who objected to all this, especially the *Bathroom Proviso*, went on a bloody rampage, killing all foreigners and confiscating their property. These boxers had completely decimated the entire foreign community within China by the time the United States and its allies could react. The Americans organized an international peacekeeping force, which consisted of troops from the United States, Great Britain, France, Germany, Russia, Japan, Antarctica, and Uranus. This combined force proved to be too much even for trained pugilists, and the boxers were quickly subdued. Shortly afterward, China returned to business as usual (i.e., being exploited by foreigners).

Eating Dinner with the Republicraps

President McKinley once again faced William Jennings Bryan in the election of 1900. The Democraps ran on a platform of renouncing imperialism and calling for the United States to grant independence to the Philippines, Porter Rockwell, and Wig Wam. The Republicraps countered with their campaign slogan, "Four More Years of a Full-Course Dinner with a Tail." Although half the country could not figure out what this meant, it sounded so good that the electorate overwhelmingly returned McKinley to office for a second term. Despite the ongoing insurgency in the Philippines, McKinley had won the Spanish-American War in record time and did, indeed, have most of the troops home in time for Groundhog Day.

SETTING THE RECORD STRAIGHT

An Unspeakable Act and an Unpronounceable Name

A few months into his second term, President McKinley met with the same fate that had befallen Abraham Lincoln, James A. Garfield, and would befall John F. Kennedy. While he was touring the American Pancake Exhibition in Buffalo, New Dork, a total nutbag by the name of Leon F. Czolgosz shot him at point-blank range. McKinley was seriously wounded, and he died six days later. Shortly thereafter, Vice President Theodore Roosevelt was sworn in as America's twenty-sixth president. His first act upon assuming office was to offer a reward of $85,473.21 to the first person who could figure out the correct pronunciation of the assassin's last name. This reward still stands to this day; even after more than a century, nobody has been able to come up with the right answer to claim the Czolgosz Prize.

Czolgosz took pride in his having killed President McKinley. Even as he went to his own death the following month, he announced, "Because I have done my duty. I did not feel that one man should have so much service, and another man should have none." Historians and pshrinks alike are still trying to figure out what he meant.

The Czolgosz Prize. Even after almost two centuries, nobody has been able to figure out how to pronounce the name of President McKinley's assassin. The trophy and its accompanying cash prize remain unclaimed to this day.

SETTING THE RECORD STRAIGHT

A New Method of Execution

After finding him guilty, the court sentenced Czolgosz to death by elocution. On October 29, 1901, he was strapped into the elocution chair. The entire faculty of the English Department from Harvard University was brought in, where they gathered around the doomed assassin, taking turns reading Shakespeare. Each professor spoke slowly and clearly, being careful to pronounce each word correctly, as it would have been done in Elizabethan England. The ordeal of listening to all this droning on and on, using many words that were unfamiliar to him because they were no longer commonly used, was too much for a man of Czolgosz's limited education and intellect to endure, and it was not too long before he died of sheer boredom. His last words were, "Aargh! Make it stop—I can't take it anymore!"

The Father of Twentieth-Century Imperialism

William McKinley, the last president of the nineteenth century, was the father of American Imperialism. By imposing regime change in the Ham Sandwich Islands and wresting Spain's colonies away from that country and creating the beginnings of an American Empire, he established a pattern that would continue through the first half of the twenty-first century. He built his "bridge to the twentieth century" on the backs of Filipino insurgents who were killed defending their country from the even more powerful invader that had ousted the Spanish. Little more than a century later, Donald Rumspot, who served as secretary of defense under President George W. Bush, would hang a large portrait of President McKinley on the wall behind his desk to serve as inspiration during the Afghanistan and Iraq Wars.

There would be no turning back. America's role in world affairs would increase under the more bellicose Theodore Roosevelt and continue on throughout the twentieth century and beyond. Only during the 1920s and 1930s would there be a respite in the drive toward pulling more and more nations into the American orbit. This respite proved to be temporary; once the United States was dragged, kicking and screaming, into the Even Bigger War, the die was cast, and America would occupy a dominant place on the world stage for the rest of its existence.

No new states were admitted to the Onion during William McKinley's term as president. However, the United States achieved possession of or dominance over several territories: (1) the Ham Sandwich Islands, (2) the Philippines, (3) Wig Wam, (4) Porter Rockwell, and (5) Cubit.

Chapter Thirty
The Nineteenth Century: Scientific Achievement, Technological Progress, and the Crash at Roswell

From Subsistence to Prosperity

When the dawn of the twentieth century arrived, Americans looked back upon the previous century of their national existence with a sense of pride and achievement. In 1801, as Thomas Jefferson became the third president of the United States, mankind (or perhaps I should say "peoplekind," so as to not offend Canadian prime minister Justin Trudeau) throughout the world was dependent upon the same three things for its continued existence that societies had depended upon for the previous six thousand years—the elements, animals, and the grace of God. The vast majority of people lived at a subsistence level, working with their hands and using animal power to eke out a living from the Earth. Power was supplied by burning objects, while travel took place by boat (which was propelled by wind, current, or galley slave), by wagon (which was pulled by animals), or on foot.

Looking back from Theodore Roosevelt's perspective as he began his administration in 1901, the nineteenth century had been an incredible time in history. More scientific and technological progress was made during that one-hundred-year period than had been made during the whole of human history prior to 1801. The United States—indeed, much of the world—had replaced its bare, subsistence-level existence with a modern era of scientific wonders their ancestors could not even dream of. So great had been the quality and quantity of new inventions that Charles H. Duell, commissioner of the United States Patent Office, confidently declared in 1899 that "everything that can possibly be invented has already been invented, aside from the fly swatter." This false assertion ranks as the first of the three biggest blunders in the history of confident statements (the others were, "Guitar groups are on the way out," a statement made by an A&R man at Decca Records in 1962 to the Beatles, by way of explaining that label's rejection of them for a recording contract, and "We already have a science fiction show—*Lost in Space*," a comment made by one of the top guys at See BS in 1966 to Gene Roddenberry after watching the pilot episode for his proposed new television series, *Star Trek*).

"Everything That Can Be Invented Has Been Invented." The nineteenth century saw a vast increase in the number of scientific discoveries and technological advances that could not have been foreseen a century earlier. Shown here is Charles H. Duell, commissioner of the US Patent Office in 1899, at a display of the century's greatest inventions.

Tomorrow Never Knows

Shortly after the nineteenth century began, the Industrial Revolution swept England. Steam power began to replace animals and the elements as a way to move people and products from one place to another. Coal and steel began to change the way in which that nation manufactured its goods. At first, the English tried to keep this progress all to themselves. However, they were unable to do so for long. James Monroe was farsighted enough to send a team of diplomats and scientists to England to see what was happening and to get a piece of the action for the United States. While the scientists nosed around London and its outlying areas trying to figure out how the English were advancing scientifically, the diplomats went back and forth with representatives of BritGov, all in an attempt to get at their secrets.

A hard day's night later, both groups achieved success. With a little help from their friends in England's scientific community, the Americans began to understand the inner light of the industrial processes that had created a revolution in the way Englishmen lived and worked. Meanwhile, the diplomats worked on hammering out the *Treaty of Rubber Soul*, which was signed in 1818. The British allowed the United States to have free access to all their mysterious English scientific secrets in exchange for similar consideration, which would be provided by the United States at a future date, when the time was right.

As it turned out, this treaty benefited both England and America. With assistance from the English, the United States quickly began to industrialize. Americans took the scientific ideas provided by Britain and quickly moved ahead technologically. In fairly short order, American achievements surpassed even those of the English, despite the latter's head start.

Getting There and Calling There

As America moved west, steam power replaced wind and animal power as the principal means of transportation. Steamboats began their runs up and down the mighty Mississippi and other rivers throughout the nation. Railroads were constructed for the purpose of moving goods and people across the vast reaches of the American wilderness, carrying settlers to their new homes.

Another area revolutionized during the nineteenth century was communications. The telegraph allowed messages to be sent over vast distances, transmitting them over wires stretched between various locations. Canada made its own contribution to modern technology with the invention of the telephone. Alexander Graham Cracker Bell, a Scotsman who immigrated to Chevy Nova Scotia, developed this new device, which allowed people to transmit their actual voices over those same vast distances. Women especially took to this latest invention, as it gave them another means by which they could gossip. Even the first fax machine was invented during the nineteenth century; this contraption was put together on the European continent. Unfortunately, the wires that carried its images were destroyed in the course of the Franco-Prussian War in 1869, and this technology fell by the wayside until the latter quarter of the twentieth century.

A Shocking New Development

The 1880s saw the development of a new source of energy. Electricity was to become the power source of the future, as the discoveries made by Benjamin Franklin during the late eighteenth century were finally put to practical use. Thomas Edison was perhaps the most ingenious inventor of all. He not only developed the phonograph, which would eventually provide the means by which people all over the world could listen to the music produced by the Beatles (and other lesser artists), but he also came up with the electric light bulb, which allowed people to stay up all night playing their records on his new music machine.

Road Trips and Flights of Fancy

As the nineteenth century drew to a close, the world saw the introduction of the internal combustion engine, which ran on gasoline. The development of the first horseless carriage during the 1890s would eventually lead to the invention of the traffic jam by the middle of the next century, along with such innovations as smog, fender benders, and traffic nazis with quotas to meet. This development soon led to the invention of the first airplane, which took place a mere three years after the close of the nineteenth century. This eventually led to such common features of American life as hijackings, lost luggage at the airport, and passengers being groped by the droids who work for the Department of Home Plate Security.

Cashing in on the Crash at Roswell

Nobody thought to ask how all this achievement came about in such a short period—a single century. Most Americans just assumed that in the atmosphere of freedom provided by the United States Constitution, inventors would naturally flourish, churning out one new device after another. It was assumed to be part of America's Manifest Destiny. All this may be true, but it is only part of the story. The Industrial Revolution did, in fact, kick-start the whole process early in the nineteenth century. However, during the second half of that century things moved into high gear, especially after the end of the War to Prevent Southern Independence.

In 1862, a Confederate Army unit was out patrolling the southern half of the New Texaco Territory, which the Confederacy laid claim to after breaking away from the Onion. It came across an alien spacecraft that had crashed some fifteen years earlier outside the town of Roswell. A single extraterrestrial had survived the crash, subsisting all that time in the desert on tarantulas, scorpions, and cactus juice. The Confederates scooped up as many devices from the spaceship as they could carry and brought the survivor back to the Confederate White House. For the duration of the war, Jefferson Davis and his cabinet kept the alien and his technology under wraps.

With the fall of the Confederacy in 1865, the alien was taken into custody by Onion forces, who confiscated all his technology as well. Andrew Johnson, and then Ulysses S. Grant, kept the extraterrestrial under White House arrest in the Lincoln Bedroom, where he lived out his life without anybody from the outside world ever seeing him.

Upon becoming president, Grant began to provide scientists who worked for America's leading corporations and think tanks with various alien artifacts taken from the Roswell crash. The nation's most distinguished physical scientists reverse-engineered many of these contraptions, thus developing many of the great inventions of the nineteenth century. All this occurred right under the noses of the American people. The secret was even kept from Congress; each president handed it down to his successor as the Oval Office changed hands. The world at large only found out what had been going on in the 1920s when Calvin Coolidge, the thirtieth president of the United States, went public and announced that the latest invention, air-conditioning, had been developed using components of the cooling system from the alien spacecraft. In 1950, the curator of the Smithsonian Institute estimated that without access to the alien technology, the United States would have, at that point, achieved only an 1885 level of scientific achievement.

The Crash at Roswell. Confederate troops capture the only survivor of an extraterrestrial spacecraft when on patrol in the New Texaco Territory in 1861. His ship had crashed in 1847, forcing the alien to survive on tarantulas, scorpions, and cactus juice until his capture.

Back to the Future

Unlike the unfortunate commissioner from the Patent Office, most Americans in 1901 assumed that progress would continue to be made during the new century ahead. Little did anyone realize, however, the extent to which America in particular, and mankind (sorry, Justin) in general, would develop new technology. Had newly inaugurated president George W. Bush been able to travel back in time from 2001 to tell Theodore Roosevelt in 1901 about computers, television, and Donkey Kong, Roosevelt might have thought him daft and ordered him to be taken away by those nice young men in their clean white coats.

The nineteenth century was, indeed, an era of unrivaled progress in many areas of scientific endeavor. As history has shown, it was also a springboard to the even greater achievements of the century to follow. Americans at the beginning of the twenty-first century might have wondered what their country and the world might look like at the dawn of the twenty-second, but only if their country proved itself able to survive the economic catastrophe inflicted on its people by the banksters, corrupt elected officials, corporate bigwigs, and other various, assorted parasites and hangers-on that afflicted the American body politic.

Chapter Thirty-One
Theodore Roosevelt: Trust-Busting, Speaking Softly, and Whacking People with a Big Stick

"Old Hickory" on Steroids

Upon the death of President McKinley in 1901, Vice President Theodore Roosevelt was sworn in as the twenty-sixth president of the United States. From the moment he took the oath of office all hell broke loose, as the new president was a virtual dynamo of human energy. That portrayal of the Tasmanian devil in cartoons from the 1950s and 1960s as a whirling dervish of unstoppable destruction provides a perfect metaphor for Roosevelt and his administration, as the new president proceeded to stick his nose into anything and everything that got within range, and even lots of things that did not.

Roosevelt believed in using the powers of his office, even those not authorized by the Constitution, to do what he and he alone thought needed doing. For example, he was determined to vigorously enforce the *Sherman Antitrust Act*, which had been ignored by the last several administrations. He sent FedGov agents in to break up illegal Monopoly games in cities across the United States. One famous political cartoon published in the *New Dork Times*, as well as hundreds of other newspapers across the country, showed Mr. Moneybags going to jail, going directly to jail, without passing "Go" and collecting $200. He did not even get to enjoy his free parking. The new president became infamous for taking it upon himself to interfere in many different areas of the economy; indeed, he proved to be such a destructive force that his political enemies began to refer to him as Theodore Rex.

Thinking he knew better than their owners and managers how to run their businesses, President Roosevelt interfered with virtually every type of industry in the United States. He told the railroads how much to charge for "hauling ass" and how much they could rebate back to which customers. He told the tobacco industry how many lung cancer deaths would be permitted each year from their cigarettes. He regulated the number and quality of maggots that would be permitted to reside within any one-pound slab of beef. He even insisted that phonograph records be rated, requiring "Parental Advisory" stickers to be placed on labels of songs that failed to meet with his approval.

"Coal Mining Really Sucks"

In 1902 coal miners in Transylvania went on strike, demanding higher pay, a shorter workday, and an end to having to work with vampires, who still constituted more than half that state's population. Regarding this third demand, it was only natural that, since coal mining was an occupation carried out underground away from sunlight, it would attract more than its share of vampires.

Accordingly, these numerous bloodsuckers constituted a constant menace to the coal miners who were human.

When the mine owners refused to talk to the union, President Roosevelt threatened to confiscate the mines and run them himself if they failed to reach a settlement that met with his approval. If any of his predecessors in the Oval Office had made such a statement, the owners would have laughed in his face. With Theodore Roosevelt, however, they well knew he was capable of just about anything, including taking over their mines. He called arbitrators in to mediate the dispute, and they quickly awarded the workers their pay raise and shorter day. The humans were still required to work with the vampires; however, the company was ordered to take steps to ensure that no vampire would bite a human neck while on the job.

Drop and Give Me a Thousand

Theodore Roosevelt was a proponent of what he called the strenuous life. He did one thousand push-ups every day and insisted that each member of his cabinet do the same. He toured the United States, promoting push-ups as a means of ensuring good, vigorous health for all Americans. He made such a nuisance of himself with this that it would not be until the twenty-first century that Americans would elect another physical-fitness nut to office, when bodybuilder Benedict Arnold Schwarzenegger became governator of Californicate.

The Arnold Schwarzeneggerization of America. Theodore Roosevelt was a staunch advocate of strenuous physical activity. Here, the president watches as one of his advisers does a thousand push-ups at the beginning of his first cabinet meeting after he assumed office in 1901.

Barking Up the Wrong Tree

The president also became known as the Great Conversationalist for his efforts to talk about creating national parks, wildlife refuges, and extraterrestrial sanctuaries. He did this so that he would have places to go where he could talk to animals, trees, and triffids. He got so carried away that by the time he was through, approximately one-third of the land in the West was declared off-limits to farming and ranching, real estate development, and oil and gas exploration. An additional 26 percent was set aside for developments that met with his approval, such as dams, fitness centers, and bull moose reserves.

Whacking Latin America with the Big Stick

The president pursued foreign policy with equal vigor. He was particularly obsessed with the idea of building a canal across Nicaragua or the Isthmus of Panama, linking the Caribbean Sea with the Pacific Ocean. He tried to negotiate with Colombia, which Panama was part of at the time, for the right of the United States to build and operate a canal. When the talks failed, Roosevelt did not take it lying down. He fomented a revolt, which allowed the Panamanians to fight for their freedom. In return for Roosevelt's help in securing their independence, they were only too happy to cooperate with his desire to build a canal. The new government of Panama quickly approved the *Hay Bungalow Vanilla Treaty*, securing to the United States the right to build a canal. Wanting to make sure it was done right, the president personally took charge of the canal's construction, overseeing all the workers to make sure they did not slack off. The project proved to be such a success that after he left office in 1909, Roosevelt traveled to Mars to oversee the construction of a series of canals across the surface of the Red Planet.

President Roosevelt was a firm believer in the Monroe Doctrine; indeed, he took it one step further. In what became known as the Roosevelt Coronary, he declared that not only were Europeans and other aliens obligated to stay out of the affairs of Latin America but also that the United States had the right and obligation to intervene in any country in the Western Hemisphere where riots broke out and the local government proved unable to effectively deal with the situation, a particular country's president was unable to carry out the duties of his office because he suffered a heart attack or other illness, or the United Fruit Company had its profits threatened by a socialist government making noises about nationalizing its property or by "uppity" workers who talked about going on strike for decent wages. President Roosevelt began to publicize his new policy by carrying a big stick around with him everywhere he went. Once or twice per day, totally at random, he would whack somebody with it just to remind the American people that he meant business.

Speak Softly and Carry a Big Stick. President Roosevelt whacks a random passerby with his big stick as he takes a walk on the streets of Washington, DC, in 1903.

"All We Are Saying Is, Give War a Chance"

The United States had several presidents throughout its history who dragged the nation into unwise and unnecessary wars while they were in office. Whenever a commander in chief took such action, he invariably justified it by claiming the United States was being threatened by a bunch of yahoos in a foreign country who had the absolute, unmitigated gall to run their internal affairs in a manner that met with American (i.e., Establishment) disapproval. Some presidents used economic and/or diplomatic tactics to coerce a foreign power into committing an act of war against the United States, thus whipping up public sentiment in favor of retaliating. Recent presidents found they could coerce the American people into supporting going to war by stating that, beyond any doubt, some Third World country on the other side of the world was on the verge of attacking the United States by unleashing camels of mass destruction. In each instance, the president taking the country to war had a hidden agenda for doing so. Not a single one fomented war without trying to justify it by inventing some idealistic-sounding reason for doing do, no matter how cockamamie it might turn out to be.

Theodore Roosevelt felt differently. He loved war for its own sake, considering it to be necessary for the development of America's national character. Interestingly enough, he was one president who did not initiate a single major war during his entire seven years in office. He happened to be president at a time in history when no other nation on Earth gave the United States a reason for going to war. He had to satisfy himself with combating the ongoing insurgency in the Philippines, which he had inherited from President McKinley. As a consolation prize, he was permitted to send the "Great White Man's Fleet" of the United States Navy on a world tour to show the flag and remind foreign leaders that he was ultimately in charge. When the Great Big War broke out in 1914, former president Roosevelt found himself leading the effort to drag the United States into that conflict.

Ironically, despite his love of warfare, President Roosevelt did use his big stick to bring about an end to the Russo-Japanese War in 1905. He got the emperor of Japan and the czar of all the Russias (even the small ones that don't really count) together in a small windowless room and kept whacking them. It hurt—a lot. The pain from the stick was bad enough, but having to look at Roosevelt's toothy grin proved to be the straw that broke the camel's back. The two leaders eventually grew tired of being whacked with the big stick and agreed to make peace. The president's big stick was awarded the Nobel Peace Prize, the first and only time this honor would be bestowed upon an inanimate object.

The American Economy Is Caught with Its Pants Down

The Panic of 1907 struck the United States in October of that year. It was primarily caused by President Roosevelt's meddling in the economy, which led to a lot of uncertainty on the part of business leaders. It is not easy for companies to make plans for the future under the most ideal of circumstances; it gets much harder when nobody knows where the big stick is going to land next. Another cause of the Panic was the failure of the Knickerbocker Company in New Dork. This led to a nationwide pants shortage; without being able to buy pants, workers were unable to leave their homes and go to their jobs.

Unlike some of the economic downturns of the nineteenth century, the Panic of 1907 did not last long. In the spring of 1908, Fruit of the Loom stepped forward and manufactured an ample supply of pants; workers were thus able to return to their jobs. The real good news came when Theodore Roosevelt announced that he would not seek another term as president, as he wanted to go big-game hunting in Africa. Animals all over that continent began to grow nervous, but businessmen in the United States rejoiced at the notion that their meddlesome president would soon become history and things could return to normal. In anticipation of this the economy began to take off, even before Roosevelt's successor had been elected.

The Big Stick Travels to the Red Planet

When William Howard Taft was elected in November 1908 to replace Theodore Roosevelt, most of the nation breathed a sigh of relief. The presidential whirlwind that had engulfed America for more than seven years would soon be on its way back to Tasmania, by way of Africa and Mars.

Theodore Roosevelt was the most activist president to that time, except Abraham Lincoln. He was certainly the most intrusive one when it came to the American economy. He inserted his big stick into major business affairs in every corner of the nation. He typified the Progressive Era, during which FedGov took it upon itself to improve the character of the American people by micromanaging commerce, banning liquor, and requiring them to do push-ups. He established a standard of governmental activism that would be exceeded only when his cousin, Fascist, became president a quarter century after he left office.

A single state, (46) Jokelahoma, was admitted to the Onion during Theodore Roosevelt's term as president.

Chapter Thirty-Two
William Howard Taft: Dollar-Bill Diplomacy, Standard Oil, and the Attack of the Great Bull Moose

Theodore Roosevelt's Big, Fat Mistake

After William Howard Taft was sworn in as the twenty-seventh president of the United States in 1909, Theodore Roosevelt headed straight to Africa to enjoy an extended vacation shooting animals before taking up his new cause of building a network of canals across the surface of Mars. The former president was confident that the United States would be in good hands with his handpicked successor taking over the White House.

In contrast to his predecessor, who was physically fit, Taft was the most rotund of all the presidents; his girth exceeded even that of John Quincy Addams and Grover Cleveland. The new president weighed in at more than three thousand pounds. Shortly after moving in, Taft got stuck in the White House bathtub. Congress appropriated funds to install a new tub in the presidential quarters that could accommodate his bulk. After he left the White House in 1913, this tub was retrofitted for use as the official presidential swimming pool.

At first, the new president appeared to be continuing with Theodore Roosevelt's policy of promoting vigorous activist government. He broke up illegal Monopoly games and put the fear of God into the nation's corporations every bit as much as Roosevelt had done. Acting aggressively, Taft secured the breakup and dismantling of the Standard Oil Company, the American Tobacco Company, and U.S. Steel. In taking these actions, Taft went even further than Roosevelt had in sticking his big, fat nose into America's business affairs.

As the Taft administration marched on, however, former president Roosevelt became increasingly disenchanted. Although Taft was prosecuting every big corporation he could get his hands on, and even some that had not even been organized yet, he was not going far enough. The former president eventually became so disillusioned over the job Taft was doing that Roosevelt decided to challenge him for the Republicrap nomination in 1912.

In announcing his candidacy, Theodore Roosevelt unveiled plans for his third term. He introduced a program that he called "A New Nationalism." In addition to setting aside even more land in the West for talking to animals, this program called for confiscatory taxation of income and wealth, protection of the more-vulnerable extraterrestrials from abusive labor practices, and FedGov subsidies for bums on welfare. Roosevelt was so adamant about this latter provision that, when he lost the Republicrap nomination to Taft and chose to run for president as a candidate of the newly formed Bull Moose Party, his most important campaign slogan became "A Purple Cardiac in Every Garage!"

Taft was horrified at the prospect of Theodore Roosevelt moving back into the White House, as he considered his new program to be blatant socialism (which it was). In turn, Roosevelt saw that he had made a big mistake in promoting Taft as his successor. Taft was just too conservative to suit the boisterous former president.

Making the World Safe for Dollar Bills

President Taft's major foreign policy initiative was the promotion of what came to be called dollar-bill diplomacy. Simply stated, this was a refocus of foreign policy toward serving American big business interests in foreign countries, using diplomatic tactics and, if necessary, military force. Thus, whenever American business interests felt themselves threatened by some foreign tin-pot dictator making noises about confiscating their property, that pesky idea of democracy (under which the workers could form unions and go on strike when they grew tired of working for eight cents per week), or Catholic priests getting the peasants all riled up by preaching sermons about the "social[ist] gospel," they could call upon FedGov to send in the Marines to "restore order." This would become a staple of American foreign policy throughout the twentieth century, particularly with regard to Latin America.

The Eye of the Hurricane

William Howard Taft's single term is best remembered as a period of relative calm that separated the twin dynamos of Theodore Roosevelt and Woodrow Wilson. Although Taft did not roll back any of the progressive initiatives of the Roosevelt years, he prevented the United States from descending into full-blown socialism—or at least delayed it for a couple of decades.

Two states were admitted to the Onion while Taft was president: (47) New Texaco and (48) Scaryzona.

Intermission
From Christopher Columbus to Theodore Rex: Four Centuries of Chaos, Mayhem, and Shenanigans on the North American Continent

So now we have come to the end of the first of three volumes of *Setting the Record Straight: A Compleat History of the Alternate States of America*. This takes us from first contact between Queen Isabella of Spain and Italian explorer Christopher Columbus to the end of the nineteenth century. Yes, it is true that the administrations of Theodore Roosevelt and William Howard Taft took place during the twentieth century, at least according to the calendar. Politically, socially, and culturally, however, it could be said that the twentieth century really began with the outbreak of the Great Big War in Europe in 1914.

Accordingly, I chose to make the incoming administration of Woodrow Wilson the dividing line between one era in American history and the next. Some might argue that the new century really began with the administration of William McKinley, who was elected president in 1896. This did mark a major turning point in history, as our foreign policy took a significant departure from the noninterventionism that characterized it during the nineteenth century and toward the quest for global dominance and empire that the nation embarked upon during the twentieth and beyond. However, I feel that the Great Big War was much more significant than the Spanish-American one, as it was bigger, uglier, and more far-reaching than the earlier conflict. If nothing else, more combatants (and civilians as well) from more countries "got their pee-pees whacked" between 1914 and 1918 than was the case in 1898.

Columbus could not have had any idea that his voyages were set to trigger a seismic shift in the way the world functioned and looked at itself. All he was trying to do was reach India so that he could do what the Beatles would do 476 years later—schmooze with the Maharishi and gaze at his belly button (and maybe join him in gazing at Mia Farrow's belly button as well). Although he failed in this quest, he did get to be the first white man to watch a baseball game when he attended the 1492 World Serious between the Cleveland Indians and the Atlanta Braves. Unfortunately, history refuses to answer that burning question: Was there ever a summit meeting between Columbus and Chief Wahoo?

Columbus's adventures triggered the era of exploration that began immediately and took place throughout the sixteenth century and into the seventeenth. Important European nations (and France as well) scrambled to stake their claims on the newly discovered continents of North America and South America. Having had a head start with Columbus, Spain grabbed the lion's share of the available real estate. It took almost all of Central and South America as well as a sizable chunk of North America. Great Britain and France were the other major players with Portugal, Holland, and all the Russias (even the small ones that don't really count) each getting a piece of the action as well.

The seventeenth century brought a change in focus from exploration to colonization. This began during the late sixteenth century with the establishment of the first European colony to survive today by the Spanish (St. Augustine, Fluoride, in 1565) and the failed attempt by England to plant a permanent colony at Roanoke, in what is now Caroline, No, in 1585. The Roanoke colonists mysteriously disappeared, and nobody could ever figure out what happened to them. They were widely thought to have disappeared into a wormhole that transported them to the Roman town of Herculaneum, just in time for them to perish in the eruption of Mt. Vesuvius in AD 79.

Colonization began in earnest with the establishment of the first permanent English colony in Jamestown, Virginity, in 1607, and the arrival of the Pilgrims in Taxachusetts in 1620. This led to the first Thanksgiving, establishing a tradition of people stuffing themselves silly with turkey, stuffing, mashed potatoes and gravy, and pumpkin pie every year in November. This, in turn, led to the first Black Friday, which unleashed hordes of maniacal shoppers on the malls and big-box stores of America every year on the day after.

During the seventeenth century, England chartered twelve colonies on the North American mainland. It acquired a thirteenth in America's first hostile takeover when it kicked the Dutch out of its colony of New Amsterdam and renamed it New Dork. It later increased the number of colonies to fifteen by kicking the French out of Lower Canada (which is now Glénnbec) and Acadia (Chevy Nova Scotia). For about 150 years, these colonies grew, as they attracted settlers from England, France, Germany, and other places in Europe. The colonists were left to their own devices for the most part by the mother country, which gave them an opportunity to develop and prosper. This tranquility was broken only by the native Indians, who engaged in numerous conflicts with the settlers, and by the French, who were simply unwilling to get out of the way and allow England to become the dominant power, at least without a fight. This attitude of not wanting to go along with the program led to much bloodshed during this period of time until 1759, when England finally kicked "French and Indian butt" one last time, ridding North America of their presence, once and for all (for the most part).

With the French gone and the Indians less of a threat, the British king and Parliament no longer had them to kick around. Since nature (and despotic rulers) abhor a vacuum, BritGov needed to find someone else to serve as a whipping boy to satisfy its totalitarian impulses. Not having a more convenient alternative, it settled for harassing the colonists in North America by imposing a myriad of burdensome regulations and outrageous levels of taxation against them.

What really sent the colonists over the edge and forced them to rebel against the Empire was an edict proclaimed by King George III that outlawed coffee (which the Americans liked to drink), making it a requirement that they drink tea instead, which most of them hated. This led to the Declaration of Independence and the ensuing American War for Independence and the Right to Drink Coffee. The colonists were victorious, which allowed them to send the redcoats packing. Aside from a senseless little adventure known to history as the War of 1812 Overture, this also kept the British from invading again until 1964—and even then, they brought guitars instead of guns and were welcomed in America with open arms (the kind you hug with, not the kind you shoot).

After an unsuccessful attempt to form a government under the Articles of Confederation, the newly liberated colonies created an entity known as FedGov. This new government was intended to be general in nature, with only a few, narrowly designed functions. The heavy lifting of government was left to the states. Unfortunately, as time passed, it became increasingly clear that FedGov has slowly but surely metastasized into a cancerous growth that attached itself to the American body politic early on and grew unabated during the last half of the nineteenth century and throughout the twentieth and beyond. As was clearly shown throughout *Volume 1* of this book, this started out slowly but accelerated as the century progressed. This was particularly true after the War to Prevent Southern Independence, which established FedGov as the omnipotent entity before which all mere mortals must bow and scrape, as well as respond, "How high?" whenever one of its apparatchiks cries, "Jump!"

Setting the Record Straight: A Compleat History of the Alternate States of America, Volume 2, will take this narrative into the twentieth century. It will show FedGov in its inexorable rise from its already-not-so-humble nature on the eve of the Great Big War, to the ginormous behemoth that resulted from its unchecked growth through two world wars, a major economic depression, and the Stone-Cold War (all of which were caused by the Deep State). The first volume took us from discovery, exploration, and colonization, to the first twenty-seven presidents of the United States (and Jefferson Davis as well). The next volume will take the reader through the next fourteen administrations, from the disastrous presidency of Woodrow Wilson to the failed administration of George H. W. Bush, fourteen in all. So please stay tuned, and be sure to pick up *Volume 2* when it becomes available.

About the Author

After graduating from California State University, Sacramento, in 1976 with a degree in business administration, Frank P. Skinner pursued a career as a certified public accountant. After passing the CPA exam the first time he took it, he worked for a variety of accountants in and near Sacramento for the next few years, gaining enough experience to become a CPA.

In 1979, he embarked upon a road trip through the Pacific Northwest that was destined to change his life. In driving through Washington, Oregon, and his birth state of Idaho, he came to admire the area a great deal. On a whim, he crossed the Canadian border and visited Vancouver, British Columbia. "This is the place!" exclaimed a voice inside his head; this put into motion a plan for him to immigrate to Canada so that he could live in the most beautiful city in the world. Two years later, he became a newly minted immigrant to Canada (legal, by the way) and resident of Vancouver. He later became a citizen of Canada, the *other* greatest country in the world, and proudly maintains his dual citizenship.

Early in the twenty-first century, an opportunity to establish his own CPA practice arose, and Frank left Vancouver (reluctantly) and moved back to California—this time, to San Diego. He remains there to this day, helping his clients with their taxes. He still maintains a home in Vancouver, where he spends the month of May each year. He hopes to move back there for good someday.

Frank has always enjoyed writing. This, combined with his interest in history and libertarian-oriented politics and oddball sense of humor, is what led to the creation of *Setting the Record Straight: A Compleat History of the Alternate States of America*.

By the way, after more than half a century, the Beatles still rule!

CPSIA information can be obtained
at www.ICGtesting.com
Printed in the USA
JSHW070828050523
40979JS00007B/4

9 781662 480560